A Laura Fleming Mystery

Wed and Buried

Toni L.P. Kelner

KENSINGTON BOOKS
Kensington Publishing Corp.
http://www.kensingtonbooks.com

KENSINGTON BOOKS are published by

Kensington Publishing Corp.
850 Third Avenue
New York, NY 10022

All Kensington Titles, Imprints, and Distributed Lines are available at special quantity discounts for bulk purchases for sales promotions, premiums, fund-raising, and educational or institutional use. Special book excerpts or customized printings can also be created to fit specific needs. For details, write or phone the office of the Kensington special sales manager: Kensington Publishing Corp., 850 Third Avenue, New York, NY 10022, attn: Special Sales Department, Phone: 1-800-221-2647.

Kensington and the K logo Reg. U.S. Pat. & TM Off.

First Kensington hardcover printing: February 2003
First Kensington mass market printing: July 2004

10 9 8 7 6 5 4 3 2 1

Printed in the United States of America

To my great-aunt,
Virginia Allen Raines,
who taught me that some mysteries
about babies can never be solved.

ACKNOWLEDGMENTS

I want to thank:

- My husband, Stephen P. Kelner Jr., for helping me find time to write this book, and taking his own time to improve it.

- My agent, Joan Brandt, for offering suggestions in her own inimitable manner.

- Elizabeth Shaw, for proofreading speed and enthusiasm.

- Fellow EMWA member D. P. Lyle, M.D., for answering my questions about isopropanol poisoning.

- Fellow North Carolinian Tim Meyers, for scouting out details about Hickory, NC.

- My mother, Peggy R. Perry, for background on collectibles.

- Troy Soos for creating Pudd'nhead Wilson and Chris Cittman for giving him his most distinguishing characteristic.

- The Mystery Babes and folks on DorothyL, for lending me their names for Byerly's denizens.

- My daughters, Magdalene and Valerie, for occasionally letting me use the computer for writing rather than for playing games.

- The amazing folks who educated and entertained Maggie and Valerie while I worked: Jan Anthony, Sue Bergemeier, Sandy Chipman, Kristin Esterberg, Jennifer Goodwin, John Haney, Dharma Noriega, Rita Murphy, Joan Rafferty, Joanmichelle Rafferty, Leanne Russell, Ashley Sippel, and Victoria Walker.

Chapter One

I looked down at the sheet-covered form and swallowed hard, grateful that my daughter Alice wasn't with me. She wouldn't have known what it was she was seeing, of course, but a seven-month-old baby has no business being around a dead body.

Even with the sheet concealing the worst, there was so much blood, and the smell . . . I swallowed again and looked away.

My great-aunt was staring at the body, too, and I'd never seen her look so pale.

"Aunt Maggie?" I said, and gently touched her back.

She looked at me, but I don't think she really saw me. Her eyes were still filled with that awful vision of death. Tears were streaming down her face, and she looked so much older than she'd looked that morning.

"This wasn't supposed to happen," she said in a disbelieving voice. "Bill said the house was safe. I wouldn't have gone to the carnival if I hadn't thought he'd be safe."

There was nothing I could say to her—I'd thought the Walters mansion was safe, too. When Big Bill Walters told me that somebody was trying to kill him, I'd been sure I could outwit whoever it was. Instead, I'd been the one outwitted. Maybe if I hadn't been so full of myself, we wouldn't have been standing next to a dead body.

Chapter Two

It had been a very different scene when I drove up to the Walters house a few days before. Actually, the Walterses like to call their house a mansion, and I suppose it's a reasonable description. The long, curving driveway; the graceful columns in front; the veranda with white-painted cast-iron furniture and trailing vines; the many, many rooms decorated out of the pages of *Southern Living*—it all added up to a picture postcard of an antebellum mansion. The fact that it was built long after the Civil War doesn't mean that it's not a darned impressive place.

I parked the rental car in front of the house and stood waiting while my husband, Richard, maneuvered Alice out of her car seat. She was sleeping, thank goodness. My nerves were still frazzled from dealing with a seven-month-old on the flight from Boston, including having to nurse her on the plane. Of course, I couldn't blame my nerves solely on Alice. The fact was, something had happened in my family that I just couldn't believe, and I didn't think I would until I heard it from the horse's mouth.

I rang the doorbell and waited. The Walterses had a full-time housekeeper, and it was she who opened the door. Miz Duffield's expression didn't quite make me feel as if I should have gone to the back door, but it came close.

"May I help you?" she asked.

"Hi. I'm Laura Fleming," I said, though I was fairly sure she already knew who I was. "Is Aunt Maggie around?"

"I'll see if she's receiving visitors."

Miz Duffield did at least let us wait in the front hall rather than outside, but I couldn't shake the feeling that an alarm would go off if we stepped out of that hall while she climbed up the gentle spiral of stairs.

"Perhaps we should have called ahead," Richard said, shifting Alice to his other shoulder.

"Since when do we have to make an appointment to see Aunt Maggie?" I said stubbornly, but I wondered if maybe he was right. Aunt Maggie must have changed an awful lot since I'd seen her last, or she'd never have done what she'd done. There was no telling what she was like now.

A few minutes later, Miz Duffield started back down the stairs, but she was passed by a reddish-brown blur of fur that ran up to us and sniffed eagerly.

"Bobbin!" I said, and crouched down to pet her. Nobody is sure how many bloodlines are mingled in Bobbin, but visibly, the dominant breed is chow chow. Though Aunt Maggie had become a dog owner fairly late in life, she'd done so as forcefully as she did anything, and Bobbin instantly became her constant companion. Seeing the dog at the mansion made me feel better.

Once Bobbin finished inspecting me, she turned her attention toward Richard, and, realizing that Richard was holding a mighty interesting package, she hopped up on her hind legs to get a better whiff of Alice.

Miz Duffield had finally caught up with Bobbin, and said, "Is it safe for it to be around a child?"

I'd been wondering the same thing myself, but the woman's tone rankled. "Bobbin would never hurt a baby. Hold Alice down where Bobbin can see her, Richard."

He looked doubtful, too, but he did it. Bobbin looked at our sleeping child and wagged her tail happily. Alice picked that moment to wake up, and when she opened her eyes, there was Bobbin's muzzle right in front of her.

"It's all right, Alice," I said comfortingly, but I needn't have bothered. After the tiniest of starts, Alice bestowed one of her rare smiles on Bobbin.

"Would you look at that?" I said, exasperated. I'd only managed to get a dozen smiles out of Alice myself, and here she was, giving one away to a dog.

Then Aunt Maggie's voice echoed down the stairwell. "Irene, are you bringing them up here or what?"

Miz Duffield sniffed. "Your aunt will see you now," she said unnecessarily, and led the way up the steps, moving her skirt aside when Bobbin brushed past her. "Mrs. Walters—Mrs. Burt Walters—would never have allowed a dog in the mansion."

I almost felt sorry for the woman. Obviously, things had changed for her, too, and just as obviously, she didn't like it.

Aunt Maggie was waiting for us at the top of the stairs, and her appearance reassured me even more than seeing Bobbin had. Her short salt-and-pepper hair hadn't been styled, and she wasn't wearing even a hint of makeup. She had on a pair of red sneakers, blue drawstring pants, and a screaming yellow T-shirt with the slogan, "I don't know, and I don't care!" In other words, she was dressed the same as always.

"Hey, Aunt Maggie." I gave her a quick hug, which is generally about as much hug as she can stand, even from family. Richard settled for a peck on the cheek.

"Y'all must have just got in," Aunt Maggie said. "I wasn't expecting to see you until the party tonight."

"We just couldn't wait to introduce you to Alice," I said brightly.

Aunt Maggie gave me a look. "You just wanted to see if it's true, didn't you, Laurie Anne?"

"Well, I was a little surprised when Aunt Nora called to tell me the news," I admitted.

Aunt Maggie snorted. "I bet Alice here could have knocked you down with a feather."

"Half a feather," I said. "Is it . . . ? Did you really . . . ? I mean, did he . . . ?"

"Yes, Laurie Anne. Big Bill Walters and I really eloped last week."

I have no idea what expression froze onto my face, but whatever it was, it made Aunt Maggie burst out laughing. "Laurie Anne, if you could see yourself!"

Richard, who is far more gracious than I, said, "Please accept our best wishes. I hope you two will have many happy years together."

"Richard," Aunt Maggie said, "at our age, we don't have many years of any description left."

It wasn't their ages that had shocked me so much. Well, that had been part of it. I'm not exactly sure how old Aunt Maggie is, but rumor has it that she's closer to eighty than she is to seventy, and the same is true of Big Bill Walters.

Even without the unusual age of the newlyweds, there was the whole idea of Aunt Maggie getting married to anybody. She'd been badmouthing marriage ever since I'd known her, and had avoided far more family weddings than she'd attended.

Of course, I'd always assumed that Aunt Maggie would change her tune if the right man came along, but for her to marry Big Bill Walters, of all people!

Ever since the Walters family opened the textile mill that's the leading industry in Byerly, they'd considered themselves the town's first family, and they had enough money and influence to support that claim. Of course, being the top dog in Byerly wasn't really that big a deal— the whole city of Byerly isn't that big a deal—but the Walterses' constant putting on of airs had grated. We Burnettes, on the other hand, were as common as dirt, and plenty of us had been dirt poor, too.

It had been a big enough shock when Aunt Maggie and Big Bill started keeping company a few years back[1], and they had survived one breakup[2], but I'd never expected them to get married. Dead relatives on both sides of the families must have been spinning in their graves, and the living ones were probably even more stirred up.

I realized I was still gawking, and pulled myself together enough to say, "We're very happy for you."

Aunt Maggie just laughed again. "Let's see this young'un you brought to meet me."

Richard handed over Alice, and for a woman who'd never had a child of her own, Aunt Maggie did a competent job of holding, jiggling, and tickling her. In return, Alice gave her a bigger smile than she'd given Bobbin, making me wonder what I was doing wrong.

After a few minutes' inspection, Aunt Maggie handed down her verdict. "She's a Burnette, all right."

Privately I agreed with her. Alice's nose, the shape of her eyes, those precious grins—all of them said "Burnette"

[1] *Dead Ringer*
[2] *Mad as the Dickens*

to me. But out of loyalty to my husband, I said, "Richard's mother says her head is shaped just like his."

Aunt Maggie looked at Alice's head, then at Richard's, and shrugged. "If you say so. She is a right pretty little thing."

"Thank you." I knew that feminism insists that looks aren't the most important thing about a female of any age, but frankly, even I would be hard-pressed to find many praiseworthy traits in a seven-month-old. Besides, Alice was awfully pretty.

"I expect y'all want to come say hello to Bill while you're here," Aunt Maggie said, leading the way. "I think his office is down this way, but I haven't gotten this place figured out yet."

"Should I call him 'Uncle Bill' or 'Uncle Big Bill'?" I asked.

"Call him whatever you want," she said, "just don't call him late to supper."

Either Aunt Maggie had exaggerated the size of the house, or she got lucky, because she found Big Bill behind the first door she tried. He was in a good-sized room outfitted like an office, but a whole lot nicer than any home office I ever expected to have. No metal file cabinets and particle-board desks here—everything was rich cherry wood, with brass accents and a thick oriental carpet. The chairs and the couch were upholstered in gleaming burgundy leather you could sink into.

Despite the nickname, Big Bill wasn't really that big a man, but he still dominated the room. Richard, who knew about the theater, said Big Bill had stage presence, on and off the stage, and my aunt Daphine said he had an air about him. Whatever it was, the man had it in spades. He still had a full head of hair, even if it was snow white, and moved as vigorously as a man many years younger.

Big Bill smiled broadly when he saw us, and abandoned the stack of papers on his desk to come give me a kiss and shake Richard's hand. "Is this little Alice?" he asked, spying the baby Aunt Maggie was holding. "Why, she's just as pretty as her mother. Richard, you're going to have to beat the boys off with a stick."

"I've already ordered the barbed wire for the fence," Richard assured him.

Big Bill put his arm around Aunt Maggie. "We're awfully glad y'all made it in town for the reception. I didn't think you'd be able to come, what with the new baby."

"We'd planned to come around Thanksgiving anyway," I told him. "Aunt Nora has been dying to see Alice. In fact, when she first called to tell me about the reception, I accused her of making it up just to get us down here."

I thought Big Bill laughed a bit more at that than was called for.

"Is the reception going to be a big affair?" Richard asked.

"Lord, yes," Big Bill said. "I think Vasti has invited half the town."

"Make that the *whole* town," Aunt Maggie said. "She even let me invite some of my friends."

Big Bill chuckled. "Vasti's been as busy as a bee, making all the arrangements."

"I can imagine," I said. Knowing my cousin Vasti, she was getting others to do the actual work, but she did have a flair for organizing.

"I don't see what we need some fancy party for," Aunt Maggie said, making a face. "There's an auction tonight I'd rather go to."

"Not me," Big Bill said. "I'm looking forward to showing off my new bride."

Aunt Maggie snorted and pushed Big Bill's arm off her shoulder.

It wasn't the usual behavior for newlyweds, but I think I would have freaked out if Aunt Maggie had gone all lovey-dovey.

"Vasti just wants a chance to show off your house," she said.

"Our house, now," Big Bill corrected her.

Aunt Maggie muttered, "I suppose," looking remarkably unenthusiastic.

"It'll give both sides of the family a chance to get better acquainted," I said. I couldn't wait to see what Big Bill's highfalutin son Burt and even more highfalutin daughter-in-law Dorcas thought of their new relations. I didn't imagine that Dorcas was happy about having Aunt Maggie in the house. Ever since Big Bill's first wife had passed away, Dorcas had played lady of the manor, but presumably that was Aunt Maggie's job now. Dorcas's and Burt's only consolation must have been knowing that at Aunt Maggie's age, she wasn't going to give Big Bill any more children to compete with Burt. "Besides, we're all disappointed we didn't get to see the wedding."

"We didn't get married to put on a show," Aunt Maggie said.

"I know that," I said, "it's just that—"

"Don't mind Maggie," Big Bill said, patting her shoulder. "She's just nervous about the party."

Aunt Maggie pushed his hand away again. "You know darned well what I'm nervous about, and it's not the dad-blamed party."

"Now, Maggie—"

"Bill, I told you before that I thought we should call Laurie Anne, and you talked me out of it, but now that she's here, don't you think we should tell her?"

"We've been all through that," Big Bill said.

"That was before, but now it's been a week and a half, and we're not a bit further along."

"That's not true. I've got some definite leads."

"Leads, my tail end! You don't have the first idea of what's going on."

"Damn it, Maggie—"

"You watch your language around this child, Bill Walters," Aunt Maggie snapped.

"Maggie, that baby can't understand a word I'm saying."

"Maybe she can and maybe she can't, but I don't want little Alice's first words to be cuss words!"

She glared at him and he glared at her, and Richard and I just watched the two of them, wondering what in the Sam Hill they were talking about.

Finally, Big Bill backed down, but he wasn't gracious about it. "Fine. Tell them if you want to, but that doesn't mean I'm giving up."

"Tell us what?" I asked.

"The real reason Bill and I got married," Aunt Maggie said.

Richard couldn't resist saying, "He didn't get you into trouble, did he?"

I elbowed him, but Aunt Maggie ignored him. "The fact is, somebody is trying to kill Big Bill."

Chapter Three

"**A**re you serious?" I said.

"Dead serious," Big Bill said, and I don't think he even meant to make a pun. "There have been three attempts so far, and I'm just lucky none of them succeeded."

"What kind of attempts?" Richard wanted to know.

"The first was three weekends ago, when I went up to my cabin to do some hunting. The first morning I was there, a bullet went right by my head. Another inch, and I wouldn't be here now."

"Hunting accidents aren't that uncommon," I said. "Somebody could have thought you were a deer."

"A deer with a bright-orange hat and jacket?" Before I could object further, he added, "I know, people get killed every year, even when they're dressed properly. The thing is, I own all the land around that cabin, and there's not supposed to be anybody else nearby."

"Nobody's ever trespassed before?" I asked skeptically.

"Laurie Anne, you're not saying a thing I didn't

think myself. I assumed it was an accident, too, until the other incidents."

"What else has happened?"

"The next weekend, Maggie and I were at an auction. We ended up staying late talking to some people, and by the time we got out to the car, the lot was nearly empty, and quite dark."

"It was Red Clark's place," Aunt Maggie put in, "and you know Red is too cheap to put up lights in the parking lot."

Big Bill went on. "We were loading boxes in Maggie's car, when a pickup truck came from nowhere and nearly hit me. If I hadn't dropped the box I was carrying and ducked behind another car, he'd have got me."

Aunt Maggie said, "That truck ran right over that box, so the driver must have known he hit something, even if it wasn't Bill; but he didn't even slow down."

I started to object to that, too, but realized that there was no explanation I could suggest that Aunt Maggie and Big Bill wouldn't have considered first. "Anything else?"

Big Bill nodded and went a little pale. "The last one was the worst. I don't know if you've heard, but I bought up that apartment building on Debbie-Carroll Road."

"I thought they were going to tear that place down," I said, remembering what an eyesore it was.

"We may as well have, considering the amount of work it's taken to fix it up. I'm converting it into condos."

A few years ago I'd have laughed at the idea of condos in Byerly, but a fair number of folks had moved to town because it was close enough to Hickory to commute, and a lot cheaper.

Big Bill said, "I went over there last week to see how it was going—I've been making a point of checking things out every Thursday morning. I don't let the foreman show me around, either. I rummage around on my own—that's the only way to be sure it's being done right. They'd just finished putting in bathrooms for the units on the first floor, so that's where I went first. The first two bathrooms looked fine; a couple of taps needed to be tightened up, but nothing major. When I got to the third one, I noticed a puddle of water coming out the door. I yelled for the foreman to get over there and went to see what the problem was. If he hadn't been nearby . . ." He swallowed visibly. "I was a split second away from stepping into that water when the foreman pulled me back because he'd heard a snapping sound. There was a live wire in the water." He paused to make sure we got the point.

"How much voltage?" I asked.

"Enough to fry me like a piece of chicken."

I wrinkled my nose at the picture that put into my head. "Do you know who's doing this?"

"If I knew who it was, do you think he'd still be walking around?" Big Bill said peevishly.

"Do you have any enemies?"

"Of course I do," he said. "Do you think I've gotten where I am without making enemies? I've got a list as long as my arm." He sounded almost pleased, as if it were something to be proud of. "All I've got to do is figure out which one of them it is."

"All *we've* got to do," Aunt Maggie corrected him.

"That's right," he said with a smile for her. "My new wife is here to help."

"What about the police?" I said. "Don't you think Junior could help, too?"

"I don't need her help."

I started to object, but Big Bill held up one hand to stop me. "She's a fine chief of police, but there're some things a man needs to do for himself."

Aunt Maggie rolled her eyes. "What he means is that if we called Junior, she'd ask a lot of questions that Bill doesn't want to answer."

"Why not? Are you doing anything illegal?" I asked.

"Absolutely not!" Big Bill snapped. "That doesn't mean I want Junior Norton sticking her nose into my business."

I wasn't convinced that all of Big Bill's dealings were completely on the up-and-up, but saw no reason to argue the point. Especially since now he was my great-uncle. "Then why didn't you call Richard and me? We do have some experience in this kind of thing. Or do you not trust us, either?"

"Of course we trust you, Laurie Anne," Aunt Maggie said. "We just figured with the new baby, y'all wouldn't want to get mixed up in something like this."

"Alice does keep me busy," I said, "but not so busy I can't help my family when I'm needed." Not to mention the fact that as much as I loved being with my little girl, after seven months of maternity leave I was getting restless to do something a little more mentally challenging than changing diapers. Alice wasn't exactly a good conversationalist, and was no good at all for gossip.

"I knew you'd come if I asked," Aunt Maggie assured me. "The other thing was that Bill doesn't want everybody and his kid brother knowing somebody has been trying to kill him."

Darned if she hadn't hurt my feelings again. "Richard and I can keep a secret!"

She gave me a look. "How many times have you been mixed up in some murder or another? Do you honestly think people wouldn't notice you asking questions? How long would it take for folks to figure out that something was going on?"

"You've got a point," I had to admit.

"Besides," Big Bill said, "we figured we could handle it ourselves. As many murderers as you two have tracked down, how hard could it be?"

"Oh, not hard at all," I said dryly. "Have you got it all figured out yet?"

"Not quite," Big Bill said, "but we're making good progress."

Though Aunt Maggie rolled her eyes, she didn't contradict him out loud.

Richard said, "Not that I'm not concerned about Big Bill's welfare, but I'm having trouble seeing how this connects to your recent nuptials."

What with all the talk of attempted murder, I'd nearly forgotten about them getting married.

Aunt Maggie looked at Big Bill, but he just shrugged and said in an irritable tone, "You've told them this much. Why stop now?"

"That last attempt shook Bill up a bit," Aunt Maggie said.

"It would have shaken up anybody!" Big Bill said angrily.

"Nobody's saying you didn't have a right to be worried. Shoot, my hair would be as white as yours if it had happened to me."

Big Bill nodded, mollified.

"Anyway," Aunt Maggie went on, "he came over to my place afterward and we talked it all out. We know it's nigh onto impossible for anybody to be on guard twenty-four hours a day. A man's got to sleep some time, so Bill needed somebody to watch his back. That's where I come in."

"Couldn't Big Bill have hired a bodyguard?" I said.

"That would have scared off the killer!" Big Bill said.

"Why would that be a bad thing?" Richard wanted to know.

"Because then I wouldn't get a chance to catch him," Big Bill said as if it were the most obvious thing in the world. "There's no way that son of a—that so-and-so is going to get away with trying to kill Big Bill Walters." He drew himself up to his full height.

"Besides," Aunt Maggie said, "Bill couldn't keep a bodyguard around forever, which means that all the killer would have to do is wait and then try again. Better to find out who it is sooner rather than later."

Aunt Maggie's explanation made more sense to me than Big Bill's reasoning, but there was still a piece missing. "Okay, I can see why Big Bill wanted you around, Aunt Maggie, but why get married? Why not just move in temporarily, or have him stay with you?"

Big Bill let out a noise that could only have been a guffaw, and at first I thought he was laughing at the idea of his staying at the Burnette home place, which was admittedly not up to the standards of the Walters mansion. Then I saw Aunt Maggie's expression.

"Move in, just like that?" she said in a scandalized tone. "Laurie Anne, maybe girls your age don't care about such things, but I'm not about to have the town of Byerly talking about me behind my back. I've got my reputation to think about."

"'The purest treasure mortal times afford is spotless reputation.' *King Richard II*, Act I, Scene 1," Richard said so solemnly that only I knew how close he was to snickering.

As for me, I did know what she was talking about, even if being a "good girl" wasn't something that I'd ever worried about myself. Of course, with her clothes and occasionally abrupt manner, Aunt Maggie already had a reputation in Byerly as an eccentric, but Southerners like a good eccentric, and I'd long suspected that Aunt Maggie took pride in being one of the best in town.

"Has it worked?" I asked. "I mean, have you learned anything? Have there been any more attempts on Big Bill's life?"

"Not a one," Aunt Maggie said, "and no matter what Bill says, we don't have any idea who's after him."

I looked at Richard with a question in my eyes, and he hesitated, looking at Alice. Then he nodded, so I said, "Do you want Richard and me to help?"

"That would be great," Aunt Maggie said, but at the same time, Big Bill was saying, "That won't be necessary."

The two of them glared at each other again. Big Bill said, "Maggie, I told you I wanted us to handle this ourselves."

"And I said I'd try, which I have, but we've got nothing."

"That's not true." He waved at the stack of papers on his desk. "We've got these threatening letters to go through—I bet we'll figure out who it is from these."

"Those are *all* threats?" I said, looking at the two-inch-thick stack. Other than bills and solicitations, I didn't get that many letters in a year.

Neither of them answered me. "We decided—" Big Bill started, and Aunt Maggie countered with, "*You* decided and I went along. But that was before Laurie Anne came to town, and I think—"

Alice chose that moment to start crying.

"I think she's picking up on the tension," Richard said accusingly, and plucked her from Aunt Maggie's arms to comfort her.

"You see, Maggie," Big Bill said, "they can't be chasing after a murderer when they've got a baby to tend to."

I was tempted to argue with him, but then I felt the tingle that meant my milk was starting to let down because of Alice's crying. Maybe Big Bill was right. "Excuse me," I said, "I've got to feed Alice."

"Do you want me to get Irene to warm up a bottle?" Big Bill asked.

"I'm not bottle-feeding," I said.

"Oh? Oh!" He started for the door. "I need to be getting back to work, anyway—I'll just use one of the other rooms."

"This discussion isn't over, Bill Walters," Aunt Maggie yelled to his rapidly retreating back.

Alice wailed again, and Aunt Maggie looked repentant. "Maybe I better leave y'all alone."

After Aunt Maggie closed the door behind her, I took a deep breath, wanting to release some of my own tension before nursing Alice. Then I settled down on the couch, undid my blouse, and reached for her.

Richard, who was used to the procedure after seven months, helped me get her situated, then sat down beside me. "It looks as if we're in for another relaxing visit."

"Sorry about that. I bet you wish you'd married into another family."

"No other family could have produced somebody as wonderful as you," he said, and kissed my cheek. "Not to mention our little princess here."

"Do all daddies call their little girls princesses?"

"Purely conceit on our part. It's our way of complimenting ourselves, since the father of a princess has to be a king."

"I never thought of that. Does that make me a queen?"

"Of course. The queen of my heart."

"I hope that when Alice learns to talk she talks as pretty as you do." Aunt Maggie had been worried about her first words being cuss words, but with a Boston College Shakespeare professor as a father, she was more likely to start spouting Elizabethan prose. Or maybe she'd speak bits and bytes first, since she had a computer programmer for a mother.

I knew it was the hormones surging as I nursed her, but I was feeling almost serene right then, despite the oddity of the situation. "I cannot believe I'm nursing our baby in the Walters mansion. Or that Big Bill is married to Aunt Maggie."

"Or that somebody is trying to kill him?"

"No, that part I can believe."

"Is that any way to talk about your own uncle?"

"He's only an uncle by marriage. Not that Big Bill isn't a nice man in his own way, or Aunt Maggie wouldn't give him the time of day, let alone her hand in marriage. But he's a lot more mellow now than he used to be. According to everything I've heard, he was a ruthless businessman in his time, and he's still a tough man to work with. I'm sure he's got plenty of enemies. Look at that stack of hate mail on his desk."

"Do you think we should?" Richard said with an impish grin.

I was tempted, but shook my head. "We better not. Unless Aunt Maggie gets Big Bill to change his mind, we're not going to get involved in this."

"You don't think she's going to give up, do you?"

"It's hard to say. We're talking about the original irresistible force meeting the archetypal immovable object. In other words, they're both as stubborn as mules."

"It must be a family trait," he said.

"Keep it up, and you can be on diaper duty all week!"

"Anything but that," he said with a mock quaver in his voice. Or maybe not mock. Alice's diapers were pretty scary. "But back to the matter at hand. Are you going to stay uninvolved just because Big Bill says so?"

"Isn't that enough?"

"Laura, no offense, but telling you *not* to do something is generally the best way to get you to do it."

"Diaper duty for sure," I said, but he was right.

"Okay, usually I would see it as a challenge, but this time I'm going to abide by Big Bill's wishes. For one, I don't see how much good we could do if he doesn't want us to help. Sure, we could snoop around and find out some of the gossip, but Big Bill is pretty good at keeping his business to himself."

"Don't forget that very available stack of letters," Richard said, starting to get up. "That would give us a place to start."

"Sit down. The other problem is that he's married to Aunt Maggie."

"Having a family member involved generally guarantees our involvement."

"I'm not talking about family, I'm talking marriages. As old as they are, Aunt Maggie and Big Bill are still newlyweds, and I don't want to add stress and strain to a brand-new marriage. This one's got enough working against it as it is."

"But they only got married so Aunt Maggie could protect Big Bill," Richard said. "It's not a real marriage, is it?"

"I don't know, Richard. I can't see Aunt Maggie promising to love, honor, and cherish Big Bill unless she meant it. Even if they did use Bill's situation as an excuse, how do we know they weren't moving toward marriage already? I don't want to mess it up."

"You're a hopeless romantic, you know?" he said, kissing me again, more thoroughly than before.

Richard was so thorough, in fact, that it took a minute for the tap on the door to register. By the time I realized that somebody had knocked, Burt Walters was walking in the door.

If nursing a baby in Big Bill's house had felt surreal, that was nothing to how I felt having Burt in the same room as me when my shirt was open. Sure, I had a cloth thrown over my shoulder so nothing actually showed, but I still wasn't completely dressed, and I could tell from the way Burt's face turned bright red, that he knew it, too.

"Uh, hello there," he stammered. "I thought you were my daddy. I mean, I thought Daddy would be in here. But he's not and you are and . . ." I think Burt is an inch or two taller than his father, but Big Bill has so much personality that he seems a lot bigger than his son. Burt kept his hair dyed dark, and I was always surprised he didn't try to bleach it to the same pure white as his father's. As far as I could tell, that hair was the only thing he willingly did differently from his father.

Before Burt could figure out what he really wanted to say, Big Bill pushed past him, with Aunt Maggie following.

"Don't you ever knock?" Big Bill said, sounding irritated.

"I did knock," Burt protested. "Nobody answered."

"Then why did you come in? Were you planning to nose around while I wasn't here?"

"Of course not, Daddy." Burt looked even more flustered. "I thought you hadn't heard me."

"So you wanted to sneak up on me?"

"No, I just . . ." Probably realizing the futility of the argument, Burt changed the subject. "I brought you those numbers you wanted from the mill."

He held out some sheets of paper, and Big Bill snatched them away. "Aren't you even going to speak to your stepmother?"

I was impressed when Burt managed to smile. "Hey, Miz Burnette." Then he caught the thunderous expression on his father's face. "I mean, Maggie." Big Bill looked even more angry. "I mean . . ." Burt swallowed. "You know, we've never worked out what I should be calling you now."

"You could call her Mrs. Walters, since she's my wife!" Big Bill growled.

Aunt Maggie took pity on Burt. "That's a mite too formal for every day," she said. "I don't think you'd feel right calling me Maggie, and I'm not your mama, so we won't even go there. Why not call me Aunt Maggie? Would that go down easier?"

"Yes, ma'am," Burt said. "I mean, yes, Aunt Maggie." Before his father could chide him again, he added, "It's good to see you, too, Laurie Anne, Richard. That must be the new baby I've heard so much about."

"Yes, sir, this is Alice."

"Now, don't call me 'sir,'" Burt said. "Like Daddy said, we're all family now." He beamed at his father, looking like a puppy hoping to be rewarded for a clever trick.

Unfortunately, the only treat he got was Big Bill barking, "What in the Sam Hill is going on down there at the mill? These numbers are a joke!"

Burt hurried to his father's side. "Let me explain what I've done," he started, and the two of them started speaking business or accounting or some other language I don't know.

While they were distracted, I decided that Alice had nursed long enough and managed to detach her, hand her off to Richard for burping, and get my shirt put together again. While I knew mothers who assured me that breastfeeding was as natural as breathing and that there was no reason on earth a woman shouldn't nurse her child anywhere, I still didn't like doing it in public.

Burt and Big Bill finished their money talk, with Big Bill looking disgruntled and Burt looking worried. But Burt managed to pull up another smile and stepped over to Richard.

"Now, that is a pretty baby," he said to Richard as he gently chucked her under the chin. "Every inch a Burnette, too."

"Her head is shaped like Richard's," I said again.

"Do you want to come to Uncle Burt?" he cooed at Alice, then stopped. "Or is it Cousin Burt? I'm all confused now."

"That's hardly news," Big Bill said sarcastically.

"Would you like to hold her?" Richard asked, ignoring Big Bill, and passed her over. Burt held her gingerly, but he looked delighted to have a baby in his arms. Maybe this mixing of Burnettes and Walterses was going to work out after all.

Then Big Bill said, "It's just as well you didn't have any children, Burt. Having a child that disappoints you is the worst thing on earth."

Burt's face went white. Not only was his father being insulting, but the reminder of his childlessness must have stung even more. Burt and his wife had wanted a family, but Dorcas couldn't carry a child, and the doctors had insisted on a hysterectomy after her last miscarriage.

In a choked voice Burt said, "I better get these reports straightened out." He handed Alice back to Richard and left without saying another word.

Big Bill stared after him, and I realized Alice was starting to get anxious again. It was amazing how much an infant could pick up on bad feelings, and there were definitely bad feelings between Big Bill and his son. Not to mention my feelings—I was appalled that Big Bill would talk to Burt that way.

Of course, I didn't think they'd ever had a normal relationship. Big Bill had always favored Small Bill, his firstborn son, even after he got word of Small Bill's death in Vietnam. Burt had spent his whole life trying to earn the regard his father gave to Small Bill unconditionally, and had never quite managed it. If that weren't complicated enough, there were facts about Small Bill's death that Big Bill didn't know, things I'd discovered almost by accident. Still, I'd never seen Big Bill treat Burt that way in public. Had Burt objected to his father's new marriage, or was there something else going on?

"Well," I said, breaking the awkward silence, "Richard and I better get going so we can get ready for the party. Aunt Maggie, are you sure you don't mind our staying at your place? At your other place, I mean." Aunt Maggie was the current owner of the Burnette home place, the house where I'd lived myself when being raised by my grandfather Paw, and we usually stayed with her when we were in town.

"Of course I don't mind," she said.

"Why don't you stay here?" Big Bill said, shaking himself out of his angry mood. "There's plenty of room."

I looked at Richard, but he shrugged, leaving it up to me. "Thanks, but we'll be fine at Aunt Maggie's. Aunt Nora's already got a crib set up for Alice."

"All right, then. We'll see you tonight."

Richard grabbed the diaper bag, and Aunt Maggie said, "I'll walk y'all out. Bobbin needs to take a trip to the yard, and I hate to think what Irene Duffield would do if she had an accident."

I was just as glad, because after seeing the way Big Bill was with Burt, I was starting to realize that there was something missing in what he'd told us, and I thought I knew what it was. The question was, did Aunt Maggie know?

Once we were outside, I let Richard get Alice settled into her car seat while I walked a piece with Aunt Maggie so Bobbin could do her business. "Aunt Maggie, Big Bill thinks he knows who's trying to kill him, doesn't he?"

"He says he doesn't," she said, but didn't meet my eyes.

"Then why this marriage?"

"We told you. So he'd have somebody to watch his back."

I hesitated, but had to ask the next question. "Has Big Bill changed his will since y'all got married?"

"If you think I only married him for his money—"

"That's not what I'm saying."

"So why bring it up?"

She was being deliberately ornery, and I knew she was trying to get me off the subject, so I held onto my temper as best I could. "The three big reasons for killing are revenge, sex, and money. Your marriage wouldn't stop anybody from killing Big Bill for revenge or sex, so there would have been no reason for y'all to get married if either of those were the motive. But money— that's a different matter."

"Anybody with as much money as Bill has is always a target," she said, but still didn't look me in the eye.

"If Big Bill had died last week, who would have benefited?"

"There are a lot of names in the will."

"I'm sure he made some bequests, but everybody in town knows that Burt is supposed to inherit everything else. Only now that y'all are married, he's left it all to you, hasn't he?" She didn't answer, but she didn't contradict me, either, so I followed the thought to its logical conclusion. "Big Bill thinks Burt is trying to kill him, doesn't he?"

Aunt Maggie didn't say anything for a long time, just watched Bobbin sniff around the grass. "He hasn't said so, Laurie Anne, not even to me, but I think you're right. He just can't say it out loud. Can you imagine thinking such a thing about your own flesh and blood?"

Seeing how cruel Big Bill had been to Burt, I didn't feel so kindly toward him. Besides, I'd realized something else. "Aunt Maggie, don't you realize that Big Bill's set you up as a target, too?"

"He's done no such thing!" Aunt Maggie snapped.

"Then what happens if you die before Big Bill, or if you die together? The money will go to Burt after all, won't it?"

"Yes, but that's not the point."

"But—"

"I knew all along that I'd be in danger if Bill and I went through with the wedding. I'm not stupid, Laurie Anne."

"I know you're not—"

"Is that right? Then why did you assume that I didn't realize what was going on?"

"I didn't assume . . ." Then I stopped, not sure I'd be telling the truth. "Okay, maybe I did. I'm just worried about you, Aunt Maggie. Big Bill's got a lot of enemies, whether or not Burt is one of them."

"I know. That's why I'm here. Bill doesn't have anybody else he can trust right now. And nobody, not even Big Bill Walters, should be all by his lonesome when there's a killer after him. Laurie Anne, when you get to be my age, you'll realize being alone is scarier than just about anything else."

I tried to understand what she was saying. I had no particular fear of being alone myself, not with Richard and Alice, plus all my cousins and aunts and uncles. But Big Bill was in a very different place, both because he didn't have as much family and because of the way he'd lived his life. It was easy to say that he deserved to be alone, but who was I to judge anybody else?

I finally said, "All right, Aunt Maggie, as long as you know what you're doing, and as long as you know you can call on me or Richard any time you need us."

"I do know that, Laurie Anne, and I appreciate it."

Then she grinned. "You know, nobody's tried to mother me since my own mama died—and she didn't try it all that often. I think your having Alice has gone to your head."

I wanted to argue with her, but she started laughing, so I figured it wasn't worth the trouble. She was still laughing at me when we left.

Chapter
Four

As I drove toward Aunt Maggie's house, I told Richard what I'd guessed and how Aunt Maggie had confirmed it.

"So Big Bill thinks his own son is trying to kill him," he said. "There's plenty of precedent for it, of course. All the way back to Oedipus killing Laius, and Goneril and Regan going after Lear."

Not to mention an incident in Byerly we'd been involved in, I thought to myself.

Richard said, "Do you think Burt is a killer?"

I considered it. "I can't know for sure, Richard, but I sure don't see it. Burt doesn't seem like the murdering kind, for one, and he's going to get Big Bill's money eventually anyway."

"Maybe he needs money in a hurry. Gambling debts or something like that. If he still has an eye for the ladies, that can cause unexpected expenses."

"Maybe," I said, "but I think he's got a fair amount of money of his own, and surely he'd be able to raise more, just by virtue of being Burt Walters. Besides, I really think he loves his father."

"Even with the way Big Bill treats him?"

"Wasn't that awful? Big Bill never used to be that bad. I think he's only acting that nasty now because he suspects him. Though he may be missing a suspect."

"Who?"

"Dorcas. Burt's wife would have just as much to gain from Big Bill's death as Burt would."

"They could be in it together," Richard pointed out.

"True." Alice picked that moment to start babbling from the backseat. I said, "Alice, please don't ever try to kill your father."

"Don't even joke about it," Richard warned me. "Come to think of it, how much longer do we have to speak freely around Alice?"

"According to Aunt Maggie, no time at all, at least where swear words are concerned. Why?"

"I was just thinking that we're going to have to be careful not to talk about the murders we've been involved in. Though I suppose she'll find out about them someday."

"In this family? Count on it."

"What do you suppose she'll think of it all?"

"If she's like most kids, she'll think we're the biggest geeks on earth, and that our entire goal in life is to embarrass her at every opportunity."

"Only when she's a teenager."

I shuddered. Having a baby had been scary enough, but a teenager . . . "Maybe she'll be a natural-born sleuth and help us."

"No way!" Richard said. "She stays out of it!"

I looked at him in surprise. "That's awfully Neanderthal of you."

"I mean it. I'm not letting our little girl put herself in danger."

"If she acts like my side of the family as much as she

looks like it, I don't know that we'll have a choice."
Seeing the fierce look on my husband's face, I reached
over and patted his leg reassuringly. "Richard, she's
seven months old. We don't have to worry about this for
a while yet."

"Maybe not," he conceded, "but I've been thinking
about it."

"I thought we had this discussion when I was pregnant. We decided that as long as we were careful, we
shouldn't let a baby completely change who we are."

"But it's not 'a baby' anymore. It's Alice."

"You lost me."

"I'm not sure I understand this myself, Laura. It's just
that I feel so protective of Alice now that she's here. I
can't stand the idea of her facing the kinds of danger
we've been in."

"Richard, we're not going to carry Alice into a shoot-
out."

"I know, but we've also got a responsibility to take
care of ourselves, for her sake. I don't want our child to
be an orphan."

"I don't want *any* child to be an orphan," I said,
thinking of my own parents, who'd died in a car crash
when I was fifteen. Aunt Maggie had talked about how
scary it was for an older person to be alone, but I
thought that it was even more terrifying for a child or a
teenager. I remembered how I'd felt, even though I'd
known I had people who loved me, and the idea of
Alice going through that sickened me.

Of course, my parents couldn't help what happened
to them—they'd been driving safely, wearing their seat
belts, when a tractor-trailer jackknifed because of another driver's antics. Still, there were things I could do
to take care of myself and Richard. "Here's what I think,"
I said. "Whether or not we get involved in Big Bill's pro-

blems, or anybody else's, we have to swear not to put ourselves in jeopardy if there's any way we can avoid it. Agreed?"

"Agreed."

A minute later, I pulled into the carport at Aunt Maggie's house. When most people think of Southern houses, they probably either think of mansions like the Walterses' or tarpaper shacks. What I think of is the Burnette home place, an old farmhouse that started out small but grew as the family did. And just as siblings don't always favor each other, the house's additions don't look much like one another. Still, they've managed to hold together well enough for an awful lot of Burnettes to be born there, live there, and sometimes die there.

I'd lived there with Paw, and when he died, he passed it on to his sister, Aunt Maggie. I wondered what she'd do with it now that she was ensconced at the Walters mansion. Whatever she decided, I knew she'd never sell it. I think any of the Burnettes would rather have sold our right arm than that house.

I had my own key, and when I opened the door, I was surprised by how empty the house felt, even though Aunt Maggie had moved out less than two weeks before. Not that there was any dust to be seen. When they'd heard Richard and I were bringing Alice down, a bevy of aunts had converged to make sure everything was ready for us—it was probably cleaner than when Aunt Maggie was living there.

There was a stack of used but clean baby toys in a milk crate in the living room, and when we carried our suitcases upstairs to the bedroom, we found a crib set up, complete with a Mickey Mouse mobile dangling overhead. Somebody had even put a changing table in the bathroom.

They'd also stocked the refrigerator: I recognized

Aunt Nora's fried chicken, Aunt Daphine's apple cobbler, and a dish of lasagna that had been made with Richard's recipe. If that weren't enough, they'd left sandwich fixings and a big pitcher of iced tea, too.

"You know, my aunts could give the people at the Four Seasons in Boston lessons in welcoming guests," I told Richard.

"I suppose we'll be having dinner at the party," he said regretfully, eyeing the fried chicken.

"Aunt Nora said they were having a buffet," I said, but I was tempted, too. "You know, it wouldn't hurt to grab a bite now. In case we get too busy visiting to eat anything later."

"Good point," he said, and reached for the chicken. "I wonder if Aunt Nora brought biscuits."

She had, of course, and we ate enough so that we wouldn't need to eat anything at the party, and probably not for breakfast, either. I almost felt sorry for Alice for not getting to share in the bounty, but decided I was only eating that much for her benefit, anyway.

Once we were finished and I fed Alice, it was time to get ready for the party. "Does this look all right?" I asked Richard. I hadn't had much of a choice when I was packing for the trip, because I only had two nice outfits that buttoned down the front so I could nurse Alice. I'd picked my aqua suit because I thought it wouldn't show spit-up as much as my navy blue dress.

"You look fine."

"Are you sure? I don't want to look bad next to the Walterses."

"Laurie Anne, how does Aunt Maggie dress?"

"She's not going to wear a T-shirt to her wedding reception."

"Are you sure?"

"No," I had to say. "Anyway, nobody is going to notice

me anyway, not as long as I'm holding this baby." Richard's mother had given me the dress I'd put on Alice, and while I objected to dressing little girls in pink and ruffles all the time, I was willing to let one slip in now and then. Besides, it had the cutest little hat to go with it.

I'd pulled the car right up to the front door when we went to visit Aunt Maggie that afternoon, but by the time we got back, there wasn't room left to get in the driveway. Instead, a woman in a Byerly police uniform waved us to a nearby church parking lot that was a third full already.

"That wasn't Junior, was it?" Richard asked.

"Not unless she's grown a foot and gained a good fifty pounds," I said. "I think it was Belva Tucker. I heard she'd come to work for Junior."

"The deputy from Rocky Shoals?"

I nodded. We'd had a disagreement with Belva a while back[3], but Junior had needed an experienced deputy after losing her own[4], and I was willing to give her the benefit of the doubt.

I recognized most of the other people who drove or walked past us. They were dressed up, too, and almost certainly on their way to the party. Aunt Maggie hadn't been kidding when she said Vasti had invited everybody in Byerly. There are so many of us Burnettes that we can fill a church hall all by ourselves, but we were going to be in the minority this time.

There was a line when we got to the front door. Dorcas Walters had just let in a pair of women and was turning to the man in front of her with a determinedly welcoming smile on her face. I didn't really blame her

[3] *Tight as a Tick*
[4] *Mad as the Dickens*

for having to work at it. Though tattoos were hip in many circles, even in Byerly, I was pretty sure that they weren't common with Dorcas's friends. Besides, even folks who like tattoos don't usually sport as many as Tattoo Bob Tyndall, the artist who plied his trade at the flea market where Aunt Maggie set up. Tattoo Bob had once told me he considered himself his best advertisement, so naturally he wore short-sleeved shirts whenever possible. I counted five visible tattoos, and knew there were more that Dorcas didn't see—and wouldn't want to. Here I'd been worrying about how Dorcas would deal with the Burnette family—I'd forgotten about some of the characters Aunt Maggie was friends with.

As Tattoo Bob went inside, Dorcas turned to Richard and me with an air of relief. "Laurie Anne, Richard. I'm so glad y'all could come. Is this the little darling Burt told me about?"

I suspected that if Dorcas had been involved in as many two-o'clock feedings as I had, she wouldn't think our baby was so adorable, but I nodded anyway. "This is Alice."

Dorcas didn't take her from me, probably in deference to the royal blue silk dress she was wearing, but she did look at her wistfully. "You're just a little baby doll," she said to her. "Yes, you are." To Richard and me, she said, "Come right in. Most of your family is already here."

I couldn't resist saying, "Don't you mean *our* family?"

Her smile tightened a bit around the edges. "Of course. Our family."

Though I was tempted to stick around to see how Dorcas would deal with the rest of the arriving Burnettes and flea market denizens, the lure of people inside was too great. After all, we had a baby to show off.

Aunt Nora must have been watching for us, because

she jumped up from her chair as soon as we walked into the living room. "Oh, my Lord," she said as she took Alice from me, "she's as pretty as an angel!"

I leaned over, meaning to hug Aunt Nora's neck, but Aunt Nora pulled away to yell, "Daphine! Nellie! Ruby Lee! Edna! The baby's here!"

I looked at Richard, who raised an eyebrow. "Do you suppose she's even noticed we're here, too?" I asked.

"Maybe she thinks Alice flew in on angel's wings," he suggested.

Seconds later, the rest of my mother's sisters arrived, all cooing and chirping. Richard and I were pushed out of the circle completely, but could tell that Alice didn't mind the attention. Maybe she knew they were all family, even if the sisters were all so different.

Aunt Nora has a figure I've always thought of as matronly. Not really fat, but definitely thicker in places than she used to be. At least her hair was the same color as always, thanks to Clairol.

Aunt Daphine also owed her dark hair to judicious application of color, but didn't resemble Aunt Nora in any other way. She was tall and thin, with well-defined cheekbones and brows.

Aunt Ruby Lee's hair is reputed to be glossy blond naturally, and her blue eyes, dimpled cheeks, and generous curves made her look like a replica of Dolly Parton done to actual human scale.

Aunt Edna was slender, and her eyes and hair were all nice enough, but it wasn't her looks that made her memorable. It was her wit and the way she moved that reminded everybody of the spitfire she was as a girl.

Aunt Nellie, the tallest of them, was a study in contrasts. Her hair was nearly black, her skin quite fair. Tonight she was wearing her trademark color of peacock blue in a striking pantsuit, with big hoop earrings.

"Hey there," I said, but my aunts kept on admiring Alice as if I hadn't spoken. "Hello?"

"You said you wanted to show her off," Richard reminded me. "Why don't we go enjoy the party? We can pick up Alice when it's time to go."

"Ha, ha," I said, but it was starting to look as if we really could leave without being noticed, when Aunt Daphine finally glanced our way. She'd only had one child herself, so maybe she wasn't as baby crazy as the others. Goodness knows that if I ever gave birth to a daughter like my cousin Vasti, I'd be leery of babies.

Aunt Daphine said, "Hey there, little mama," and gave my neck a hug. "And hello to the new daddy, too," she added, hugging Richard. "Will she be calling you that? I don't know what folks in Massachusetts call their daddies."

"So far we haven't even gotten a 'Da-da' out of her, so it's still a moot point," Richard said.

We laughed, but I'd already decided that what Alice called me was *not* a moot point. I'd called my mother Mama, and she'd called her mother Mama, and so on. Alice was going to call me Mama, even if she had to say it with a Boston accent.

Aunt Daphine chatted with us a little longer, but I could tell she was dying for a chance to hold Alice; so I told her she could go ahead and get in line while Richard and I hunted up something to drink.

It didn't take much hunting. Tables with soft drinks, wine, beer, and iced tea had been set up in several corners around the bottom floor of the house, and there was plenty of food around, too, from finger food to serious munchies on a long buffet table. I had to admit that Vasti knew how to throw a party—I almost regretted eating that fried chicken.

The decorations were nicely understated, too. Since

Vasti isn't known for her subtlety, I'd expected her to festoon the place with tissue-paper wedding bells and such, but maybe she'd decided that the Walterses' rich furnishings were impressive enough. She'd settled for placing flower arrangements designed to look like bridal bouquets here and there, and the buffet table featured a four-tier wedding cake draped with luscious pink icing flowers.

It was next to the buffet table that I spotted my cousin in heated conversation with Miz Duffield.

Vasti was saying, "You were supposed to rent glass plates and cups, not use paper."

Miz Duffield sniffed. "I thought paper would be more appropriate." She looked pointedly at my cousin Linwood, who was noisily sucking the filling from a celery straw. "Besides, all the available rental items had already been reserved. Most affairs of this style are planned months in advance."

Vasti sniffed back at her. "Some of us don't need that long to plan a nice party. I mean, *affair*. And what about the band? I told you to leave room for the Ramblers to set up, and you've got a bunch of old guys with violins in their corner."

"Those 'old guys' are the area's finest string quartet. Mrs. Walters—Mrs. Dorcas Walters—is particularly fond of string quartets. She prefers not to drown out the conversation of her guests with raucous music. Though in this case . . ." She looked over at Linwood again, who was loudly telling a raunchy joke about a preacher and a traveling salesman to some of my other cousins. "We've never had the kind of 'music' you're talking about."

"That's because I've never been in charge before. I am now, and I say that the Ramblers are going to play here tonight. Roger is part of the family, after all." The look she gave Miz Duffield emphasized that *she* was not.

Miz Duffield drew herself up to her full height. "In the Walters home . . ."

Big Bill appeared next to them, looking particularly genial. "Ladies, what's the problem?"

"Just a disagreement over the arrangements, Mr. Big Bill," Miz Duffield said smoothly. "Nothing for you to concern yourself with."

"Is that right, Vasti?" Big Bill said.

"Apparently, your maid here doesn't think Roger's Ramblers are good enough to play for the party."

"I said no such thing. I merely pointed out that in the past, we've—"

"Things change, Irene. Do what Vasti says."

"But Mr. Big Bill—" She visibly stopped herself. "Yes, sir. However, I'm concerned about the champagne Mrs. Bumgarner selected for your toast. It's not the label we've used before, and I know how particular you are about your champagne. If you like, I can get a case of the correct label delivered right away."

"I'm sure Vasti's champagne will be fine," he said in a tone that left no room for argument. Then he smiled again, took a tiny quiche from the buffet table, and wandered away.

Vasti looked smug, but poor Miz Duffield looked as if she was going to cry. So I popped up with, "Why don't y'all use both bands? The quartet can stay where they are, and the Ramblers can set up somewhere else."

"Where?" Vasti demanded.

"Isn't there a gazebo out on the grounds? There'd be a whole lot more room for dancing out there." Vasti looked stubborn, so I added, "On a nice night like this, folks will be able to hear the music for miles around."

I hoped Vasti would go for the idea of letting the few people who hadn't been invited know exactly what they were missing. "All right," she said. "Set it up that way,

Irene." She turned her back on the woman so she could give Richard and me quick hugs, asked a couple of perfunctory questions about Alice, and pasted on her party smile so she could go greet some of the people she wanted to impress.

I turned to Miz Duffield. "I'm afraid this marriage is going to mean a lot of adjustments for both sides of the family."

"Clearly," Miz Duffield said. "I am glad to see that *some* members of the Burnette family were brought up properly." She walked away as stiffly as if she had had a broomstick tied to her spine.

"I'm not too well brought up to smack somebody who insults my family," I said to Richard.

"Laura," Richard said, "be nice."

"Hey, I fixed it so she could keep her string quartet, didn't I? It's bad enough that the Walterses have looked down on us Burnettes for years, but to have a servant do it gripes the tar out of me."

"Now who's being a snob?"

I stopped. "You're right, that was uncalled-for. Miz Duffield would irritate me no matter what she did for a living."

We finally got our drinks—iced tea for me and Coke for Richard—then went to retrieve Alice. I'd like to pretend that she'd missed us, but in fact she was having a grand time being made much of. So we went in search of others who would admire her. We hadn't gone far when my cousin Thaddeous's fiancée found us.

"Laura!" Michelle squealed, and gave me a loud smack on the cheek. "Or should I call you Laurie Anne, since I'm a bona fide Southerner now."

Michelle, with her olive skin, jet black hair, and Boston accent, was about as likely to be mistaken for a native Southerner as I was to be taken for a French poodle. But ever since she'd moved to Byerly to be closer to Thaddeous, she'd thrown herself into Southern life with a vengeance. I'd heard her refer to the Civil War as the War Between the States, and she claimed to have come up with a recipe for grits with marinara sauce.

"Let me see that baby!" she said, taking Alice out of my hands. "She looks just like you."

I thought I heard a muffled sigh from Richard, so once again, I pointed out that Alice's head was shaped like his. Michelle nodded politely but clearly had no idea what I was talking about.

"So tell me everything about being a mother. Is she sleeping through the night? Are you exhausted? You are nursing her, aren't you? Have you started her on solid foods yet?"

"Not yet, yes, yes, and yes," I said, counting them off on my fingers. "You know, I think I ought to get a T-shirt printed with the answers to the standard questions."

Michelle dimpled. "I know, everybody must be asking you the same things over and over again." She pinched Alice's chubby cheek gently, and while Alice looked confused, at least she didn't cry. "I shouldn't do that. I used to hate it when my aunts and uncles pinched my cheek, but I just couldn't help myself."

"I understand," I said. "I find myself making raspberries on her tummy, myself."

"What about you, Richard?" Michelle asked. "What family traditions do you inflict on your poor child?"

"We don't really have any traditions like that," Richard said.

"Oh yeah?" I said. "What about—?"

"Look, there's Augustus and Willis. I think I'll go say hello." He beat a hasty retreat.

"All right, what does he do?" Michelle had to know.

"He talks baby talk."

"So what? Everybody talks baby talk."

"Yeah, but Richard quotes Shakespeare in baby talk."

She burst out laughing. "You are kidding me."

"I swear. He stops if he hears me coming, but I'm going to hide a tape recorder one of these days and catch him at it."

We spent a few minutes more extolling Alice's many virtues, and then moved on to office gossip. Michelle had been the receptionist at my company before Thaddeous lured her to Byerly, and even though I was on maternity leave, I had news that was current enough to satisfy her.

Then I asked, "What about the mill? Anything juicy going on there?" With a little family help, Michelle had landed the plum job of secretary to Burt Walters. "How is Burt to work for?"

"Not bad, once I got him straight on a few things."

"Like what?"

"Like the fact that I'm engaged, and even if I weren't, I wouldn't mess around with him."

"He made a pass at you?"

She shrugged in a very Italian way. "Please, he makes passes at everybody. Which I used to think was because of what a cold fish his wife is, but now . . ."

There was no way I could resist an opening like that. "But now?"

"Now I've got to wonder if maybe he wasn't just making passes at women to hide what he's really interested in." She waggled her eyebrows. "I think Burt has lace on his drawers, as Thaddeous would say."

"You think Burt Walters is gay!" I said in astonishment.

"Shhh! Keep your voice down!"

We looked around, but as far as we could tell, nobody had heard my outburst.

"Come on, Michelle, he's been married for years,

and he always chased women like crazy. Including my mother, as a matter of fact."

"As if no man ever covered up that way. Not to mention the guys who don't want to be gay, so they work so hard at being straight that they go after anything in a skirt."

"Sure, that happens," I acknowledged. "But Burt? Why on earth do you think he's gay?"

"If you saw his new protégé, you wouldn't ask. About three months ago, Burt hires this guy young enough to be his son. Good-looking, too—half the single girls at the mill are in lust with him. Anyway, Burt takes a personal interest in him and starts telling him all about running the mill. He takes him to lunch all the time, and some folks have seen them together after working hours."

"Really?"

"Now, I don't ask any questions about things that aren't part of my job—"

"Of course not," I said, even though I knew darned well that Michelle took every possible opportunity to find out what went on in the places she worked.

"But I do ask why it is Mike—that's his name, Mike—I ask Burt what I'm supposed to tell people who wonder why Mike isn't working his way through the ranks like anybody else. And Burt tells me that Mike is too smart to waste his time that way. That he's Mike's mentor, and he's training him to take over the mill. Which has all the other managers ready to go ballistic. Some of them have been there forever, going up one step at a time, and the idea of Mike bypassing them is making them crazy. Tavis is running himself into the ground trying to keep everybody happy."

"Tavis?" Tavis Montgomery was Burt's second in command, and his ambition was well known. "I'm surprised he's not as mad as everybody else."

"Oh, he was furious, but it didn't take him long to realize that there's nothing he can do about it. So now he's pretending everything is okay, and hoping Mike screws up badly enough for Burt to get rid of him. Then he can get his old place at the conference table back."

"Does Dorcas know?"

"Of course she knows—she's not blind!"

"Has she said anything? Or done anything?"

"Her? Of course not. But listen, have you ever seen Dorcas Walters at the mill?"

"Never."

"That's right. A society woman like her has more important things to do. But a few weeks after Mike started at the mill, here comes Dorcas, wanting Burt to take her to lunch. She started showing up at quitting time to remind him of their plans for the evening, and one time she even came during coffee break to bring him fresh donuts. And dressed to the nines every time. A new hairstyle, too, and I think she's lost ten pounds."

"Poor Dorcas," I said.

"It's a waste of time, anyway. How can any woman compete with a guy? Let alone a guy so much younger than she is?"

"Do you think Burt is going to leave her? Or that she'll ask for a divorce?"

"Who knows? Burt doesn't need to do anything—he's getting it both ways, if you know what I mean, so why rock the boat? And Dorcas is so big on being Mrs. Burt Walters that it's going to take a lot to get her to give that up. Me, I'd dump him out on his ear. I've got nothing against gays, but I'm not going to waste my time playing camouflage for anybody. Not that I've got anything to worry about with Thaddeous."

"Not hardly," I said. Thaddeous was so much in love with Michelle that his feet had barely touched the ground since she moved to town. So it was no big surprise that he happened to come by right then, and conversation turned back to how wonderful Alice was. From the gleam in his eyes when he watched Michelle cradling her, I had a hunch that marriage and babies would be in the very near future for those two.

While Michelle and Thaddeous played peek-a-boo with Alice, I speculated on whether or not Burt's newfound leanings had anything to do with the attempts on Big Bill's life. Did Big Bill know about Mike? Would he accept it if he did know, or would he disinherit Burt? I hadn't been able to picture Burt committing murder just to get his money a little sooner, but it was a different story if Burt was worried about losing everything.

By the same token, Dorcas might want to get rid of Big Bill before he found out. Her lifestyle was as much at risk as Burt's. If it came to divorce, she'd be able to get a lot out of Burt, but not if Big Bill took it all away first.

Then there was this Mike character. I found it hard to believe that an attractive young man, gay or not, would find Burt all that appealing unless money was involved. Could he be trying to kill Big Bill so as to make a bigger haul? Or even to protect his lover's interests?

I shook my head, trying to get my thoughts elsewhere. Big Bill had made it plain that my assistance was not wanted. It was silly to keep worrying about his problems. Fortunately, the party provided plenty of other things to think about. I'd caught up with all the aunts, but there were still the uncles: Uncle Buddy, Uncle Ruben, and Uncle Roger of Roger's Ramblers. Then there were the cousins. I'd already seen Thaddeous and Vasti, but there were still Thaddeous's brothers, Augustus and Willis; Vasti's husband, Arthur, who had their little girl Bitsy in tow; Aunt Ruby Lee's kids, Ilene, Clifford, and

Earl; Linwood and his wife Sue, who had mercifully left their four kids at home; and Aunt Nellie and Uncle Ruben's triplets, Idelle, Odelle, and Carlelle. Plus there were more folks on the path to joining the family: Aunt Edna's beau, Caleb, who'd recently given her a lovely diamond; Clifford's girlfriend, Liz, a local nurse that everybody in the family was crazy about; and Ilene's boyfriend, Trey Norton, who was my friend Junior's little brother.

There were friends to talk to, too, like Aunt Maggie's other flea market cronies and the rest of Roger's Ramblers. Plenty of the mill employees had come, including the ambitious Tavis Montgomery, but if Burt's "friend" Mike was there, I didn't meet him. Despite all the people I did know, there were plenty I didn't, and it was tempting to guess which folks were Burnette connections and which ones were friends of the Walterses. When I had to sneak into a corner to feed Alice, Richard and I had a wonderful time speculating about who was who. Of course, the two groups weren't mingling much, so that made it easier.

"That old guy in the suit with his back to us?" I said. "Burnette."

"Who is he?" Richard asked.

"No idea. But nobody connected with the Walterses would wear a suit off the rack, and that one looks brand-new." Just then he turned in our direction. "Ow! Do you see that scar on his head? Definitely a Burnette—any of the Walterses' friends would have plastic surgery or wear a rug to cover it up."

"The woman in the black dress?"

"Are you kidding? That dress is silk—it must be a Walters."

We went on that way for a while until Richard pointed out a woman in a lovely Oriental blue pantsuit with her back to us. "Burnette," Richard said.

"No way. She's got shoes that match her outfit. Walters."

"Want to bet?"

"Absolutely. The loser has to change Alice's next three diapers."

"You're on." Richard approached the woman, tapped her on the shoulder, then gave her a quick hug. Then they looked in my direction and waved. It was Aunt Maggie! Big Bill pulled her away then, and Richard sauntered back to me with a satisfied smile on his face.

"You cheated!" I said. "You knew it was Aunt Maggie all along."

"Guilty as charged," he said. "Of course, you could have asked me if I knew who it was, but since you were so sure you were right . . ."

"Okay, you win. I just wonder who helped her pick that outfit. Vasti or one of the aunts?"

"Want to bet on it?"

"No, thanks. You probably already know that, too."

Richard just grinned.

Alice finished nursing a minute or two later, and we went to catch up with Aunt Maggie, who was standing with Big Bill and Tavis Montgomery. The usual hugs were exchanged, and naturally political animals like Big Bill and Tavis couldn't miss an opportunity to kiss a baby. Tavis was a tall, trim man, and his silver-gray hair always seemed a bit too distinguished to be true. Rumor had it that he had two different wardrobes, one of "regular guy" clothes for when he was fulfilling his duties as local union president, and one of Brooks Brothers suits for when he wanted to deal with the power people in town. Obviously, Big Bill counted as powerful, so Tavis was in a suit that night.

"Isn't this a lovely party?" Tavis said once the preliminaries were taken care of. "Mrs. Walters, you've done a remarkable job."

It sounded so strange for him to call Aunt Maggie "Mrs. Walters," and I guess it was strange to Aunt Maggie, too, because it took a couple of seconds for her to answer. "Thanks, Tavis, but you know doggoned well I didn't arrange any of this. If it'd been up to me, we'd be eating fried chicken out of a bucket."

Tavis laughed in that hearty way people do when they don't really have anything to say. "Mrs. Walters, your very presence adds to the elegance of the event."

Big Bill beamed his approval, but Aunt Maggie inelegantly rolled her eyes.

"That is a pretty outfit, Aunt Maggie," I said. Aunt Daphine must have picked it out, I decided. Vasti would have tried to get her into a dress and pantyhose—Aunt Daphine had more tact.

"Thank you," she said, "but between these fancy clothes and all this makeup, I feel like I'm already dressed up for Halloween."

As far as I could tell, she was wearing lipstick and maybe mascara, but for Aunt Maggie, that was a lot of makeup.

"Speaking of Halloween," Aunt Maggie said to Tavis, "have you decided which room I get for the white elephant sale at the carnival? I could fill the whole library, but I can make do with two classrooms as long as they're next to each other. I've already got my nephew Augustus lined up to help man the table."

Tavis furrowed his brow. "I didn't realize you were planning to supervise the white elephant. You haven't attended any of the planning meetings, and—"

"Tavis Lee Montgomery, I have been running the white elephant since you were in diapers. There wasn't any need for me to come to some meeting to decide what color paper cups y'all are going to use!"

"I understand, but I assumed that you newlyweds

would have other things on your mind." He tried for an indulgent smile.

Aunt Maggie gave him a look. "Maybe your mind stays in the gutter, but Bill and I know when it's time to do our part for Byerly."

"I appreciate your civic-mindedness, but you really don't have to worry about the white elephant. Mrs. Roberts has volunteered to—"

"Marlyn Roberts? Lord, Tavis, that woman doesn't know McCoy pottery from Fiesta ware. She'll price cheap Taiwan junk like it's gold just because it's new, and pure give away the good stuff."

"I'm sure she'd welcome your help."

"I'll bet she would, if she could take all the credit. No, you can give Marlyn the lemonade stand or the craft table. The white elephant is mine."

Tavis looked at Big Bill, presumably trying to decide which was the best way to please him. Then he looked at Aunt Maggie, and her expression made it plain that the choice wasn't his, anyway. So he went back to the meaningless laugh, followed up with, "You'll have the library, of course."

Big Bill grinned as if he'd enjoyed seeing Tavis taken down a notch, which he probably had. "Laurie Anne, are y'all going to be staying in town long enough for the carnival?"

"I hadn't thought about it, to tell you the truth," I said. The Byerly Halloween Carnival had been a high point of my childhood. Always planned for a night or two before Halloween so as not to interfere with trick-or-treating, it was the next best thing to the actual holiday. The town went all out, transforming the high school into a spooky delight, with games that always gave prizes, a scary-but-not-too-scary haunted house, cakewalks, a costume contest, and of course, the white elephant sale.

One of my fondest memories was seeing Big Bill himself in the dunking booth, and for once in my life, lobbing a softball with enough accuracy to drop him into the water. I knew the carnival had continued after I moved north, but we'd never managed to be in town at the right time to attend. "Richard, are you interested?"

"Do we get to dress up in costumes?" he asked.

"Most people do."

"Alice, too?"

"Of course."

"Then I'm in."

Richard had done a lot of theater, especially Shakespeare, and he loved nothing better than a chance to put on something outrageous. I could only imagine what he had in mind for Alice. I made a mental note to have a camera handy.

Dorcas and Burt came up then, and I noted that Dorcas had her arm firmly tucked into Burt's. After what Michelle had told me, I thought I knew why, and I could see that she really had made an effort. She'd always been a pretty woman, but tonight she was positively stunning. For her sake, I really hoped the rumors about Burt were wrong.

"Daddy, Aunt Maggie," Burt said, "can I get y'all anything?"

"I'm not so old that I can't pick up a cup of punch," Big Bill said, his eyes narrowed, and I knew he was still worried that Burt was trying to kill him.

"I didn't mean—" Burt started to say, but Dorcas interrupted him to say, "I hope you're happy with everything at the party, Big Bill. And you, too, Aunt Maggie." She stumbled a little over the "Aunt Maggie" part, but it was a good try.

"The party did turn out nice, Dorcas," Big Bill said. "A lot more lively than what you usually do. I'll have to

let Vasti do all of the party planning from now on."
Obviously, Big Bill had come to the same conclusion
that I had, that Dorcas was just as likely to want him
dead as Burt was.

Dorcas's face froze, and I was impressed that she
managed not to say the things she had to be thinking.

"I've always enjoyed Dorcas's parties," Tavis said, but
when he saw the beginnings of a frown from Big Bill, he
quickly added, "Of course, there's nothing like a new
perspective to let in a little fresh air." Then, with just a
hint of malice, he said, "Speaking of new perspectives,
where's that young protégé of yours, Burt? I wouldn't
have thought he'd blow off an important event like
this."

If anything, Dorcas froze even more—so much I was
afraid her face would crack. She'd heard the rumors, all
right.

"Mike had a prior commitment," Burt said. "He sent
his regrets. I'm looking forward to introducing him to
Daddy some time soon."

That was something I'd pay to see.

Big Bill looked uninterested. "If y'all will excuse me,
I think I hear the Ramblers getting started up. Maggie,
are you in the mood to dance?"

"I might be," she allowed, and let him lead her off.

It was about then that I caught a whiff of something
unpleasant from Alice's diaper, and knew it was time to
start paying off my bet with Richard. I excused myself
and went looking for someplace to change her.

Some people don't mind changing their babies wherever they happen to be, and I'd been known to pick a
quiet spot and change her in public, too. But the last
thing I wanted to do was give the Walterses or Miz Duffield
any more reasons to think we Burnettes weren't raised
right. Unfortunately, the first bathroom I found had a

line, and the next didn't have anything big enough to lay Alice on. I could have gone upstairs, but nobody else was leaving the first floor; and it seemed rude to act as if I owned the place. Finally I found Miz Duffield rearranging platters on the buffet table.

"Miz Duffield," I said, "I need to change Alice's diaper, and the bathrooms are taken. Is there a room I can use?"

As usual, Miz Duffield sniffed to show her distaste, but I bet she regretted it when she got a whiff of Alice. "There's a utility room off of the kitchen. I suppose it would be all right for you to change her in there."

Though I was tempted to find Miz Duffield's bedroom and change the baby right in the middle of her bed, in the interest of family happiness I went looking for the utility room. "But if it's not clean in there," I told Alice, "we're going to find someplace else to fix you up."

As it turned out, the utility room was quite clean. In addition to a huge washer and drier, there was a long table, probably for folding clothes, but it was a good height for changing the baby. I wouldn't leave Alice's stinky diaper under Miz Duffield's pillow after all.

After we finished up, I stepped back into the kitchen and, out of the corner of my eye, thought I glimpsed somebody else leaving the room. When I saw what had been left on the table, I reconsidered my kindly thoughts toward Miz Duffield. There was a bottle of rubbing alcohol on the counter. Had that woman expected me to leave baby poop all over the place? Well, if she thought I was going to swab down the table just because I'd changed a diaper on it, she had another think coming!

I glanced around for Miz Duffield when Alice and I rejoined the party, meaning to give her a stern look, but didn't spot her. Instead, the triplets spotted me and rushed over to get their turn with Alice. Since Carlelle, Idelle, and Odelle were dressed alike, I don't know if my baby realized she was being held by three different women or not, but she didn't seem to mind either way. They cooed over her enthusiastically and declared that Alice was the cutest baby they'd ever seen. Of course, I knew darned well that they said that to all the babies, but I was willing to accept that they'd finally gotten it right.

They were still passing her back and forth when Vasti stationed herself in the center of the room and started tapping on a glass with a butter knife. When the room quieted, she said, "I just know y'all are dying to toast Uncle Big Bill and Aunt Maggie, and if Irene will hurry up and pass out the champagne, we'll get started."

Miz Duffield looked mutinous but dutifully walked through the room with a tray of filled champagne glasses. Vasti herself handed two sterling silver goblets engraved with roses to Aunt Maggie and Big Bill.

"You know I don't drink, Vasti," Aunt Maggie said.

"You have to make a toast," Vasti objected.

"I don't see why."

"But Aunt Maggie . . ."

Aunt Maggie rolled her eyes. "Fine. Pour this mess out and get me some sweet tea."

"I'll take that," Big Bill said, pouring the offending liquid into his own cup. "It's going to take a whole lot of champagne to properly toast the charms of this lady here."

Aunt Maggie rolled her eyes again, but from her tiny smile, I thought she rather liked the compliment. If not, she'd put up with it as long as she could drink iced tea instead of champagne.

Once everybody had a glass, Vasti said, "Burt, I know you're going to want to be the very first to toast your father and stepmother."

If Burt had wanted to go first, you couldn't tell by his blank expression, which looked as if it had been glued on to hide what he was really thinking. Big Bill glared at him for a moment, and Burt finally got out, "Best wishes to the happy couple," and choked down a swallow of champagne while the rest of us in the room touched glasses.

I noticed that Big Bill frowned just a touch at the taste of his champagne, which probably pleased Miz Duffield. Of course, she wasn't happy enough to keep from sniffing as she picked up Aunt Maggie's champagne goblet and took it away. Presumably, she thought that if Big Bill drank champagne, everybody should drink champagne.

"Now Uncle Buddy," Vasti said. She'd probably picked him for the next toast because he was the oldest male on the Burnette side, but obviously she hadn't bothered to warn him, because he went white as a sheet. Uncle Buddy rarely speaks in private, let alone in public.

Still, he's not a man to shirk his duty. He held his glass high and said clearly, "Getting married was the smartest thing I ever did. Here's hoping it's as good for y'all as it's been for me and Nora."

Aunt Nora blushed, and darned if Uncle Buddy didn't kiss her in front of all of us.

After that, Vasti let people toast on their own, though she did glare at various folks when the pace started to slow down. Richard quoted an appropriate bit of Shakespeare, Aunt Daphine recited a little poem, and Linwood told an inappropriate joke. As a nursing mother, I didn't drink any champagne myself, but if I had, my glass would have been drained long before Big Bill spoke up.

"I don't know that I've ever heard a finer tibute—er, tribute. It does a man's heart good for all you fine, fine,

fine people to speak on our behalfs—behalf. Even those
of y'all who aren't that fine. 'Cause y'all know who y'all
are." He laughed as if he'd said something witty, and I
winced, wondering if he was about to accuse somebody
of trying to kill him. Instead, he drank more from his
goblet and said, "It hasn't been easy catching Maggie
Burnette, but I've never been one to stop when I want
something. Somebody. So I didn't. Stop, that is." He
laughed again.

"The old fool's drunk," a woman behind me whispered.

"Don't be silly," a man's voice said. "He's only had
one glass of champagne."

"He must have started drinking early," the woman
answered, "and I don't blame him. If I'd just tied myself
to that old battle-ax, I'd get drunk, too."

The triplets stiffened, and I was about to turn and tell
the snobs off when a couple of things came together in
my mind. Carlelle was still holding Alice, and I snapped,
"Watch the baby," and pushed my way through to Aunt
Maggie and Big Bill as quickly as I could.

By the time I got to them, Big Bill was mumbling
something about Aunt Maggie's eyes, slurring his words
so badly I couldn't understand him, and Aunt Maggie
was tugging at his sleeve, looking disgusted.

Big Bill lifted his goblet as if to drink again, then
blinked at me in astonishment when I slapped it out of
his hand and knocked it onto the carpet. "It's poisoned!" I said. "You've been poisoned!"

Chapter Five

Big Bill's mouth opened, but he didn't speak. He just slumped into a chair and put his hand to his throat.

Aunt Maggie shouted, "Somebody call for an ambulance!" To me she said, "What do we do? Should we make him throw up?" She looked ready to stick a finger down his throat herself.

"I don't know," I said helplessly, seeing the panicked look on Big Bill's face. "Does anybody know the number for the poison control center?" Then I remembered. "Liz! Somebody find Clifford's girlfriend Liz. She's a nurse—she'll know what to do."

Liz must have heard the commotion, because she showed up then. "What did he drink?"

"Isopropanol," I answered.

"Rubbing alcohol? Are you sure?"

"Pretty sure. The symptoms fit. He's acting drunk even though he's only had one glass of champagne."

"Mr. Walters, have you had any other alcohol to drink tonight?" Liz asked in a clear voice.

He shook his head.

"Okay, then. We're going to get you a glass of water to drink while we wait for the ambulance."

I was going to send somebody to fetch the water, but I didn't know who I could trust. So I ran to the kitchen myself, ignoring the sea of wide, frightened eyes that surrounded me. I grabbed the biggest glass I could find from the cabinet, filled it from the tap, and rushed back to Big Bill.

Liz was taking his pulse, and in a pitiful voice Big Bill asked, "Am I going to die?"

"No, sir, not if I can help it," Liz said firmly. "You just hang on." She took the glass from me and held it so Big Bill could drink. "Keep it coming," she said.

Richard was there by then, and said, "I'll get more."

As Big Bill drank, Aunt Maggie stood behind him, her hand on his shoulder, watching the people in the room. I knew what she was thinking, because I was thinking it, too. Somebody there had tried to kill Big Bill. Again.

Big Bill was on his third glass of water when the ambulance arrived, and Liz efficiently informed the attendants of the situation. The rest of us stood back as they started an IV and loaded Big Bill onto a stretcher. Burt, who'd come to stand by his father, said, "Daddy? I'm coming with you."

"No," Big Bill said. "Just Maggie."

I could see the hurt in Burt's eyes, but all he said was, "All right. I'll meet you at the hospital." Then he looked around for his wife. "Dorcas, you stay and take care of things here. I'll call you as soon as we know anything."

Dorcas nodded and gave him a quick peck on the cheek as he turned to go. It was probably the first real sign of affection I'd seen between them all night.

People moved out of the way for the ambulance attendants to wheel Big Bill away, with Liz, Aunt Maggie, and Burt following. As they left, Junior Norton came in with her deputy Belva. When Junior spotted her brother Trey, who was a part-time deputy, she told him to follow the ambulance to the hospital and stay with Big Bill. Then she surveyed the room.

Junior and Belva made an interesting team. Junior was short, and Belva tall. Junior was trim, and though Belva wasn't fat, she was bulky. But even though Junior was the smaller of the two, it was obvious from the way she moved that she was in charge. She'd been young when she became Byerly's chief of police, but she came from a long line of police chiefs, and that gave her a lot of the authority she carried like some cops carry a gun.

"Okay, people," she said, "I've got some questions to ask—let's keep it calm and this won't take long."

"The bottle!" I said, suddenly remembering. "The rubbing alcohol bottle. It's on the kitchen counter."

"Hold on a minute," Junior said. "Belva, you stay in here and keep an eye on folks. Don't let anybody leave."

"You got it, chief."

"Laurie Anne, lead the way."

I did, but the bottle was nowhere in sight when we got to the kitchen.

"Damn, damn, damn," I said. "I should have grabbed it, but I was helping with Big Bill."

"Do you want to tell me what's going on here?" Junior said patiently. "Assume I wasn't here when it happened, because I wasn't."

"Sorry, Junior." I explained everything that had happened since I'd gone to change Alice's diaper, including the facts that I'd seen a bottle of rubbing alcohol on the kitchen counter before, and that I'd seen somebody leaving the room in a hurry.

"But you don't know who it was?" Junior asked.

I shook my head. "At first I thought it was Miz Duffield, but that's just because she was the one who sent me to the utility room to change Alice. I didn't actually see her, or anybody else."

"And just from looking at that bottle, you knew that Big Bill had been poisoned?" Junior said doubtfully. "Kind of a stretch, if you ask me."

I bristled. "Maybe so, but the symptoms fit, and Liz thinks I'm right."

"You just happened to know what happens when somebody drinks rubbing alcohol?"

"It's because of the parent magazines Richard and I have been reading," I explained. "One of them had articles about common household dangers, including isopropanol."

"I thought you said it was rubbing alcohol."

"I did. Isopropanol is the same thing as rubbing alcohol. It's in a lot of aftershaves and cleaning solutions, too. Anyway, the article said what the symptoms are, and when Big Bill started acting funny after drinking his champagne, I put two and two together."

"Pretty smart work," Junior said, "but I'm surprised you thought of poison right off, and not a stroke or something like that. Unless you expected somebody to try to kill Big Bill, of course."

I hesitated. Though I thought Big Bill should have reported the attempts on his life right way, I wasn't sure I should go against his wishes. Then again, Junior already knew that there was no way that rubbing alcohol could have gotten into Big Bill's goblet accidentally. Besides which, it wasn't fair to let her go into the case blind. So finally I said, "You'll want to talk to Aunt Maggie and Big Bill, because I don't know the details, but I do know that Big Bill is worried about some things that have happened." I briefly described the incidents, concluding with, "Of course, they could all have been accidents."

"Is there any particular reason that Big Bill hasn't told me about these accidents himself?"

There was no way I was going to repeat my idea that Big Bill suspected his son. Big Bill would have to tell her, or she'd have to figure it out for herself. "Because he's Big Bill," was all I would say.

From the way Junior looked at me, I could tell she knew I was holding something back, but she let it pass. "All right. What did this bottle look like?"

"Just a regular bottle," I said. "I didn't pick it up or anything."

"Brand name? Color?"

"I didn't notice the brand, but it was brown. A plastic bottle, not glass."

"That's something to look for."

"Where do we look first?"

"*We* don't. I'll look while you go back in with the others." Before I could argue with her, she said, "Laurie Anne, I've got a house-full of people out there, and some of them are pretty big wheels in this town. They aren't going to be happy when Belva won't let them leave, so I need to do this just as fast as I can, without having to keep an eye on you. Now if you should happen to overhear anything suspicious in there, I'd be glad to hear about it later."

That was more like it. "You got it, chief," I said, and headed back into the living room.

Chapter
Six

It seemed odd to me that the same people were in the same room, still dressed up in their glad rags, but the gathering looked nothing like the party that had been going on just a little while before. Partially it was because it was more crowded—Belva had herded everybody in from outside. Partially it was because nobody was going near the refreshment tables. But mostly it was because of the way people had divided themselves and were looking suspiciously at one another. The game Richard and I had been playing earlier seemed kind of creepy now. I didn't think it was an accident that the Burnette crew had ended up on one side of the room, with the Walterses' friends on the other. Tavis Montgomery was the only one who seemed willing to cross the great divide—I guess he figured that a Burnette's vote was as good as anybody's. I looked around for the man with the funny dent in his head, wondering which side he'd ended up on, but didn't see him.

Junior came out then to confer with Belva, and then started taking people into the Oriental study to question them. I noticed that the Walters contingent pushed forward immediately, and have to admit that I resented their assumption that they'd get to go home first.

Richard had gotten Alice from the triplets and was sitting on a chair jiggling her on his knee, which almost certainly meant that she was hungry. I checked my watch, realized how long it had been, and went over to him. Some things took precedence over detective work.

"Feeding time?" I asked him.

"And how," he said, standing up to let me take the chair. He stood where he could shield me while I got my blouse unbuttoned, and then handed me Alice. The poor little thing grabbed hold of me as if she hadn't eaten in months. I could have gotten Junior to let us go somewhere more private to nurse, but since I was hoping to do a little eavesdropping, I didn't even ask. On those occasions when I'd nursed Alice in public, I'd noticed that people tended to talk over me as if I weren't there—maybe that would help me overhear something useful.

It might have worked, too, if it hadn't been for Vasti. I'd just finished telling Richard what I'd told Junior when she stepped past him and said, "You're not still nursing that baby, are you?"

"She just got started," I said indignantly.

"I mean, why haven't you got her on a bottle yet? Isn't she eating solid food?"

"We're working on it," I said defensively. "She eats cereal in the morning and baby food at dinner." Then I reminded myself that I didn't have to answer to Vasti. "Besides, the doctor says it's healthy to nurse a baby for the first year."

"A year?" She rolled her eyes. "Doctors! What do they know? A bunch of men who probably don't even know how to change a diaper."

"My doctor is a woman."

"Oh, I'd never go to a woman doctor," she said, with complete disregard for logic. "You're not really going to breastfeed for a solid year, are you?"

"Probably not," I admitted. "I expect it will be too hard once I go back to work."

Vasti gasped theatrically. "You're going back to work? When you've got a baby?"

I started trying to explain how Richard and I needed my income, and that we'd found a wonderful day-care provider, and that Richard himself would do a lot of the parenting during the summer, but Vasti was too busy being appalled to listen. Normally I let the worst of Vasti's comments roll off me like water off a duck's back, but this time it was harder. The idea of leaving Alice with somebody else didn't thrill me, either.

Various other Burnette women heard the discussion and came over to join in, which reminded me just what the term "old wives' tales" means. I had to hear when each of their children had been weaned, started on solid foods, and cut their first teeth, plus advice on how to get Alice to attain those milestones as soon as possible. Then there were debates as to whether a child as young as Alice should be in day care. I had to grit my teeth during most of it—I've never been good at taking advice, no matter how well meant.

The only reason they stopped telling me how to raise my child was because Vasti said, "Can we talk about something important now? Laurie Anne, you and Richard are going to find out who tried to kill Uncle Big Bill, aren't you?" Being Vasti, she'd spoken so loudly that everybody in the room heard her.

I sighed. So much for covert eavesdropping. When I finally got Alice fed, I did try to wander over toward people on the Walters side of the room, acting as if I were trying to get Alice to burp, but after Vasti's announcement, conversation stopped the second I got close enough to hear anybody.

Richard, who'd escaped during the seminar on motherhood, came back to find me. "Anything?" he asked.

"Not after Vasti shot her big mouth off."

"Don't blame her. I started sneaking around even before she blew the gaff, but people avoided me with great determination. I think our reputation as Byerly's premier crime solvers has preceded us."

Maybe I should have been complimented, but mostly I was annoyed. It didn't help that Junior was clearly giving Richard and me a chance to work, because she left the interview with us for absolute last. Alice had long since fallen asleep on my shoulder, and I'd nearly done the same on Richard's, when Junior finally came out to talk to us.

The first thing she told us was that she'd checked on Big Bill and that it looked as if he was going to be just fine.

Then I had to tell her that I hadn't found out a darn thing she could use. "I wish we had something for you," I said apologetically.

"That's all right. I don't expect you to do my job for me. Though I expect that's what you're planning to do."

"I am not," I said.

Junior just gave me a look.

"Okay, maybe I am, but it's not because you're not good at it."

"I know, I know. It's because it's your family. Laurie Anne, why is it that you're the only one who has to be convinced that you're going to get involved when something like this happens. Everybody else knows you're going to."

"I just hate to be so predictable."

"Well, now we both know you're going to be running around asking questions, and since you're related to Big Bill, you might hear things that people wouldn't tell me for love or money. Naturally, I'm going to be investigating, too, and I've got access to information you don't have. Chemical tests and fingerprints and all. You wouldn't be interested in that stuff."

"Junior . . ."

She just grinned. "Seriously, you and I work differently. If I hadn't known it before, I knew it after last Christmas.[5] So I'll go my way, while you and Richard can go yours, and if y'all get anything I can use, y'all let me know. Deal?"

"Deal," I said, and we shook on it. Junior and I had come a long way since I'd had to talk her into investigating a case, or she'd tried to talk me out of it. Her only interest was in putting the bad guys away, and competition didn't seem to come into it. That's one of the reasons she was a real cop while I was just an eager amateur.

"Speaking of police methods, have you found out anything?" Richard asked.

"Not a doggone thing," she said wearily. "Nobody admits to pouring Big Bill's champagne—as many people as there were milling around, our poisoner was either mighty lucky or mighty careful. Since nobody else got sick, we're guessing the isopropanol went into the goblet, not the bottle, but that's about all we know."

"What about Aunt Maggie's goblet?" I told her about Aunt Maggie switching to iced tea. "Was her champagne poisoned, too?"

Junior made a face. "I don't know if even the folks at

[5] *Mad as the Dickens*

the lab will be able to tell us that. Miz Duffield washed the goblet out before Big Bill got ill—she's mighty irritated that she can't start washing up the rest of this mess." She shook her head. "The lab isn't going to be too happy with me, either. I've got Belva bagging and tagging every glass and champagne bottle she can find."

I probably shouldn't have asked the next question, because it wasn't any of my business; but I was curious. After making sure Belva wasn't close enough to hear, I said, "How did you come to hire Belva? I got the impression you didn't care for her." Belva and Junior's former deputy had slugged it out over a previous case, and Junior had said then she thought Belva was lazy, and none too bright.[6] I hadn't liked her much myself, mostly because she'd accused Aunt Maggie of stirring up trouble.

Junior shrugged. "Belva started out pretty green, but she's learned a lot, and I think it's going to work out. I just wish she'd quit calling me 'Chief.' "

Junior let us go after that. Alice was still asleep, and Richard nearly was, so I decided to forgo any serious conversation that night. Instead, I loaded them into the car, drove them home, and put all of us to bed.

---

[6] *Tight as a Tick*

Chapter
Seven

The next morning was beautiful and crisp, just cool enough to convince me to pick out long-sleeved shirts for Alice and me. "Of course, this isn't going to seem at all chilly to you," I crooned to her as I got her dressed, "because you're my little Yankee baby."

"I heard that," Richard said.

"Hey, she's the first Burnette born above the Mason-Dixon line; that's worthy of note."

We lay down on the bed on either side of her to cuddle and talk.

"Any word about Big Bill?" Richard asked.

"I called while you were in the shower. Aunt Maggie says he's doing fine."

"Thanks to you."

"Thanks to serendipity. If I hadn't read that article on poisons in the home, or happened to be in the right place to see that bottle of rubbing alcohol, or had wandered off before Big Bill started to show the effects . . ." I shook my head, wanting the awful thoughts to go away. "It was too close, Richard, way too close."

"I know," he said, closing his hand over mine.

"Anybody could have drunk some of that champagne: Aunt Maggie, you, even Alice."

He looked at our daughter skeptically, no doubt trying to figure out how, when she wasn't even walking yet.

"Okay, maybe not Alice, but Aunt Maggie could have. We have to find out who's after Big Bill."

He didn't even blink. "Duh! I knew the minute Big Bill said somebody was trying to kill him that eventually we'd step in. We always do."

"I wasn't sure this time, not with Alice here. Can you picture me trying to ask questions while I'm nursing her, or when she's fussy? 'Hush now, Alice, we need to get this nice lady's alibi.' "

"It's not the way Sherlock Holmes would do it," Richard said.

"More importantly, we can't put her in any danger."

"We won't. What we're going to do is make your aunts and cousins very happy."

"How's that?"

"We're going to let them take turns baby-sitting."

It sounded a bit like Tom Sawyer whitewashing the fence to me, but when we started calling around, my aunts were several steps ahead of us. Like everybody else, they'd assumed that Richard and I were going to help Big Bill, so they'd already started scheduling who got Alice when. Aunt Daphine was that day's lucky winner.

As I packed Alice's bag with diapers, formula, baby food, and teething rings, I had to admit that I was feeling pretty darned good. I was worried about Big Bill and Aunt Maggie, of course, but I couldn't help but look forward to having time alone with Richard. As much as I loved Alice, and as much fun as motherhood was turning out to be, I still got tired of being "Mama" all the time. The baby books all assured me that my feelings were completely natural, which was even more depressing. As I'd told Junior, I hated being predictable.

I was a little concerned about how we were going to handle breast-feeding. Though Alice had started on solid foods, I still nursed her several times a day, not to mention the dreaded two A.M. feeding. But, as I told Richard, there was no reason we couldn't arrange our interrogations around the baby's schedule.

The main obstacle still in our way was the fact that Big Bill didn't want us involved, so Richard and I did a lot of plotting during the drive to drop off Alice at Aunt Daphine's, and then on to the hospital in Hickory. By the time we got there, we had our approach worked out.

"Do you think they'll go for it?" Richard asked as we waited for the elevator to take us to Big Bill's floor.

"Do you think I'm going to give them a choice?" I'd said before that Big Bill and Aunt Maggie were as stubborn as mules, but as Richard had pointed out, it was a family trait. I wasn't planning to take "no" for an answer.

There was a cluster of people in the waiting room nearest Big Bill's room. Burt and Dorcas were there, of course, plus some folks I had seen at the party, and Hank Parker, the star reporter from the *Byerly Gazette*. In fact, he was the only full-time reporter for the twice-weekly paper, but he took his work all the more seriously for that. When he saw Richard and me, he rushed right over, notebook in hand.

"Miz Fleming, is it true that Big Bill Walters was poisoned last night? And that you were the one to foil the murder attempt?" Hank must have grown up watching B movies, because he dressed like the relentless reporter characters in thirties and forties detective pictures, right down to the straw boater with a press pass in the brim, which he wore even after Labor Day. That didn't mean that he wasn't sharp as a tack—he'd stayed in Byerly because he liked it, not because he couldn't have gotten a job at a big-city newspaper.

"Hank, why are you asking me questions when you already know the answers? Didn't y'all have a reporter at the party?"

He grimaced. "A stringer, and she only does society news. I don't need to know what color shirt Big Bill wore in the ambulance."

Poor fellow—Big Bill was always big news in Byerly, and for Hank to have missed out on seeing an actual murder attempt must have really hurt.

"All right," I said, taking pity on him. "We'll answer a few questions."

"Great! So how did you know it was poison?"

"Pure, dumb luck." I explained the article I'd read that described the effects of isopropanol poisoning.

"Household poisons? That might make a good sidebar for my piece," he said. "How did Big Bill react? Did he turn to his new bride for comfort? Was he angry, frightened, panicked?"

He had been a little frantic, but I could hardly blame him for that. "He was quite calm, considering, and did everything Liz told him to. That's Liz Sanderson. She's an RN, works over at the nursing home. She's the one who really saved his life, you know."

"Sanderson," he said, writing it down. "Is she young?"

"Young, blond, and pretty. She looks great in pictures."

"That's what I want to hear." Then, careful not to offend, "You're quite photogenic, too."

"Thanks so much," I said. "Is there anything else?"

He looked at his notebook. "Not now. Can I count on

you two for an exclusive interview once you've solved the crime?"

I sighed—even Hank knew what I was going to do before I did. I didn't know which was more peculiar: that everybody else in town accepted Richard and me as Scooby-Doo surrogates, or that I couldn't seem to.

Richard said, "You bet," and Hank went away happy.

Once he was gone, Burt came over and we exchanged air kisses and handshakes.

"How's Big Bill?" I asked.

Burt said, "He's doing better, but he doesn't want anybody else in there except Aunt Maggie." Then, as if realizing that that might sound insulting to Aunt Maggie, he added, "Which is only natural."

"I'll just let them know we came by," I said, though in fact I had no intention of leaving until we'd spoken to the newlyweds. I tapped on the door, and after Aunt Maggie peered out, she turned back into the room and said, "It's Laurie Anne and Richard."

"Let them in," said Big Bill.

His father allowing us in and not him had to have hurt Burt's feelings, but he just said, "Tell Daddy we're out here if he needs us."

Richard and I went inside, and Aunt Maggie closed the door behind us.

Big Bill had managed to get what must have been the biggest room in the hospital. Private, of course, and with the dark wood furniture it looked more like a good hotel room then a hospital room. Only the crank on the bed gave it away as hospital equipment. Well, that, the rack of monitors, and the IV stand holding the fluids that were dripping into Big Bill's arm.

Big Bill was propped up in the bed, and as we came in he turned down the sound on the TV he had tuned to the Business Channel. His color wasn't great, but he looked alert, and the monitors all seemed to be happy with his condition.

"Hey there," I said. "How are you doing?"

"A whole lot better than I would be if you hadn't figured out what was going on," he said. "I want to thank you, Laurie Anne. You saved my life, and I won't forget it."

"Liz was the one who knew what to do," I reminded him.

"She wouldn't have realized there was anything wrong with me if you hadn't told her. No, I owe you my life, and Big Bill Walters always pays his debts."

If the situation had been different, I'd have politely demurred and told him that it was nothing anyone else wouldn't have done, but this time I intended to take advantage of his gratitude.

"If you really mean that . . ." I said.

"I never say anything I don't mean."

"Good. Then there is something I want."

He looked surprised—I guess he hadn't been expecting me to ask for a favor quite so quickly—but he said, "Just name it."

"Richard and I want to go after the one who's trying to kill you," I said. "And we want you and Aunt Maggie to stay put until it's all over."

"Me?" Aunt Maggie said. "I'm not the one in danger."

"We don't know that. The question is, did the killer know that you don't drink? If he didn't, then that rubbing alcohol could have been meant for you, too. Until we're sure, I want both of y'all out of harm's way while Richard and I take over the investigation. That means that we're going to be sticking our noses into all kinds of places, including that stack of threatening letters."

"I don't know about this," Big Bill said. "There's a lot of things in my files I don't want coming out."

"You said *anything*," I reminded him.

Big Bill huffed and puffed, but Aunt Maggie looked pretty darned tickled. "She's got you there, Bill," she said. "After all, you said yourself that Laurie Anne saved your life. You trust her, don't you?"

"It's not a question of trust," he said hurriedly, "it's just that . . . well, we were making progress on our own."

That was baloney and we all knew it, but I didn't think it would be very tactful to say so. "I'm not saying y'all couldn't have tied up all the loose ends yourselves, given time, but you can't investigate when you're on guard every minute. Nobody could."

"Can you two investigate while carting around a baby?" Big Bill said skeptically.

"We won't have to. I have four aunts fighting over Alice, not to mention cousins and friends. She'll be just fine." And though I wasn't doing this just to get a break from infant care, it wasn't something I minded, either.

I figured if I gave Big Bill more chances to argue, he'd do just that, so I began acting as if it had all been decided. "Richard and I have already started trying to eliminate suspects, and I don't want to offend you, but the first one we thought about was Burt."

I paused to see what he'd say, but his only comment was, "Is that right?"

"After all," I said, "he's your only real heir. But it doesn't work for us. For one, he's clearly devoted to you."

"When you get to be my age, you'll learn that people can hide their real feelings," Big Bill said regretfully.

"True, but it still may not make sense, depending on whether or not there was poison just in your goblet. Why would Burt kill you, knowing that Aunt Maggie would get everything?"

"He could have been meaning to kill me later on," Aunt Maggie suggested.

"But then Big Bill's money would have gone to your heirs, right? Burt isn't your heir."

"That's right," she said.

Big Bill said, "If we had both died, the money would have gone to Burt."

"Only if Aunt Maggie died first, and there's no way Burt could have been sure of that. It would have been too big a risk."

"You're right," Big Bill said, almost happily. "It doesn't make sense for Burt to try to kill me that way. Or Dorcas, either."

I felt obligated to add, "Of course, that only applies if the motive was money. Either Burt or Dorcas could have some other reason for wanting you dead."

"Horsefeathers!" Big Bill said. "Anybody can see that they love me. I don't know why you even wasted time thinking about them."

Trust Big Bill to chastise us for thinking something he'd suspected all along. Of course, since he'd never spoken his fears about his son out loud, now he didn't have to take the words back. "You're probably right," I said, "but I still want y'all to be careful. That's why I want somebody with you."

"A bodyguard?" Big Bill said, shaking his head. "I can't do that. Not now."

"Why not? Before, you were trying not to let the killer know you were watching for him. Now everybody knows somebody is trying to kill you."

"That's exactly why I can't hire a bodyguard. People would think I was afraid. Big Bill Walters is not going to be afraid in his own town!"

I'd been worried that this would be a sticking point, knowing how much pride the man had. "Lots of men have bodyguards," I pointed out. "The president doesn't even go to the bathroom without the Secret Service, and movie stars always have guards. It doesn't mean that they're afraid—it means that they're smart."

"That's different," he said stubbornly. "This is Byerly. If I don't go about my business despite this coward trying to cut me down, I'll never be able to hold my head up again."

I sighed, cursing the myth of Southern manhood. Or maybe all men. Of course, Richard wasn't like most men, which is why he came up with the right answer.

"That would be reasonable if you were completely recovered from the poison," he said.

"What do you mean?" Big Bill said. "The doctor says I can go home tomorrow."

"I don't know," Richard said. "I borrowed Laura's laptop this morning and did some research on the Web. Isopropanol poisoning can be tricky. Sometimes people go into comas."

"I'm not going into any coma!" Big Bill said.

"People can slip into them unexpectedly," Richard said, "but even if you don't, you might take a long time to recover. Nobody would expect a sick man to think about business. In fact, an important man like you should get round-the-clock care, even if you're not in the hospital. You'll want to get a staff of private duty nurses to watch you at home, and of course your new wife will want to stay with you, too."

I looked at Richard admiringly, then added, "If you weren't really as sick as people thought you were, it would make a dandy trap for the killer. If you wouldn't be scared of setting yourself up that way, that is."

"Let him come!" Big Bill said. "I'll show him what a sick old man can do." But he added, "Of course, these nurses might better be a little tougher than average."

"As a matter of fact, I have somebody in mind, and she's considerably tougher than average," Richard said.

Big Bill nodded at me, I nodded back at him, and Richard nodded at both of us. Aunt Maggie just grinned. We were in business!

Chapter
Eight

We still had details to iron out, of course. For one, if Big Bill was going to pretend to be sicker than he really was, his doctor was going to have to be involved. When I brought it up, Big Bill said, "I can handle Dr. Patel." I didn't know if he was going to bully Dr. Patel or bribe him, but either way, I didn't have to worry about that detail.

Then there were the nurses. I'd thought that Richard intended to enlist some of my aunts or cousins, but he had an actual nurse in mind. Vivian Foster was a retired Army nurse Richard had met a while back, and they'd become friends when they discovered that they shared a love of English literature.[7] True, Vivian preferred Jane Austen to Shakespeare, but Richard didn't hold that against her. Anyway, like Dr. Patel, Vivian was going to have to know that Big Bill wasn't as sick as we wanted people to think, and if she was going to successfully play bodyguard, she had to know what was going on. Besides, it wouldn't be right to put her in the line of fire without warning her.

[7] *Dead Ringer and Tight as a Tick*

Richard called her, and in the course of a messy five-way conversation, we told Vivian enough of the story to get by. Byerly being Byerly, she'd already heard about Big Bill's poisoning and had already figured that he might still be a target. She agreed to watch him, and knew a couple of other ex-Army nurses who could work shifts with her. She even said that she'd arrange for some medical equipment to have at the house as camouflage. The only kicker was that in addition to her usual pay rate, Vivian wanted Big Bill to help raise money for the VFW's veterans support group. Since my cousin Augustus was in that support group, Aunt Maggie told Big Bill he ought to help the group anyway, so he was willing to go along.

Once all that was arranged, Richard and I started picking Big Bill's brains for people who wanted him dead. Unfortunately, he said he didn't know of anybody. Though he freely admitted he had plenty of enemies, and had made an awful lot of sharp business deals during his career, he just couldn't conceive of anybody wanting him dead as a result.

"What about disgruntled employees at the mill?" I asked.

"Burt's been running the show over there for years," Big Bill pointed out. "If it was anything to do with the mill, it would have happened long ago."

"What about something from that far back, like with the union?" Big Bill had fought hard against the union coming to the mill, and he hadn't always fought fair.

But Aunt Maggie said, "Laurie Anne, if anybody from the union has reason to hold a grudge against Bill, it's me, and I can guarantee I'm not trying to kill him."

"Of course not," Big Bill put in. "There's no way she could have been driving the truck that tried to run me over."

Aunt Maggie turned on him. "You suspected *me?*"

He looked embarrassed. "Not for very long."

She didn't look angry, just exasperated.

Given the circumstances, I couldn't blame him for considering everybody a suspect.

"Is there anything more recent?" Richard asked.

Big Bill shook his head. "Not a thing. I've got some deals going, of course—there's always deals going—but nothing to get anybody stirred up. The biggest one right now is renovating that apartment complex I told you about, and I've not heard one complaint about that."

The first thing I needed to know was who would benefit from Big Bill's death, and I already had the answer to that. At least, I thought I did. Maybe other people had a financial interest. As much money and all as he had, his will was likely to be a complicated document. "What about your will?" I said. "Who gets what?"

Big Bill didn't answer until Aunt Maggie said, "Bill, if you're not going to answer their questions, they're not going to be able to help."

"All right," he said, though I could tell that he hated the idea of talking about such things.

"If it's any help, Laura and I promise to keep whatever you tell us completely confidential," Richard said.

Big Bill waved it away. "I know you two won't spread my business around. I'm just used to keeping my business to myself." Then he smiled fondly at Aunt Maggie. "Of course, I need to change that now that I've got a wife to think of."

Aunt Maggie snorted.

"Which will do you need to know about?" Big Bill said. "I wrote a new one after Maggie and I tied the knot."

"Since the murder attempts started before y'all were married, let's start with the old one," I said.

"Good enough. It was pretty simple. Most of the money,

the house, and all the businesses were left to Burt. My wife's—that is, my first wife's—jewelry and furs were to go to Dorcas, along with a couple of personal things of mine and some money." Richard raised one eyebrow, and Big Bill looked almost embarrassed as he named a dollar amount. He quickly added, "Dorcas has been taking care of the house and entertaining for me ever since my first wife died, and I wanted to give her a little something of her own."

I kept my face straight, but I couldn't help thinking that if that was a *little* something, I wondered what a *big* something would be.

"Was anybody else named in the will?" I asked.

"Irene was going to get some, but not much because I figured she'd keep on working for Dorcas as long as she could walk—that woman pure worships Dorcas. Some small amounts for the woman who cooks for us, and the man who does our yard work, and our lawyer, and financial advisors. There were a handful of things I wanted given out to my cousins, the ones that are left, anyway. Nothing big, just some family heirlooms." I started to get interested, but he added, "It's all been appraised, and none of it is worth more than a thousand dollars or so. They're all in good shape, financially speaking—one of them probably has nearly as much as I do."

"Are your cousins your only other family living?" I asked.

He nodded. "The rest of the will is charity bequests." He counted them off on his fingers. "Something for the church, and the library, and the historical revival committee, and Burt's alma mater."

I was impressed. Not just by the amount of money Big Bill had to divide up, though that was pretty impressive, but that he'd thought to leave things to the people who worked for him, and to some of the most worthy charities in Byerly. Even though he gloried in having enemies, he was making sure he had plenty of friends to remember him.

Hearing the list also got me to thinking that Richard and I needed to make our own wills, to make sure Alice was taken care of in case anything happened to us.

"It doesn't sound as if your will adds anybody to the list of suspects," I said. "How did the new will change things?"

"Everything goes to my wife," he said, "unless she predeceases me. Then it all changes back to the original plan."

So much for the money. We still had sex and revenge as motives, or some combination thereof. Though I really didn't want to think about Big Bill's sex life—especially not where Aunt Maggie was concerned—I had to ask. "I know you've been seeing Aunt Maggie for a while now, but I was wondering if—I mean, is there anyone else—maybe somebody who thought you were interested, even when you weren't . . ."

Big Bill looked blank, and I didn't blame him.

Fortunately, Aunt Maggie saw through my ineptitude. "She wants to know if you've been stepping out on me."

"Lord, no." Then he grinned. "Not that there haven't been plenty of women willing—some young ones, too. The older a man gets, the less competition there is."

"Of course, the size of your bankbook doesn't make a bit of difference," Aunt Maggie said.

"Of course it does," Big Bill said, "but it didn't matter why they wanted me. My heart belongs to this lady here."

I expected her to snort again, but Aunt Maggie permitted herself a tiny smile. It must be nice to know that she'd beaten out so many others, including younger women. I was just glad I didn't have to pursue that subject any further.

"That leaves revenge," Richard said, echoing my reasoning.

But try as he might, Big Bill couldn't think of anybody who was mad enough at him to want him dead. Finally, he asked, "Don't you think I've been racking my brains over this? I don't know who would want to kill me. Why do you think I've been going through fifteen years' worth of threatening letters? For my health?"

That reminded me that Big Bill's health wasn't currently all that good. Somebody had poisoned him less than twenty-four hours before, and he wasn't a young man. Even though he was doing fine, he still needed to rest. Aunt Maggie looked tired, too. So I told them both that Richard and I appreciated their trust, and that we would get started snooping.

Chapter Nine

Our first step was to look very solemn when we left Big Bill's hospital room, and when Burt anxiously asked how his father was, I said, "He's still very weak. They think the doctor is going to let him go home, but he'll need nurses on duty constantly."

"He'll get whatever he needs," Burt said stoutly.

I felt guilty about deceiving the man about his own father, but knew it wasn't half the amount of guilt I'd feel if I let something slip and it turned out that Burt really was trying to kill Big Bill.

If Burt was the one, it sure didn't show on his face, because I was watching him carefully. In the meantime, I knew Richard was scoping out the other folks in the waiting room, hoping to catch a hint of what they were thinking. As soon as we were alone in the elevator, I said, "How did they react? Did anybody give anything away?"

He shook his head. "If the killer was there, he or she has an excellent poker face. No flash of triumph at Big Bill's incapacitation, no disappointment that he's still alive, nothing."

"Oh well, it was a long shot. You'd think we'd know by now that killers don't look like killers."

"'One may smile, and smile, and be a villain,'" Richard agreed. *"Hamlet,* Act I, Scene 5."

Next we headed for the Walters mansion. Big Bill had given us permission to go through that file of threatening letters, and I was itching to get at them. It was petty of me, but Big Bill had been a source of speculation my whole life, and I couldn't wait to see just what kind of wheeling and dealing he did in that fancy office.

Miz Duffield opened the front door but only gave token resistance when we told her we had permission to use Big Bill's office. The poor thing looked miserable—her dress hadn't been ironed, and at least three hairs had escaped the bun on her head. She seemed so relieved when I told her Big Bill was doing better that I was feeling sorry for her until we got into Big Bill's office.

That's when Richard said, "What about Ms. Duffield?"

"What about her?"

"Could she be trying to kill Big Bill?"

"Are you serious? She's worked for the Walterses for as long as I can remember. If she's not devoted to them, she's been putting on an awfully good act."

"According to what Big Bill said, it's Dorcas she's really devoted to. Big Bill is just part of the package."

"True. What motive could she have?"

He thought about it. "What if Dorcas had been worried about Big Bill marrying Aunt Maggie even before it happened? She could have told Ms. Duffield that she might have to move out of the mansion, and Ms. Duffield would have known how much that would upset her. Why not get Big Bill out of the way so that Dorcas could live happily ever after? With Ms. Duffield in attendance, of course."

"Then when Big Bill did marry Aunt Maggie, she went after both of them, thinking that Burt and Dorcas would get to keep the house. Or just for revenge for Big Bill snubbing Dorcas. He was just as mean to her at the party as he's been to Burt, not to mention how rude he's been to Miz Duffield."

"Right," he said. "I don't know about the other attempts, but Ms. Duffield certainly had opportunity to poison the champagne."

"The problem is that she knew that Alice and I were in the laundry room. Why would she have risked me catching her with the rubbing alcohol?"

"What risk? If you'd seen her, she could have come up with any number of excuses for having rubbing alcohol handy. She does work here, after all. And that would explain why she was in such a rush to rinse out Aunt Maggie's champagne goblet. I bet she'd have gotten Big Bill's washed before anybody realized he was sick if you hadn't been so quick on the uptake."

"That's not bad. We'll put her on the list." Looking at the stack of letters on Big Bill's desk, I added, "Of course, it could be a long list." We divided the stack into two piles, and we each took one and settled down on the couch.

Even though I'd been relishing the idea of rooting through Big Bill's business, it wasn't long before I felt kind of sick to my stomach. Big Bill hadn't been kidding when he bragged about how many enemies he had—if anything, he'd been underestimating! The worst part was that a lot of the people who'd written letters seemed to have legitimate grievances.

"Look at these, Richard. People laid off after working at the mill for ten years or more. Unfair hiring practices. Race discrimination. Sexual discrimination. Sexual harassment. It's like a primer for how to be a robber baron."

"These are allegations, Laura. We don't know that they're true. As the Bard said, 'The devil can cite Scripture for his purpose.' *The Merchant of Venice*, Act I, Scene 3."

"And as my granddaddy said, 'Where there's smoke, there's fire.'" I waved a handful of letters at Richard. "There's an awful lot of smoke here."

"Granted. So what if they're all true?"

"What do you mean?"

"Well, if they're true, should we go back to Boston and let Big Bill get what's coming to him?"

"Of course not."

"Even if he . . ." Richard picked up a letter and quoted from it. "Even if he 'allows his delivery trucks to run past sleeping people's houses in the middle of the night, ruining their sleep'?" He picked up another letter. "Or 'sold inferior socks that caused blisters on the big toe and ankle'?"

I couldn't help laughing. "Okay, some of these are clearly cranks. I know Big Bill didn't let space aliens use his warehouse for a staging area for world domination. But some of these other letters . . . Brown lung really happens, and so do industrial accidents."

"They do, and maybe Big Bill has things to answer for. But Aunt Maggie married him, and I've always known her to be an excellent judge of character. Maybe most of these letters aren't true and Big Bill never was as big a scoundrel as people said he was, or maybe he's changed and isn't as big a scoundrel as he used to be. I don't know, but I do know that we promised Big Bill and Aunt Maggie that we'd help."

"You're right. As usual. Remind me to let you handle all the morality lessons with Alice."

"Laura, reading these letters wouldn't bother you if you weren't a moral person. I just think I've got a bit more objectivity about the Walterses than you do—I didn't grow up under their shadow."

"They do cast a big one. Kind of like Harvard and Cambridge."

"Now you've lost me," he said.

"We both know Cambridge wouldn't be nearly as interesting a city without Harvard, and Harvard wouldn't be the same kind of place if it weren't in Cambridge. Harvard provides jobs and students with money to spend and intellectual cachet. Cambridge provides a funky, eclectic city for students to fall in love with. Right?"

"Right."

"But the city has been fussing about Harvard for years: they don't pay enough taxes; they use up all the good land; the students cause problems. Ad infinitum."

"Ad nauseum," Richard said.

"Spoken like a true Harvard man. The real reason Cambridge fusses about Harvard is the fact that they've got so much money and clout, making them the biggest target. Maybe that's why so many of us in Byerly fuss about the Walterses. If it weren't for the mill and the bank, Byerly might have dried up and blown away like so many of the other tiny farm towns, and if Byerly weren't such a nice place to live, the Walterses wouldn't have anybody to work in the mills or live in their apartment buildings. But the Walterses have money and clout, and the rest of us resent them."

"Well, I wouldn't say Big Bill was an angel," Richard said.

"No arguments here, but we don't want him to be dancing with the angels, either, at least not for a good long while. So let's get back to work."

The letters weren't sorted—apparently Big Bill had just stuffed new ones into his file as they arrived. So we started by alphabetizing them by the name of the sender. That left a big stack of anonymous letters, but since we didn't know how we could trace those people anyway, we figured we might as well start with the people we could identify.

Once the letters were alphabetized, we counted how many had come from the same person. Our reasoning was that if somebody wasn't mad enough to send Big Bill more than one letter, he or she wasn't likely to be mad enough to kill him. So we eliminated folks who hadn't sent at least two letters.

Next we eliminated the people who hadn't sent a letter since the first of the year. Some of those people from further back had sounded mad enough to chew nails, but it didn't seem reasonable that somebody would have nursed a grudge without taking action sooner.

Then we edited for severity of grievance. Yes, there were many letters from the woman who said that the change she got from the bank was filthy, and the last one had arrived only a few weeks before, but I just didn't think she'd go after Big Bill. If she thought pocket change was nasty, surely she'd find murder unsanitary.

After reading for a while, I got thirsty. Big Bill would just have rung the buzzer for Miz Duffield to carry him something, but I couldn't bring myself to do that. Instead, I left Richard to keep on working while I went foraging. The house was uncomfortably quiet. Even Aunt Maggie's dog, Bobbin, was gone—Thaddeous had taken her home the night before, figuring Aunt Maggie would have enough to handle with Big Bill. I tentatively called out, "Hello?" but when I didn't get an answer, made my way to the kitchen.

Nobody was in there, so I found glasses and opened cans of Coke for Richard and me. There was a pitcher of iced tea in the refrigerator, and while I knew logically that it must have been tested to make sure it wasn't poisoned, I just didn't have a taste for it right then. I was looking for a recycling bin for the empty cans, when I had that funny feeling of being watched, and turned around to see Miz Duffield staring at me. She'd changed her clothes and forced her hair back into a bun, but her disposition hadn't improved.

"Hi," I said.

She continued to glare.

"I didn't know where you were, so I helped myself. I hope you don't mind."

"Why should I mind? I'm just the hired help."

If that was going to be her attitude, the last thing I wanted to do was chat with her, but I had reasons to try. For one, she could be a useful ally in that house. For another, I felt bad about the way she'd been treated by Vasti and Big Bill. And most important, she was a suspect, too. So I plastered on my most ingratiating smile.

She came the rest of the way into the room, eyeing me warily, and I wondered if she was checking out my pants to see if there was room for me to hide the good silver in my pockets.

I said, "I never got a chance to tell you how nice everything looked for the party last night."

"Mrs. Bumgarner was in charge, not me." The disdain with which she said Vasti's name would have made her my chief suspect if Vasti had been poisoned.

"Vasti can be a bit hard to take," I allowed, which was true enough. "Especially with all the commotion you've already had to deal with, what with Aunt Maggie moving in."

"And that dog!"

"Oh, Bobbin. I guess the Walterses don't have any house pets."

"Certainly not."

I tried again. "Now you're going to have an invalid to contend with, too."

"What do you mean?"

"Big Bill is supposed to come home from the hospital tomorrow, but he'll need constant care. Private duty nurses, special equipment, the whole bit."

"Nurses? I don't see why we need to bring in more strangers. I'm perfectly able to tend to Mr. Big Bill, just as I've been doing for years."

"I'm sure you are," I said quickly, "but it wouldn't be fair, would it? You've got so much to take care of already. I don't know how you keep a place this big so immaculate—I can't keep our little place half this clean."

"All it requires is organization and routine," she said with a sniff. But she did add, "Of course, we use a service for the heaviest cleaning tasks."

"Naturally," I said, as if I had a staff of cleaning folks myself, "but you still have to supervise them to make sure the job is done properly."

She nodded in acknowledgment.

Figuring that this was as friendly as she was likely to get, I decided to see if I could get anything useful out of her. "I was wondering, do you have a few minutes? I'd like to ask you some questions."

"What kind of questions?" she said suspiciously.

"Big Bill and Aunt Maggie have asked Richard and me to help find out who wants to harm him. You may have heard that we've done this kind of thing before."

"There has been some talk of your unusual inquisitiveness."

That almost sounded insulting, but I let it pass. Maybe she always talked that way. "It occurred to me that you're in an excellent position to know about anything odd going on here at the mansion." She looked doubtful, so I added some butter. "You've got such a personal relationship with the family, and I know Dorcas thinks the world of you."

Her bosom swelled with pride. "Yes, Mrs. Walters—I mean Mrs. Burt Walters, of course."

"Of course." I suspected that Aunt Maggie would never be "Mrs. Walters" to Miz Duffield, but since I was having problems with that myself, I couldn't very well hold that against her.

Miz Duffield went on. "Mrs. Walters does rely on me. A woman in her position has so many obligations."

"Absolutely," I said, nodding as if I had some idea of what obligations she was talking about.

"She's been working with Mr. Montgomery on the Halloween Carnival for months and has already started arrangements for this year's Jingle Bell Ball. Then there's her work with the Junior League membership committee." She cut her eyes at me. "Your cousin has been proposed for membership, but I'm not sure that she'd be a good match."

I thought that was mighty snotty for a woman who had less chance of gaining entrance into that archetypal ladies' club than Richard did, but I didn't want to destroy our tenuous rapport. So I settled for, "Vasti isn't always the easiest person to get along with, but everybody knows how hard she'll work on whatever project she's involved with, and she's had some amazing successes."

Miz Duffield sniffed once again, but only at half power, so I decided that I'd been diplomatic enough. "Obviously, I picked the right person to talk to. It sounds as if you know just about everything that goes on in and around this house."

"That I do. And the Walterses trust me to respect their privacy."

"Of course, and I wouldn't dream of asking you to violate that if Big Bill hadn't asked me to get involved." Okay, he hadn't really asked me, but he had agreed, which was close enough to satisfy my conscience. "Have you seen anything suspicious, any signs that somebody would want to harm Big Bill?"

"Big Bill Walters is one of the leading citizens in Byerly," she said. "Everybody knows that."

"Granted, but that doesn't make him an easy man to work for." I was watching her carefully when I said that, but she didn't show signs of any emotion other than indignation.

"On the contrary," she said, "I've always found Mr. Big Bill to be an exemplary employer."

Clearly, if she was disgruntled about anything, she wasn't going to admit it to me. "I'm glad to hear that. What about other people? We both know that any man in Big Bill's position attracts enemies, like . . ." I struggled for an appropriate metaphor. "Like hyenas trying to bring down a lion." Okay, it wasn't Shakespeare—it wasn't even good Disney—but it seemed to satisfy her.

"That's true. There are always lesser individuals trying to denigrate him. There's one woman—of course, I hate to indulge in idle gossip . . ."

The look she gave me was as good as an engraved invitation to push, so I obliged her. "I'm sure you wouldn't have taken note of simple gossip."

She smiled tightly. "There is one woman who's been a frequent visitor to the house, a Mrs. Marlyn Roberts. Though she's perfectly polite when Mrs. Walters is in the room, the second she steps out, Mrs. Roberts makes impertinent comments about her and speculates about the family's finances and business practices in the most vulgar fashion imaginable."

"That's terrible," I said. "Do you think she has anything against Big Bill?"

"Apparently so. Mrs. Roberts's former husband had business dealings of some sort with Mr. Big Bill, and the result was not what she hoped for."

"That's interesting." I didn't know much about the Roberts family, though I'd heard the name. They were relative newcomers, having moved to Byerly after I went up north. "Is there anybody else? Somebody who left irate messages for Big Bill, perhaps?"

She considered it but said, "No, nothing I can think of."

The next part was the most delicate, which was why I'd saved it for last. "What about the Walterses themselves? Do they get along well?"

She stiffened and sniffed all at the same time. "Surely you're not suggesting—"

"Of course not," I said quickly. "It's just that people's actions at home often indicate stresses elsewhere." I kept going, hoping she wouldn't think about that piece of psychobabble too hard, because goodness knows it wouldn't withstand the scrutiny. "Of course, Mrs. Walters's behavior is always above reproach, but Burt . . ."

This time I paused significantly to let her prompt me.

She did so eagerly. "Yes?"

"It's probably nothing, but I've heard that Burt hasn't been paying his wife the attention she deserves, that perhaps he's developed another kind of interest." It was amazing how many words I could use without saying a darned thing, but I was fairly sure Miz Duffield could keep up.

"Then you've heard about that . . . that pretty boy at the mill." She'd gone from indignant to angry. "Mrs. Walters is far too refined to speak of him, but from what Mr. Montgomery has said, it's plain just what kind of man he is. If you can call him a man. Mr. Burt and that creature have been having a ridiculous number of meetings since the day he arrived in Byerly. *Private* meetings," she added, in case I hadn't gotten the message.

"Do you really think Burt and he are seeing each other?"

"So far, there have been no signs on Mr. Burt's belongings," she said, which was tantamount to a confession that she'd been checking his clothes for evidence, "and certainly Mr. Burt has never shown such leanings before, but he wouldn't be the first man to have been led astray."

The rumor about Burt and his friend was old news, but I realized that this was the second time Miz Duffield had mentioned Tavis Montgomery.

"Is Mr. Montgomery here often?" I asked.

"Quite often. As I mentioned before, Mrs. Walters has been working on the Halloween carnival with him, and they've become good friends. He's been such a comfort to her, what with the situation with Mr. Burt. He's a very personable man, Mr. Montgomery, and quite handsome."

I couldn't tell if Miz Duffield had a crush on Tavis herself, or was merely sizing him up as an appropriate next marriage for Dorcas. I also had to wonder if Tavis was just being a good friend to Dorcas, or keeping her busy so Burt could do whatever it was he was doing, or something else. With Tavis, it was almost certainly something that would help him advance in the world.

"Thank you, Miz Duffield. You've certainly given me food for thought," I said.

"I'm always happy to do anything I can for Mr. Big Bill or Mrs. Walters."

She hadn't included Burt's name, making it painfully obvious where her loyalties were. That actually made Burt look less likely as a suspect. If Miz Duffield had known about him doing anything remotely suspicious, she'd happily have spilled the beans.

Chapter
Ten

"I know this place is big," Richard said when I finally got back upstairs with our Cokes, "but I didn't think it would take you this long to find the kitchen."

"As a matter of fact," I said loftily, "while you were lounging around, I was interrogating one of our suspects."

"Got out the rubber hose, did you?"

"No, but I thought I was going to have to for a minute. Getting information out of Miz Duffield was like pulling teeth."

"She couldn't have survived working for the Walterses all these years if she wasn't discreet."

"I suppose not. I did pry some stuff out of her." I told him about Mrs. Roberts, the additional gossip about Big Bill and his protégé, and how Tavis was spending a lot of time with Dorcas. "I don't know if any of it helps, but—"

"Is that Marlyn Roberts?" Richard asked.

"I think that's what Miz Duffield said her first name is. Why?"

"Because while you were gadding about, I read a

number of irate letters from a Marlyn Roberts." He held up a stack of perhaps a dozen.

"Let me see!" He handed them over, and I started skimming. When I was done, I said, "I don't know, Richard. She's threatened legal action, not personal violence."

"True, but you have to admit that the letters get progressively more angry."

According to the letters, Marlyn's husband had bought some land from Big Bill, land that had previously been leased by a fuel oil business. The husband had established several other businesses on that land, but they'd all failed. The husband and Marlyn then got divorced, and I had to wonder if the business failures and the divorce were related. In any case, as part of the divorce settlement, the land went to Marlyn, and she wanted to sell it. The problem was, it flunked the prospective buyer's inspection. The land was contaminated with oil, and it would cost a small fortune to clean up. Marlyn was blaming Big Bill, and wanted him to pay for the cleanup or, failing that, to buy the land back. Big Bill refused to do either.

"You're right," I said. "This last letter is pretty nasty. Marlyn is threatening to send the EPA, the newspaper, and a pack of lawyers after Big Bill." I wrinkled my nose. "Do you suppose he really sold contaminated land?"

"Don't ask me; he's your uncle."

"Only by marriage. And he wasn't my uncle when this happened."

"A technicality. Besides, it doesn't matter if he did it or not. Mrs. Roberts believes that he did."

"True, but it still doesn't seem like a good motive for murder. What good would killing him do? He can't pay for the cleanup or buy her land if he's dead."

"No, but his heirs could. Didn't you say that Marlyn is

a friend of Dorcas's? Maybe she was counting on Dorcas to do the right thing once Big Bill is out of the way."

"Good point. We'll put her on our list. What else have you found?"

"I was hoping you'd ask." He hefted a thick sheaf of letters. "These are all from one guy, and the last one came last month."

"One guy?" I said. "Who?"

"Andrew Herron. Do you know him?"

The name sounded vaguely familiar, but I couldn't place it. "I don't think so."

"Good. This one makes me nervous. Take a look."

I read the first letter on the stack. "I see what you mean. He's angry, all right, but I can't quite figure out what he's fussing about. Big Bill stole his ancestral lands?"

"Apparently. As far as I can tell, Herron's mother sold her house and some farm land to Big Bill."

"And?"

"That's it. Herron wants the land back."

"Why? I mean, why does he think Big Bill should return it?"

Richard pulled out a letter and read from it:

> *"On the grounds of human decency and humanity, if a man like you can understand those most meaningful of concepts. Or are you a man at all, and not just a vampiric monster, sucking the blood from defenseless women? The Bible says not to suffer a witch to live, and surely an undead fiend is even less worthy."*

"Both threatening and badly written. How long has this guy been sending letters?"

"As long as Big Bill has been keeping this file. Herron sends another every few months, with especially nasty ones near Christmas and Mother's Day. He's added a web site to the letterhead in the most recent letters, and I shudder to think about what's on it."

"Okay, put him on the list, too."

"At the very top," Richard said. "That's what I've got so far."

I looked at the stack of paper still remaining and sighed. "Okay, let's keep at it."

That's what we did for the next several hours, other than a short break for lunch. Richard went down to the kitchen that time and managed to charm Miz Duffield into fixing us some sandwiches.

We finally made it through the stack at three-thirty or so and had three more reasonable candidates: a woman suffering from brown lung after working at Walters Mill; a man whose home had been foreclosed on by Byerly First National Bank, which Big Bill owned; and a contractor who said Big Bill had fired him without cause. There was also a list of people we didn't think were all that likely, but who might rate some consideration.

"I wonder if all business tycoons have this many enemies," I said when we finished.

"And I thought academia was cutthroat. Some of these make the latest debates between Stratfordians and Oxfordians sound almost civilized."

"It just makes me feel dirty."

Richard waggled his eyebrows. "I know of a much better way to make you feel dirty."

He reached for me, but I said, "Not in Big Bill's office. Nursing in here was strange enough."

"Then might I remind you that Aunt Daphine still has Alice, and Aunt Maggie is probably still at the hospital, which leaves our nice bed at her house available."

"I'll drive."

We hadn't asked Big Bill if we could take the letters with us, and knowing how particular he was about his privacy, we didn't risk it. Instead, we made photocopies of the pertinent ones and left the originals on his desk, where we'd found them. Miz Duffield wasn't in sight, so we left her a note and rushed to Aunt Maggie's house.

After seven months of parenthood, we'd realized that there's nothing like having a baby to make you appreciate a little stolen time.

Chapter
Eleven

After an extremely pleasant interlude, I called the hospital to check on Big Bill. Aunt Maggie told me that the necessary arrangements had been made for him to return to the mansion the next day, and I told her that Richard and I would be there to meet him.

Next I called Aunt Daphine to let her know we were on the way to get Alice. She suggested dinner, and we accepted only under the condition that she let us take her out to pay her back for watching Alice all day. That way, I got to go to Pigwick's Barbecue for Eastern North Carolina-style pulled pork barbecue and claim it was for Aunt Daphine's benefit.

I'd originally planned to ask Aunt Daphine if she had any thoughts or gossip about the attempts on Big Bill, but the conversation turned to Alice and stayed there for quite a while. Next Aunt Daphine had to brag on Vasti's little girl, Bitsy, her only grandchild. Then we had various other bits of family news to chew on along with the barbecue.

We might eventually have moved on to Big Bill's situation if it weren't for the fact that Pigwick's is owned by

Tim Topper, a friend of ours, and when he spotted us he had to come hear all about Alice and parenthood.

By the time all that was over with, we'd ordered thick slices of apple pie for dessert, and I was no longer in the mood to talk about murder. Part of it was reluctance to discuss such things in a crowded restaurant, and part of it was what Richard had said about our having to watch what we said around Alice. All parents do, of course, but some of our topics of conversation were a little bit different. I wondered how cops and private detectives handled the problem with their families.

There was only one thing that happened that was even remotely related to Richard's and my investigation, and at the time, I didn't realize it. Alice got cranky when I was about halfway through with my pie, and I refused Aunt Daphine's offers to take her, assuring her that I was used to eating while soothing a baby. As I arranged Alice on my lap, I noticed a man sitting by himself in the corner. I probably wouldn't have if he hadn't been polite and taken off his ball cap. An awful lot of men seem to think it's okay to wear their caps inside, but this man had put his on the empty chair beside him. Still, manners weren't so rare that I would have paid any attention to him if he hadn't had the oddest-shaped head I'd ever seen. His hair was thinning, and there was a crescent-shaped dent in his head, maybe half an inch deep. Even odder, the man looked familiar.

"Richard," I said, "wasn't that man over there at Big Bill and Aunt Maggie's party?"

"I believe there was more than one man at that party," he said, but took a look without being obvious. "Oh, the man with the unusual head. That's him."

Now I was sure he was a Burnette connection. Friends of the Walterses might get takeout from a barbecue place like Pigwick's, but they wouldn't eat there unless they were campaigning for office. Only when I asked Aunt Daphine, she said she didn't know who he was. I was feeling nosy enough that if he'd paid with a credit card, I might have asked Tim to find out his name, but when the man got up to go, he left cash on the table. I didn't think about him again, at least not that night.

After dinner, we dropped Aunt Daphine off and headed back to Aunt Maggie's. By the time I got Alice ready for bed and nursed her, she was sound asleep, and Richard and I weren't far behind.

Big Bill returned home around midmorning the next day, and I don't think there was a soul in Byerly who didn't know it. He was riding in an ambulance, for one, and though I thought they were only supposed to run their sirens during an actual emergency, Burt must have slipped the driver a little something. The lights were flashing and the siren blaring the whole way. Junior was leading the way in her squad car but mercifully kept her siren shut off.

Richard and I were waiting at the house, having picked up Bobbin for Aunt Maggie when we dropped Alice with Aunt Nora. Big Bill's new nursing staff was there, too, all three dressed in pastel blue drawstring pants with patterned smocks. We'd already exchanged introductions with them and chatted a bit.

Richard had told me about his friend Vivian Foster, but he'd never mentioned that the ex-Army nurse was at least six feet tall and built like a tank. Her dark-brown hair was curled as tightly as if she'd ordered it to stay that way.

Vivian was going to be sharing shifts with Anne and Jan Shuford, a much more petite pair who looked remarkably alike. I'd assumed they were sisters, but found out that they had the same last name because they were married to brothers. Apparently they'd gone to Myrtle Beach on leave and fallen for two vacationing Byerly boys. They regularly worked private duty in the area.

The ambulance pulled up, and I took my fingers out of my ears when they finally turned off that noise. Big Bill's doctor and Aunt Maggie had ridden along, and walked alongside as the attendants wheeled Big Bill into the house. I thought Dr. Patel looked uncomfortable, and wondered if he was completely happy with deceiving people about Big Bill's condition.

Junior joined Richard and me as we watched the attendants wrestle Big Bill up that lovely spiral staircase. The doctor and Aunt Maggie followed along, and Bobbin had abandoned us to accompany Aunt Maggie.

"Big Bill looks a lot better than I expected him to, considering what I'd heard about his physical condition," Junior said, looking right at me.

"He's a tough one," I said. Then I whispered, "We'll talk later." I hadn't asked Big Bill if it was okay to confide in Junior, mainly because I expected him to tell me not to. So as long as I didn't ask him, I could tell her what I thought she needed to know, without any arguments. Junior nodded and went upstairs.

Burt and Dorcas must have followed the ambulance from the hospital, because they arrived a minute later, and Burt huffed and puffed his way past us to be with his father. Dorcas stopped to ask, "Did Big Bill make the trip all right?"

"He's fine," I assured her.

"Thank goodness. I'll tell Irene to fix him something to eat. Are you two going to be staying for lunch?"

"You're sweet to ask, but Richard and I have some things to take care of. We just came to make sure everything was all right, and to bring Bobbin home."

Her nose wrinkled when I said "Bobbin," but just a

tiny bit. "You're welcome any time, and bring that little girl of yours along, too. As far as I'm concerned, the best part about Big Bill's marriage is having babies around." She stopped herself. "I mean—"

"I know what you mean," I said. "It's been a big change for you, especially now, with Big Bill being ill."

She smiled gratefully, then asked, "Laurie Anne, are you and Richard going to be helping Big Bill find out who wants to hurt him?"

Junior was right. Everybody in town had figured it out before I did. "Yes, we are. I hope that doesn't bother you."

"No, not at all. I know we can trust you to find out whoever it is, and to do the right thing. No matter who it is." She said the last part as if it meant something specific, but I didn't know what.

So I just said, "I'll do my best."

She nodded and headed toward the kitchen.

"That was rather touching," Richard said. "I was afraid she'd resist our being around. Instead, she's put her trust in us."

"At least she wanted it to seem that way. Maybe she just wanted to find out whether or not she has to watch out for us. She would have known that it would make her look suspicious if she tried to chase us off."

Richard took a deep breath. "I love the smell of paranoia in the morning."

"Even paranoids have enemies," I told him, but I was wondering if Dorcas's last comment had meant something more. Did she suspect somebody? Had she seen something? I made a mental note to talk to her soon.

The ambulance attendants came down then, followed by Dr. Patel and Burt, who was quizzing the doctor about Big Bill's treatment. Richard and I headed on up. Jan and Anne were tucking in Big Bill's sheet while

Vivian wrapped a sticky contact around one of his fingers as he watched in fascination. That done, she pushed a button on a gadget sitting on a cart next to the bed, and a low-pitched *boop-boop* started as the number *99* flashed onto the machine's display.

"Come see what I've got," Big Bill said. "This here is a pulse oximeter—that noise you're hearing is my pulse. Vivian, what's that number again?"

"The percentage of oxygen in your blood," Vivian said. The number flashed to *100*. "Which you want to keep right there. If it goes much below that, you're not getting enough oxygen."

"Isn't that something?" said Big Bill, as happy as a child with a new toy. "Look at all this stuff," he said, waving his hand around. Suddenly, the pulse oximeter started beeping loudly, and the number display flashed *00*. "What's that mean?" Big Bill asked, sounding as alarmed as the pulse oximeter.

"It means you're moving around too much," Vivian said, and pushed his arm down. A second later, the machine went back to steady pulse sounds and the number went back to 100. "You're supposed to be sick, remember?"

"Right." He settled back in the bed, and as the nurses fiddled with various things, I took a look around. On Big Bill's instructions, Irene had cleared the furniture out of a guest bedroom so they could move in a hospital bed, a rolling tray table, and enameled carts to hold the equipment and various supplies sealed in plastic bags. There was a television on top of a high rack, where Big Bill could see it from his bed, just like in a hospital, and there were several comfortable-looking chairs, presumably for the nurses and Aunt Maggie.

Aunt Maggie was already in one of them, patting

Bobbin, and I thought I heard her apologizing to the dog for leaving her so suddenly. When she saw I was listening, she acted as if she hadn't said anything. I don't think she wanted anybody to know she talked to the dog.

Vivian closed the door to the room and said, "Most of this is just for show, though it could come in handy if there really was an emergency. One of the three of us is going to be in here at all times. Jan's got first shift, seven to three. I come in for three to eleven, and Anne will take eleven to seven. At some point, we'll need to get somebody to relieve us for days off, but not for a week or two."

"I'm hoping we won't need to keep this up that long," I put in.

"Are you women armed?" Big Bill asked.

"No, sir, we're nurses, not snipers. But we're all up to date on hand-to-hand combat, and if that's not good enough, you'd be surprised at what can be done with a scalpel or a hypo." She bared her teeth, and I made a mental note to be scrupulously polite to the nurses the next time I was in the hospital. "We'll carry in our own food, and only eat it or what Mrs. Walters here brings to us. Big Bill and Mrs. Walters should do the same thing."

"Call me Maggie," Aunt Maggie said.

"Maggie it is. The only time we'll leave Big Bill alone is for bathroom breaks. There's an adjoining bathroom, and we'll lock the door to the bedroom before we go, so it should be reasonably safe."

"I'm planning to stay here most of the time, too," Aunt Maggie said.

"Good enough."

With that decided, Vivian and Anne left, leaving Jan to finish out her shift. A few seconds later, Miz Duffield came in with a heavily laden tray. "It's too early for lunch, but I thought you might want a snack, so I made a batch of those pecan rolls you like."

They smelled wonderful, and I could see Big Bill eyeing them, but he looked over at Jan. She shook her head.

Big Bill sank into the bed and mumbled, "I'm tired—don't think I could eat a thing."

"Don't bother bringing him lunch, either," Aunt Maggie said. "I'm going to be taking care of Bill's meals from now on."

Miz Duffield bristled. "I have been cooking meals in this house for over two decades, and there have never been any complaints with my cooking."

"That was before Bill was poisoned here," Aunt Maggie said flatly.

"Are you implying that I was involved with that?" Miz Duffield said.

"I'm not implying a thing. I'm just saying that Bill's not going to eat anything that comes out of your kitchen until we know it's safe." She gave Miz Duffield a look. "I'd think you'd understand that, if you're all so concerned about him."

"Of course I'm concerned about Mr. Big Bill," Miz Duffield snapped. "I'll do anything I can to ensure his safety."

"Good. Then don't bother fetching any more food up here."

About half a dozen emotions flitted across Irene's face before she finally said, "Very well." She didn't so much stomp as march out the door.

"Was that necessary?" Big Bill asked after Miz Duffield was gone. "Irene's not all that bad, and she makes mighty fine pecan rolls."

"We're not taking any chances," Aunt Maggie said. "All I've got to do is figure out how I'm going to keep you fed, because you know I don't cook. I hope you like pizza. Domino's is the only place in town that delivers."

Seeing the grimace on Big Bill's face, I said, "Why don't I talk to Aunt Nora? She probably won't mind fixing some of your meals, and she can get one of her boys to bring them over."

That cheered them both up, and I called Aunt Nora, who said she'd be delighted to cook for them as often as they wanted, and started planning which of her specialties she'd fix first: fried chicken, country-style steak, or chicken and dumplings. By the time I got off the phone, I was ready to start planning Richard's and my schedule so we could be around at mealtimes.

Burt tiptoed in next. "Hey, Daddy, are you doing all right? Can I get you anything?"

"I think I've got everything I need," Big Bill said gruffly, but it was his usual gruffness, not the way he'd been when he thought Burt was trying to kill him.

"Do you want me to keep you company?"

"No need for that. I think I'm going to take me a nap. I imagine you want to get out to the mill before the day is completely gone."

"I was planning on staying home today."

"Is that right?" Big Bill said. "If you've got that much free time, maybe I could make some suggestions. . . ."

Burt quickly added, "But if you're doing all right, maybe I will go on into the office. You let me know if there's anything you need."

"Burt," Aunt Maggie said, "have you ever known Bill to keep quiet when he wants something?"

Big Bill and Burt both grinned. Then Burt leaned down and kissed his father on the cheek before he left. Big Bill blinked a couple of times, and darned if I didn't think there were tears in his eyes.

Being Big Bill, he immediately cleared his throat and

said, "So what have you two found out? I don't aim to spend the rest of my life in this bed."

"We went through the letters in your file," I said, "and came up with some names to ask about." Richard pulled out his notepad with a flourish and handed it to me. "Andrew Herron, Marlyn Roberts, Molly Weston, Jack Morris, and Kevin Dyer. Do any of them sound like likely candidates?"

"Andrew Herron? Isn't he that nutcase out in the woods?"

"You mean Crazy Sandie?" I said, remembering a name I hadn't thought of in years.

"That's him. He's too crazy for me to worry about."

Actually, if half the stories I'd heard about the man were true, he was just crazy enough. "What about Marlyn Roberts?"

"It's a shame about Marlyn," he said, but didn't sound all that sympathetic. "She used to be married to Dyson Roberts, and he managed to cheat her during the divorce settlement. Dyson went broke, so she can't get anything out of him, so she's hoping I'll give her some money to shut her up. Which is never going to happen. Don't worry about her, either. Who else have you got?"

"Molly Weston?"

"No idea—doesn't ring a bell."

"There were two letters from her in your files. She has brown lung."

"If you say so. I can't remember everybody who writes to me."

"How about Jack Morris? You foreclosed on his house."

"Damned right I did—that idiot was two years in arrears on his payments, and it turned out he had twenty-seven cats in that house. Do you have any idea how much it cost to clean that place out? Anyway, he moved to

Rocky Shoals, and when he died last year, darned if they didn't find another dozen cats in his apartment."

"Do any of his people blame you for his death?" I asked.

"I never heard that he had any family, just the cats."

Richard looked at the last man on our list. "Kevin Dyer. He's a contractor who—"

"I remember Dyer. He used substandard materials and charged premium prices. After he tried to cheat me, I spread the word all over the state, so he had to move out west."

"Could he be angry at you for ruining his chances around here?" Richard asked.

"I doubt it. He found much easier pickings out in Kansas. One of the men he cheated called to ask about him, but he'd waited until too late. The man had paid Dyer in advance without bothering to check his references, and then was surprised when he got rooked." He shook his head over the man's lack of business acumen. "Anybody else?"

Unfortunately, those were the best of the lot. Just to be thorough, I read out the names on our second-tier list, but Big Bill pooh-poohed them just as thoroughly. Finally I handed the notebook back to Richard and said, "You better get used to that bed, because you've just shot down every idea we had, and you haven't supplied anything in their place."

"Now, don't get mad," Big Bill said. "It's not my fault that more people don't want to kill me."

"Are you kidding?" I said. "Don't you realize how many people you've riled up over the years?"

"Of course I do, but most of them don't matter. You see, Laurie Anne, this is how I do business. If I run up against somebody weaker than I am, I win because I'm stronger, and they learn not to mess with me again. If I run up against somebody as strong as I am, I win them over so they'll do business with me. If I run up against somebody stronger than I am . . . Well, I've only done that twice, and I married both of them."

Aunt Maggie looked gratified by the compliment, but I was still exasperated. "There must be another category out there, because somebody wants you dead."

Big Bill sighed. "I'm sorry, Laurie Anne, but I just don't know who it could be. Go ahead and talk to those people if you want—maybe I'm wrong about one of them."

I looked at Richard, who nodded, and as we got up to go, I said, "We may as well get to it." I know I didn't sound very optimistic, but then again, I wasn't feeling all that optimistic.

Chapter Twelve

As Richard and I were on our way out the front door, I spotted Dorcas looking through the mail and whispered, "Richard, why don't you go on out to the car? I want to talk to Dorcas." There'd been so many movies where the sleuth had been given an enigmatic hint, only to have the hinter killed before the sleuth could follow up. I intended to talk to Dorcas while she was still alive and kicking.

"Mrs. Walters, can I speak to you for a minute?" I said.

"Certainly," she said, putting down the mail. "Shall we go into the study?"

She led the way into what I thought was one of the lovelier rooms in the house, a study decorated in Chinese-style furniture with a gorgeous Oriental rug and massive Ming vases. Dorcas took one of the chairs flanking the fireplace and gestured me toward the other. "How can I help you, Laurie Anne?"

"I've been thinking about what you said earlier, how you trusted me to find out who was trying to kill Big Bill,

no matter who it was. It sounded as if you had somebody in mind."

"I'm afraid I do." She paused.

"Can you tell me who?"

"Let me ask you a question first. Suppose you knew
an older man—a wealthy older man—who suddenly married a woman who was not nearly so well provided for. If
somebody tried to kill that man just a few days after
he'd changed his will in favor of his new bride, who
would you suspect?"

I swallowed my initial reaction and counted to ten
three times before saying, "I can see why somebody
might suspect the new bride. But there's something you
don't know."

"Oh?"

"There were three attempts on Big Bill's life before
he and Aunt Maggie got married."

"Really? I had no idea."

"Big Bill and Aunt Maggie were keeping it quiet,
hoping to find out who the person was themselves."

"Why didn't Big Bill tell Burt and I?" A second later
she answered her own question. "He was afraid it was
Burt, wasn't he? Or me?"

I just couldn't lie to her, so I nodded.

"I suppose I can't blame him," Dorcas said, "but I'd
thought Big Bill was as fond of me as I am of him."

"He is; he really is. He's just scared. Not that he'll
ever admit it."

"Never," she said. "That's the kind of man he is. I remember the first time I met him . . ." She looked into
the distance. "He was such a vital man, even more so
than now. I nearly fell in love with him that night—if it
hadn't been for Burt's mother, I very well could have."

It didn't sound like much of a foundation for her
marriage to Burt, and she must have realized that.

"Then I met Burt," she added with a small smile, "and realized he was the right man for me. Big Bill was a force of nature, as impossible to tame as a hurricane, and just as impossible for me to live with. Burt was something else—I knew who he was, and what we could do together." Then she looked down at her hands, and I thought she was studying her diamond-encrusted engagement ring and wedding band. "At least, I thought I knew him." She seemed to pull herself together. "If it's any help to you, Laurie Anne, I can assure you that I would never harm Big Bill."

I nodded, though I knew she could have been lying. I also found it interesting that she didn't add a similar comment about Burt. She really was afraid she didn't know her husband anymore.

"There must be other suspects," Dorcas said. "Big Bill is a good man, but any man as powerful as he is has enemies."

"That's putting it mildly," I said ruefully. "Richard and I spent hours going through his file of threatening letters. A lot of them are from nuts, but some are worth investigating." Dorcas looked interested in hearing more, but I realized that I might already have said too much. "If it makes you feel any better, we're doing our best for Big Bill."

"Thank you, Laurie Anne; that is a comfort. If there's anything I can do to help, just let me know."

"I will," I promised.

The door to the room opened then, and Miz Duffield stuck her head in.

"Yes, Irene?" Dorcas said.

"Mr. Montgomery is here, ma'am."

"Is it that time already?" Dorcas said, checking the slim gold watch on her wrist. "Please show him in." To me, she said, "You'll have to excuse me, Laurie Anne.

Tavis and I have to go over some last-minute decisions for the Halloween carnival."

"Richard and I need to be going, anyway."

Irene brought Tavis in. "Hello, Dorcas," he said, and gave her a peck on the cheek. "How's Big Bill?"

"Still very weak," Dorcas said, "but the doctor has every expectation that he'll recover completely."

"Thank goodness," Tavis said. "Are you sure you're up to this meeting? I don't want to intrude."

"No, I need to keep busy. Besides, I don't want to put an extra burden on you."

"You're too conscientious," he said admiringly.

I shouldn't have been watching the two of them so blatantly, but I was thinking about what Miz Duffield had said about Tavis. Tavis noticed right away and, as I stood up, came over to give me the exact same kind of kiss he'd given Dorcas. Since we'd never been kissing friends before, I didn't know if he was covering his tracks or just being a consummate politician. Then again, maybe I was still being paranoid.

"I better let y'all get to work," I said.

"I'll walk you out," Dorcas said, and escorted me to the front door. In a low voice, she said, "I apologize for suspecting your aunt, Laurie Anne. You may not believe it, but I do like her very much."

"You just didn't want her to marry Big Bill," I said.

Dorcas was far too well bred to agree explicitly. "It was unexpected," was all she would admit to, and she even added, "Perhaps Maggie is just what Big Bill needs." Then, as she closed the door behind me, she sadly said, "But that dog of hers . . ."

Once I got into the car with Richard, I told him what Dorcas had told me.

"Do you believe her?" he asked when I was done.

"She seemed sincere. Of course, acting convincingly sincere is a survival skill for pillars of society."

"Did you consider the idea that her accusing Aunt Maggie was a clever ruse to find out if we knew about the other attempts on Big Bill's life?"

"You mean, did I just feed her information she needed? Shoot, I never thought of that. I should have let you talk with her."

"I probably would have done the same thing," he said kindly. "Besides, I can't see how the information could be that vital."

I didn't either, but that didn't mean that I should go around blabbing everything to our suspects. Maybe seven months of baby talk had caused my brain to atrophy.

"Where to next?" Richard asked.

"How about Aunt Nora's house? Big Bill wasn't much help with our potential suspects, but maybe Byerly's gossip connection will have more for us."

"I smell ulterior motives."

"It is getting on toward lunch time, if that's what you mean. Aunt Nora might have some spare servings of whatever she's making for Big Bill and Aunt Maggie."

"Always an attraction, but I think there's even more to it than that. You miss Alice, don't you?"

"I'm sure she's fine."

"But you miss her!"

I sighed. "Yes, I miss her."

"Why are you so embarrassed about it?"

"I don't know, Richard. Maybe because I promised myself I wouldn't be one of those clingy mothers who doesn't think anybody else can take care of her child. It's not like an infant Alice's age even knows who's changing her diaper."

"Not true," Richard said. "According to the literature, seven- month-olds are able to recognize their parents, both by sight and scent."

"I wouldn't dream of arguing with the literature," I said. "Still, I've been dying for a chance to be alone with you, and Aunt Nora is perfectly willing to babysit for as long as we want, but all I can think about is Alice. It's making me crazy. I feel like such a . . ."

"A woman? A mother?"

"A cliché! I'm a cliché new mother!"

"Egad, can the horror of driving a minivan be far behind?"

"I'm serious, Richard. Right now, I can't even stand to think about going back to work." My company's policy, created at the height of the Internet boom as an inducement for recruiting employees, was incredibly generous, and I'd augmented it with vacation time and unpaid leave, but I was going to have to go back someday if I wanted to keep my job.

"Is this what this is about? Are you feeling guilty because of what Vasti said? Do you want to quit your job and stay home with Alice?"

"No. Yes. I don't know."

He put his hand on my shoulder. "Laura, we don't have to decide anything right now. And whatever we do decide isn't carved in stone—we can change courses as many times as necessary until we're comfortable."

I nodded, but I still felt confused. Making the decision to go up north to school had been so easy for me, and even deciding to stay in Massachusetts hadn't taken too long. Though it had taken Richard and me a while to get around to having a baby, once we decided, I hadn't questioned myself. Now I didn't know what to do with myself or with Alice.

Aunt Nora shushed us as soon as we came in the

back door of her house. "Alice is sleeping. I've got her laid down in Thaddeous's room."

I knew Alice was fine, of course, but that didn't stop me from sneaking back there to take a peek. Aunt Nora had made a pallet of blankets to lay her on, and the baby was flat on her stomach, as limp as only a baby can be.

When I got back to the kitchen, Aunt Nora had already set two places for lunch and was pouring me a glass of iced tea. Richard, who just can't overcome his Northern roots enough to appreciate iced tea, was drinking Coke.

"As long as y'all are here, I thought y'all might want a bite to eat," Aunt Nora said.

"You'll get no argument from me," I said. "Aren't you eating?"

"I can't eat when I'm cooking. I nibble and taste enough to make three meals."

Knowing that Aunt Nora preferred not to have anybody getting in her way in the kitchen, I took my chair and watched as she cut thick slices of ham to make two enormous sandwiches with mayonnaise. Then she put the sandwiches and generous scoops of potato salad onto our plates and waited for us to take a bite. "Is it all right?" she asked anxiously.

"It's perfect," I said as soon as I could speak. "When are you going to believe us when we tell you you're the best cook we know?"

She dimpled. "You're just saying that."

Richard and I assured her that we were completely serious, but she continued to deny the compliments. It was a familiar ritual that we all enjoyed.

Aunt Nora finally allowed that the food wasn't too bad, and sat down with a glass of iced tea for herself. "I hope Big Bill doesn't mind ham sandwiches. I know he's used to eating better than that, but I didn't have anything else in the house to cook."

"I'm sure he'll be tickled to death," I said.

"Well, at least it will keep him from going hungry until I can fix him something worth eating for dinner. I'll go by the store as soon as Alice gets up from her nap, and if it's not too late, run by the farm stand to see what they've got."

"Do you want us to take her back while you run your errands?" Richard asked.

"Absolutely not," Aunt Nora said. "I'm looking forward to showing her off around Byerly. And I imagine y'all have things to do for Big Bill this afternoon."

"We might," I said, "but we wanted to pick your brain a bit first."

She grinned conspiratorially. "I love it when I can help y'all—it makes all my gossiping seem worthwhile. Who do you want to know about?"

"What can you tell us about Andrew Herron? That's Crazy Sandie's real name." Herron seemed like the best place to start because he'd written the most letters, and because his were the most ominous. Besides which, now that I knew that Andrew Herron was Crazy Sandie, I was curious. Even in a town like Byerly, that was proud of its eccentrics, Crazy Sandie stood out. In fact, from reading his letters to Big Bill, I was pretty sure he'd gone way past eccentric. Though I'd never met him myself, I knew some of the stories about him and was sure Aunt Nora would have more details.

"Sandie Herron," Aunt Nora said, shaking her head sadly. "He was a wild one when he was growing up, always getting into scrapes. He drank and he caroused and he messed with women. All the things that drive mothers crazy—his mama had it rough. Augustus was just a little thing when Sandie went through the worst of his escapades, and I used to pray that he wouldn't turn out like that. Miz Herron was a widow, and Sandie was her only child. Which might have been a blessing, come to think of it. He was only nineteen or twenty when he just up and left town.

"Nobody in Byerly would have blamed Miz Herron for being relieved, but she was his mama and she worried about him something fierce. She spent a lot of money trying to find him, even though she didn't really have it to spend, but never found a trace of him. A few years later, she got cancer, and the bills started to pile up. That's when Big Bill came calling, wanting to buy her land. The Herrons were farmers once upon a time, and they had a good-sized piece of property on the side of town closest to Hickory. Miz Herron hadn't given up hope that her boy would come back, so she didn't want to sell the only thing she had to leave him, but her health got worse and the bills got bigger, and Big Bill was mighty persuasive. Eventually, she gave in and sold him the land."

"Bullying a sick widow?" I said. "That's awfully cold."

"It wasn't like that, not exactly. Big Bill gave her a fair price, even if it wasn't top dollar, and Miz Herron used the money to spend the rest of her life in a real nice extended-care facility. There was a good bit of money left over, which she left in trust for Sandie, hoping that the bank would be able to find him."

Richard said, "I take it that they did, or we wouldn't be having this conversation."

But Aunt Nora shook her head. "No, they never did. One day a few months after his mother died, he just showed up, as suddenly as he'd gone. Nobody knew where he'd been or what he'd done. He did have some scars on him that hadn't been there before, but as far as I know, he's never explained anything."

"Very mysterious," Richard said.

Aunt Nora went on. "The first thing he did was head for his mama's house, only to find out that the house was gone. Big Bill had put in a housing development on that land, all nice split-levels."

"Big Bill must have made a pretty penny off the deal," I said.

"Probably," she agreed. "Somebody told Sandie about his mother's death and how she'd sold the land, and he was beside himself! He accused Big Bill of terrible things, but Big Bill had bought the land fair and square, and there wasn't a thing Sandie could do about it. Eventually, he calmed down enough to go get the money his mama had left him, and he built himself a house out in the woods. I say house, but it's not much more than a shack—he's got electricity and a phone, but I don't know that he uses either very often. There he sits, and I guess he's still living off his mama's money, because as far as I know he never leaves there if he can help it. He's got no family or friends, not even a dog."

"A modern-day hermit, only without the religious overtones," Richard said. "Would it be safe to go see him?"

"I think so. He's never really hurt anybody."

"That's reassuring."

I added, "I used to hear all kinds of stories about him when I was younger."

Aunt Nora waved that away. "Kids have to have a bogeyman to tell tall tales about. Now, Sandie once chased some boys off his property, but only because they were throwing rocks at his house. And he was pretty rude to the census taker a couple of years ago, but he didn't attack him or anything."

He still didn't sound like somebody I'd want to spend

time with. "We may as well not bother going out there. There's no way he's going to talk to us."

Aunt Nora grinned widely. "That's where you're wrong. I've got a way to get you into his house right here." She got up to rummage around in some cardboard boxes on the hutch, then held up a thick booklet labeled *Byerly First Baptist Church: Legacy of Faith.* "The church put together a memory book with ads for a fund-raiser. Sandie was on my list, so I sent him a note about it and mentioned that one of the pictures we were going to use was of his mama. I didn't expect anything to come of it, but darned if he didn't send in money for an ad. Cash, mind you. I don't know that he's even got a checking account, what with Big Bill owning the bank. Anyway, Sandie's entitled to a free copy of the book, which I was planning to mail this week, but maybe you'd like to deliver it in person."

"That sounds like an excellent idea," I said.

Richard still looked doubtful, but agreed to go.

Alice woke up then, so I took the opportunity to nurse her before we left, which went a long way toward reassuring me that I wasn't a terrible mother.

I learned to drive on Byerly's roads, and know most of the town's streets and shortcuts, but if it hadn't been for Aunt Nora's detailed directions, I'd never have found Sandie Herron's place. He'd worked hard to find the most isolated spot he could, and even the spread of housing developments hadn't reached him yet—I wasn't sure it ever would. The long driveway was barely more than a path, and from the height of the weeds filling it, I didn't think Herron had left the place in a month. At least, not by car.

Aunt Nora had been kind when she called Herron's house a shack. I'd seen tree houses that looked sturdier than that place. It had been built of scraps of wood and asphalt shingles, and instead of a porch or stoop, it just had a pile of concrete bricks to step on to get to the front door. I couldn't tell if the windows were clean, or even unbroken, because they were covered with wooden shutters. The building didn't seem to be in immediate danger of falling over, but that was as much of a recommendation as I was willing to give. The mold-green pickup truck parked beside the house was so battered that I was surprised it wasn't up on blocks.

Not surprisingly, there was no doorbell, so Richard had to pound on the front door with his fist.

A minute passed, and we were about to knock again when the door swung inward, the hinges creaking loudly as if rarely used. A man peered out from the dim interior, his eyes blinking at the early afternoon sunlight, even though it was overcast that day. "Can I help you?" he said politely but with no warmth in his voice.

Crazy Sandie didn't look at all the way I'd expected from his reputation and the appearance of his house. I'd thought he'd be a mangy-looking biker, or maybe a wild-eyed militia type. Instead, he seemed oddly familiar, and after a few seconds, I realized that he looked just like Opie on the old *Andy Griffith Show.* Not the man that actor Ron Howard had become, but the child character morphed into a grown-up. His hair was red, his face freckled, and he was even neatly dressed in the kind of dungarees and shirt I remembered Opie wearing in the show. The only thing at war with the illusion was a puckered scar running along one cheek.

"Mr. Herron?" I said.

He nodded.

"I'm Laura Fleming, and this is my husband, Richard. My aunt Nora Crawford asked me to drop this off for you." I held up the memory book.

"Mama's picture!" he said, and grabbed it from me. He thumbed through it, muttering, "Where is it? Where is it?" Finally he stopped at a page and held it out so we could see it. "That's Mama," he said proudly.

The picture was a grainy black-and-white shot of a ponytailed young woman posed holding out a frozen turkey to a child. Sandie read the caption out loud: "'Eva Marie Volin (later Eva Volin Herron) demonstrating Christian spirit at Thanksgiving.'" He let out a deep sigh. "That was Mama all over—spending her time helping others."

"Bless her heart," I said. It's an expression with no real meaning, but sometimes it's the only proper thing to say.

Herron flipped through the book to the section of ads at the back. "Here's the ad I put in for her." It was a full page, and in print so ornate it was hard to read, it read, *God couldn't be everywhere, so he created Mothers. In honor of the finest mother ever, Eva Marie Volin Herron.*

"Isn't that sweet?" I said, relying once again on verbal white noise. Herron didn't seem to mind, or even notice.

He turned back to the picture of his mother and moved the book closer to his face to examine it. "They just photocopied this, didn't they? Why on earth didn't they scan it?"

Taken aback, I said, "I didn't have anything to do with producing the book. Aunt Nora just asked me to deliver it."

He nodded absently. "I can probably clean up the image in Photoshop, if I can get my new scanner up and running."

"Scanner problems?" I said, then looked at Richard, who shrugged. We hadn't expected such a convenient opening, but we'd be fools not to take advantage of it.

"As a matter of fact, I'm a programmer, and I'm pretty good with troubleshooting. Would you like me to take a look?"

"Would you?" He broke into a grin. "I'd love to up-load this picture onto my web site, if I can get halfway decent resolution. Come on in!" He opened the door the rest of the way and stepped aside so Richard and I could enter.

It was a pretty big room, and I guessed it was the only room in the house, other than the bathroom I could see through a partially opened door. There was a small fire-place, a scarred single bed that looked as if it had been left on the street for Goodwill, and one armchair with the stuffing coming out on one side. One corner of the room had a cabinet nailed to the wall over a sink, and there were a card table and metal folding chair to play the part of dining room furniture. There was no televi-sion, and the bare bulb overhead was the only light.

Clearly, Sandie wasn't spending his money on luxuri-ous furniture, but I could tell he wasn't so stingy when it came to his computer. Aunt Nora had mentioned that Sandie had electricity and a phone, and he was making use of both to power a PC, as well as a modem, scanner, laser printer, and color ink-jet printer. The particle-board tables everything was laid out on looked homemade, but the equipment itself was top notch.

Though the computer was the first thing I noticed, what really caught my eye was the opposite wall. It was covered in photos of every description: formal portraits, blown-up snapshots, newspaper clippings, school photos, fuzzy Polaroids. And every one of them was of Sandie's mother, at every age from infant to grown woman. It was obvious that some of the shots had originally included others, probably her parents or husband or Sandie himself, but everybody but Eva Marie had been carefully cropped out. No wonder he'd shuttered the windows— he was using the extra wall space for more pictures.

"That's my mama," Herron said unnecessarily. "I broke her heart, but I don't think she ever stopped loving me. I hope she didn't, anyway."

"I'm sure she didn't," I said. "Richard and I have a little girl, and there's nothing in this world that would ever make me stop loving her."

" 'If I were damned of body and soul, I know whose prayers would make me whole, Mother o' mine, O mother o' mine,' " Richard quoted. "Rudyard Kipling."

"I like that," Herron said. "Maybe I can put that on my web site with the picture." As he sat down in front of his computer and started pressing keys, he said. "It's a site about Mama."

Somehow I wasn't surprised. "Kipling?" I whispered to Richard.

"The Bard didn't have much to say about mothers," he said, "and the only other quote I have is 'A boy's best friend is his mother.' "

"That's nice."

"It's from *Psycho*, so I thought it might not be appropriate."

Then again, maybe it was a little too appropriate. I forced myself to turn away from Sandie's wall of tribute and said, "Let's see what we can do with that scanner."

The problem turned out to be fairly easy to fix. The software that had come with Sandie's scanner wasn't compatible with his system, so all I had to do was download the right version from the manufacturer's web site and install it. Once that was done, Sandie wasted no time in scanning the photo and ad from the church memory book and printing them out to add to the wall of pictures.

"The resolution still isn't as good as it should be," he said critically, "but I guess it will do."

"If you like, I could ask Aunt Nora to track down the original photo," I said. "You'd get a much clearer image that way."

"You think you could? I sure would appreciate that." He beamed just like Opie had when offered a big piece of apple pie. "Do you want to see my web site?"

"Sure," I said. I wasn't sure if I should applaud the Internet for letting a man retain some contact with the world, even in isolation, or complain that it was allowing him to maintain his isolation. Then again, I didn't figure that Sandie would have been a people person whether he had a computer or not.

Once he got the site open, he took us on a virtual tour of his mother's life, from pictures of his grandmother pregnant with her to shots of the flowers surrounding her coffin. "I need to figure out when this new one of her was taken, so I can put it in chronologically." He looked delighted at the prospect. "I'll give you the URL so you can come back and take a look later." Judging from the low numbers on the site's "Number of visitors" counter, we were likely the only ones other than Sandie who would ever visit it. He said, "I'll warn you, it's a pretty big site. It takes me forever to open it, but of course, I can't get broadband out here."

"That's one of the advantages of living in Boston," I said. "We get these things pretty early on."

"I guess you would at that."

Sandie and I started talking about file compression utilities, and I saw that Richard had lost interest and gone back to look at the pictures of Sandie's mother. That reminded me that we hadn't come by to indulge in a geekfest. I'd managed to get comfortable with Sandie. Now I was ready to try asking him some questions.

"You know," I said, "with all the new development going on, maybe they will get broadband out here. Didn't Big Bill Walters just break ground on a new project?" I didn't know if Big Bill was doing anything nearby, but considering his history, it seemed like a fair bet.

Sandie's face darkened, and he glowered at me, for the first time looking like the Crazy Sandie I'd imagined. "Don't talk to me about that son of a bitch!"

"I'm sorry," I said. "Do you know Big Bill?" I knew he did, but I figured asking it that way didn't count as a lie.

"I don't need to know him—I know what he did to Mama."

"I'm sorry," I said again, but Sandie needed no further prompting to pour out the story.

"I was away from home when it happened," he said, leaving out the fact that he'd been gone for years. "Mama was bad sick, and she needed money, but Big Bill Walters wouldn't loan it to her like a decent man. No, he wanted her land, land that had been in our family for generations. Even though she didn't want to sell, he badgered her and badgered her, and finally she didn't have any other choice. She had to go to some home to live out the rest of her days among strangers, and she died alone." He inhaled raggedly. "You'd think the law would be able to do something to a man like that, but he's smart; I'll give him that. He put up a bunch of cracker-box houses on Mama's land and started raking in the money. The bastard wouldn't so much as talk to me when I went to tell him what I think about him, and he doesn't even have the decency to answer my letters."

Having read those letters, I didn't see what Big Bill could have said in reply, but I didn't think it would be a smart thing to say, so I made sympathetic sounds. Richard had rejoined us, and I knew he was trying to figure out what to do if Sandie lost control.

Sandie growled, "If that man was on fire, I wouldn't bother to piss on him to put it out!" Then he shook himself. "Pardon my French. Mama never wanted me to cuss, but it's a hard habit to break." He looked fondly at the wall of pictures, as if apologizing to his dead mother.

"That's all right," I said with a weak smile.

Richard said, "Well, I think Laura and I need to be going. We've got some more stops to make."

"We sure do," I agreed, edging toward the door. "Very nice meeting you, Sandie."

"Y'all, too. I sure appreciate your help with my scanner."

"Any time." I thought about giving him my e-mail address in case he needed help again, but remembered the expression on his face when he talked about Big Bill, and decided against it. "You take care."

He walked us out the few steps to the door and waved as we went to the car. The last thing he said as we climbed in was, "You'll ask your aunt about that picture of Mama, won't you?"

"You bet," I assured him. He had his front door closed tightly before I even had time to turn the car around.

"That was scary," I said as we drove out. "Remember how you said Sandie was like a hermit without the religion? Well, he does have a religion after all. He worships his mother."

"What do you think? Guilt over not being here when she got sick?"

"I guess." I shuddered. I thought a lot of my late mother, but I'd never considered papering the walls with her pictures. "Richard, I want Alice to love me and respect me, but if she ever starts to act like that . . ."

"I'll have her in therapy before you can say *Oedipus Rex.*"

Chapter
Thirteen

"So," Richard said as we drove, "do you think it was him?"

"He sure hates Big Bill enough, but he doesn't fit all that well. He could have handled the attempted shooting, assuming he has a gun . . ."

"I saw a rack in his pickup truck," Richard said, "and a box of ammunition mixed in with the canned goods."

"Good catch. Then he could easily have done that part, and Big Bill did say it was a pickup that nearly ran him over. Since Sandie apparently built that house of his, he'd probably have been able to rig the trap at the apartment complex. The problem is, how could he have known where Big Bill was going to be?"

"I hadn't thought of that," Richard said. "I suppose he could have followed him."

"No way. People would have started talking if they'd seen Crazy Sandie around town."

"If they recognized him," Richard pointed out. "You'd never seen him before."

"True. I bet most people don't know what he looks like. Which means that he could even have snuck into the party. He could have found out about that in the *Byerly Gazette*—even if he doesn't get the paper, there's an online version. I think I'd remember him if I'd seen him, but I'm sure there were people I didn't see."

"So he stays on the list?"

"I'm afraid so."

"Okay, but if it comes to that, we're letting Junior arrest him. That guy makes me nervous."

"You and me both," I said. "Where to now?"

"What about the desperate divorcée?" Richard said. "Marlyn Roberts."

"That might be worthwhile. Miz Duffield says she comes over to the Walters house a lot, which would have given her the opportunity to check on Big Bill's schedule. And I bet she was at the party, too. Do we have her address?"

"It's on her letters," Richard said, "but do you think we should just barge in on her?"

"Probably not." I frequently use my aunts and cousins to help me find my way into strangers' houses, but none of them traveled in Mrs. Roberts's social circle. Fortunately, I knew somebody who did. "Richard, why don't you get the cell phone out of my pocketbook and call Dorcas? She might be able to set something up for us."

"Don't you think using a murder suspect to approach another suspect is, well, suspect?"

"If Dorcas is innocent and really wants to protect Big Bill, she'll be happy to do it. If she's guilty, then she'll be happy to point us in the wrong direction. Either way, we'll get a chance to talk to Marlyn Roberts."

Richard called the Walters house and explained the situation to Dorcas. For whichever reason, she was willing to help, and since she was going to a committee meeting at Marlyn's house the next morning, she suggested that Richard and I meet her there.

By the time that was all arranged, it was too late in the day to go after anybody else. "Should we sneak back to Aunt Maggie's house?" I asked Richard with a leer.

"Tempting, but we might run into Aunt Maggie. Dorcas said she had gone over there to pick up some things for the white elephant sale."

"Rats!" I was about ready to head back to Aunt Nora's to get Alice when I had a thought and made a sudden turn, catching the poor guy in the Taurus behind us by surprise.

"How about a little warning next time?" Richard said, picking up the papers my sudden turn had flipped into the floor.

"Sorry. I was just thinking that we should go visit Junior. She said she'd share information if we would. What we've got is fairly useless, but she might have something better."

Byerly's station was a far cry from the massive police complex in Boston. The front room held two desks, one for Junior and one for her deputies to share, a photocopier, and the radio equipment. As I knew from previous visits, the room's closed door led to the two cells and a large storage closet I assumed was used for weapons, evidence, and such.

Junior's new deputy, Belva, was at her desk, and had just hung up the phone when Richard and I walked in. Though Belva wasn't the prettiest woman I'd ever seen, I did envy her those soft blond curls.

"Hey there, Deputy Tucker," I said.

"Mrs. Fleming, Mr. Fleming. What can I do for y'all?"

"We were looking for Junior," I said. "Is she around?"

"No, she's taking the afternoon off. Is there anything I can help you with?"

"I'm not sure." Though Belva and I had disagreed in the past, she was working for Junior now, and it only made sense for me to make nice with her. "I don't know if Junior told you, but Richard and I are kind of investigating the Big Bill Walters case on our own."

"She did tell me, and she also said that I was to share information with you, as long as it isn't too sensitive."

"Really? Great."

"The thing is, I'm not supposed to tell you anything until after you tell me what you've got." She chuckled. "The chief sure does have a suspicious mind."

"That's why she's the chief." I took a seat and, with Richard adding pieces as I forgot them, told Belva what we'd been doing and who we suspected. "It's not much," I admitted once I was done.

"It gives us some more backgrounds and alibis to check, so that's something. The fact is, we don't have a whole lot, either. Lab reports verify that the isopropanol was in Mr. Walters's cup, not the champagne bottle, so he was definitely the target. Results on Mrs. Walters's cup were inconclusive—that housekeeper did too good a job of washing. No useful fingerprints anywhere, and we can't find the bottle you saw in the kitchen. We questioned purt near everybody at the party, but we still aren't sure who poured the champagne, and nobody saw anybody doing anything suspicious."

"With all the people around, I'd have thought somebody would have seen something," I said.

But Belva said, "Sometimes it works out that the bigger the group is, the less likely anybody is to notice anything. Too much confusion makes details like pouring champagne nigh onto impossible to keep up with."

"I can see that," Richard said. "Lately, I don't seem to notice anything but what Alice is up to."

Belva went on. "So basically, we've got zip from the party. The chief and I checked out the other places where Mr. Walters says he was attacked, but there was nothing we could use. We couldn't find the bullet from where somebody shot at him, so that lets out ballistics, and any tire tracks that might have been left from when he was nearly run down are long gone. As for the trap at the apartment complex, we talked to everybody who lives in that neighborhood or who had business there, but nobody saw anything useful. The materials used in the trap all came from the site, and they've all been moved around since then, anyway.

"We checked out the alibis for the most obvious suspects, Mr. Walters's son and daughter-in-law, but they're not in the clear for any of the times we were interested in. Mr. Walters can't come up with anybody else who might want him harmed, which is why I'm glad to have those other names to check into."

"I'm glad we could help," I said, "but I swear it seems like this many intelligent people could come up with something better. At this rate, we may as well wait for whoever it is to try again."

Belva just shrugged, and I suspected she was thinking the same thing.

"Thanks for your time, Deputy," I said as I got up, and Richard added, "May I say that it's much more pleasant to work with you than against you."

"I hear that. But call me Belva."

"Gladly. I'm Richard."

I started to tell her to call me Laura, but figured I might as well bow to the inevitable. "You can call me Laurie Anne."

"All right. Y'all take care, and I'll pass on what y'all told me to the chief."

Since we were all being so friendly, as we started to leave I said, "You know, this is probably none of my business, but Junior really doesn't like you to call her 'Chief.' "

Belva's face broke into a wide grin. "I know. I'm just

waiting to see how long it's going to take for her to tell me that herself."

I grinned back. Belva and Junior were going to get along just fine.

Chapter
Fourteen

Since Mrs. Roberts traveled in more elevated circles than Sandie Herron did or, admittedly, than I did myself, the next morning I abandoned my jeans for a nice pair of black slacks and a purple knit top. Richard was wearing his usual khakis, but he had dressed them up with a button-down shirt. Alice was more casual in a pair of green overalls with a polka-dot T-shirt, but since she was spending the day with Aunt Nellie and Uncle Ruben, she was perfectly in style.

The Robertses' house wasn't as big as the Walterses' place, but it looked a lot nicer than any house I ever expected to live in, at least from a distance. As Richard and I walked up the sidewalk, I noticed that the place could have used a coat of paint, and while the lawn had been mowed, it didn't have the look of having been weeded with a pair of eyebrow tweezers that the neighboring yards had. The two cars in the driveway were high-end Saabs but looked at least a couple of years old. Maybe Richard's description of Marlyn as a desperate divorcée was more accurate than we'd realized.

There was no counterpart to Miz Duffield, either. Instead, a teenaged girl in jeans, an oversized PowerPuff Girls T-shirt, and clunky clogs answered the door. She had a backpack slung over one shoulder.

"Hi, I'm Laura Fleming and this is my husband, Richard," I said. "We're here to help out with the Halloween carnival."

"My mother's expecting you," she said politely, and like any other teenager in America would have done, she turned and yelled, "Mom! Some people are here to help with the posters. I've got to go—I'm meeting Brittany at the mall!"

She held the door for us to come in. "Mom will be here in a minute." Then she clomped down the sidewalk and climbed into the more beat-up of the cars in the driveway.

"Tell them I'll be right there," said a voice from upstairs, and a minute later, a woman dressed in a perfectly pressed pair of tan slacks and a rose blouse came down. Her hair was a lovely shade of ash blond that matched her daughter's, but from the lines in her face, I had a hunch that she'd had help keeping it that way.

She smiled graciously when she saw us. "I'm sorry. Did Katelyn just leave y'all standing there?"

"No problem," Richard said. "She said she had to meet Brittany at the mall."

The woman rolled her eyes and sighed. "The mall isn't even open yet, so I don't know what difference another two minutes would have made." She held her hand out to me. "I'm Marlyn Roberts. I don't think we've met."

"Laura Fleming," I said, taking her hand, and murmured that I was pleased to meet her, though I'd just realized where I'd seen her before. She was the woman who'd called Aunt Maggie a battle-ax at the party. I immediately moved her to the top of my mental list of suspects, just out of spite. Then I introduced Richard.

"Dorcas Walters asked us to come—she said y'all were a little short of help. I hope we're not too early."

"Oh, the others will be along. Volunteers always come late, or even change their minds about helping at the last minute, but what can we do? It's not like we can fire them." She started down the hall. "We'll be working in the kitchen, so we don't have to worry about the mess. Come on in and get comfortable."

We'd just passed the doorway to the living room when the doorbell rang again. "Go on ahead, and I'll get that," Marlyn said.

Richard obediently went into the kitchen, but I was feeling nosy and stopped to peek into the living room.

It was enormous. One whole wall was taken up with a white leather sectional sofa, and the armchair, end tables, and coffee table were all glass and shiny chrome. At first I thought the relatively sparse amount of furniture and accessories was a style, but when I looked more closely, I was convinced that things had been removed here and there. Had Marlyn's ex-husband gotten the missing items in the settlement, or had Marlyn been selling them off?

Marlyn came back down the hall with Dorcas Walters.

"Hey, Laurie Anne," Dorcas said. "I'm so glad you and Richard could make it. We appreciate your taking a morning to help us out."

"Glad to do it," I said, which was true, if not for the reasons Marlyn thought. "I always loved the Halloween carnival, so it only seems fair to help out. We're looking forward to taking Alice this year."

Marlyn finally got us to the kitchen, which didn't look quite as bare as the living room. I wondered if that was why she had us working there. She got our drinks just in time for the doorbell to ring again, and the rest of the volunteers arrived over the next few minutes.

Our job was to make posters to use at the carnival: signs for the booths, price lists for the ticket sellers, directional arrows for the bathrooms, menus for the snack bar. One woman had brought stacks of poster board with glue and markers, and Marlyn had a computer with a laser printer to use.

All of the volunteers except us were the kinds of ladies who tended to volunteer for these kinds of things, partially because they didn't work outside the home and partially because they liked volunteer work. I was surprised at first that Vasti wasn't involved, but then realized that making posters wouldn't be high-profile enough for her. Since the women were experienced volunteers, they got things organized with a minimum of fuss and went to work with more efficiency than most of the companies I've worked with. Richard was the only man present, which amused the ladies no end, but when they discovered he had a flair for painting, they handed him a brush and put him to work. I got the computer and stayed busy entering text and finding clip art on the web.

It turned out to be a lot of fun, with plenty of chatter, but I wasn't sure how I was going to delicately bring up the subject of Big Bill. Then somebody asked how he was doing, which got the ball rolling.

"He came back home from the hospital yesterday, and he's doing much better," Dorcas said. A minute or two later, she stepped out to go to the bathroom.

"Is it true?" one woman asked timidly once she was gone. "Did somebody really try to kill Big Bill?"

"Oh, yes," someone answered her. "He was poisoned."

There was much shaking of heads, and many *tsk-tsk* sounds. Then Marlyn said, "I don't know why everybody is so surprised. Big Bill must have more enemies than I have earrings." Somebody gasped, but Marlyn went on,

"Let's not be hypocrites. We all know what kind of man Big Bill Walters is. Is there anybody in Byerly he hasn't cheated?"

Richard and I kept carefully quiet, hoping nobody would remember our connection with Big Bill.

A large woman with a determined chin said, "Has Big Bill not made good on your land, Marlyn?"

"He won't even return my phone calls!" she said angrily.

"I didn't realize you had any business dealings with Big Bill," the timid woman said.

"It wasn't me, it was my idiot ex-husband. Back before we split up, he bought the plot of land where Capital Fuel Company used to be. He said he had it inspected before he signed the papers, but either he was lying or the inspector was in Big Bill's pocket. All I know is that I ended up with the land after the divorce, and it was supposed to be worth at least what my ex paid for it. Except that when I went to sell it, I was told the land had been used as a dump for used oil, and that it needed an expensive cleanup."

This matched what she'd said in her letters, other than the implication that Big Bill had paid off an inspector.

"I still say you should make your ex-husband pay for it," the woman with the chin said. "Didn't he put other businesses on that land? How do you know the dumping wasn't his doing?"

"He doesn't have the money. At least, not on paper, and I don't think he's smart enough to hide it from me. He's got nothing, and he left Katelyn and me with . . ." She bit her lip to stop herself, and the other ladies managed to look elsewhere. "Anyway, Big Bill should take care of it!"

"I hope you're not holding your breath waiting for

that to happen," Dorcas said, coming back into the room.

Marlyn looked abashed at having been caught. "I'm sorry, Dorcas, I know he's your father-in-law."

"And Laurie Anne's uncle," Dorcas reminded her.

Marlyn shot a look in my direction, and the other women wriggled uncomfortably. They had forgotten about us.

"I hope I haven't spoken out of turn," Marlyn said, "but it's not a thing I haven't said before. Dorcas, can't you talk to Big Bill?"

But Dorcas shook her head. "I learned a long time ago that I can't change Big Bill's mind about anything. I don't ask him about his business, and he doesn't ask me how much I spend on my dresses."

Marlyn still looked vexed, but the rest of the women used it as an excuse to talk clothes, particularly how much it was costing them to outfit their daughters for the upcoming homecoming dance at Byerly High School.

I was surprised by how much more expensive the process was compared to my high school days, but then again, I hadn't been in the running for homecoming queen.

"I think the whole thing has gotten out of hand," Marlyn declared. "Have you counted up how many events the homecoming princesses are supposed to attend? Katelyn wants a brand-new outfit for every one of them—she's at the mall right now, picking out dresses. Well, I've put my foot down. I'll buy her some new things, of course, but there's no reason she can't wear outfits she already has, and I've got dresses that have barely been worn that will fit her just fine."

"I think that's very practical of you," Dorcas said, but I could tell from the sidelong glances of the other ladies that they were all thinking something else. I was thinking it, too. Marlyn wasn't economizing to make a point—she was doing it because she had to.

Conversation wandered this way and that, but not in any direction I cared about. The only subject of interest to me was when Dorcas broke the news to Marlyn that she wasn't going to be in charge of the white elephant sale. Now that she'd been reminded of who Richard and I were, she didn't dare say anything against Aunt Maggie, but I could tell how annoyed she was. The woman definitely had a temper, but whether it was hot enough to make her kill wasn't a question I could answer.

I finished the computer end of things before most of the others were done with their assignments, and after I confessed that I had no skill at all with a paintbrush, Marlyn asked if I'd pack up the items she'd collected for the white elephant sale. She managed to resist bad-mouthing Aunt Maggie, though she did make a point of mentioning how much work she'd done to get it all. I was exiled to the garage with a stack of newspapers, but since I knew Richard would keep his ears open for anything useful, I wasn't concerned.

Most of the stuff Marlyn had pulled together was about what you'd expect at a white elephant sale: used copies of Grisham and Koontz paperbacks, cheap vases that had come with flower arrangements, costume jewelry, battered toys, jigsaw puzzles that were probably missing pieces, and miscellaneous knickknacks. I dutifully wrapped them in newspaper, knowing that Aunt Maggie would be able to guilt somebody into buying them.

Then I got to a Mayflower moving box filled with what looked like old toys, still in their original boxes. I could have left them alone, of course, but I was far too nosy for that, so I started pulling them out to get a better look. The box was packed tight with GI Joe figures and vehicles. There were four other Mayflower boxes, and each one was stuffed with GI Joe and his militant friends, with all kinds of accessories. There were GI Joe playing cards, three different GI Joe board games, and a desert-patrol Jeep that looked brand-new. I blinked several times, not believing that anybody would just give that stuff away.

I wasn't the expert Aunt Maggie was, but I had attended plenty of auctions with her. One time, a box of GI Joe stuff came up for sale, and though Richard and a couple of other men admired them as things they remembered from childhood, not one dealer so much as looked in the box. Then, when it came time to bid, those same dealers nearly came to blows over that box. The amount it had eventually gone for was so high that people broke into spontaneous applause afterward as the auctioneer wiped sweat from his forehead.

These boxes were twice as big as that one had been, and as far as I could tell, the contents were in much better condition.

Marlyn came into the garage and said, "We're about finished. Do you need any help out here?"

"I think I'm done," I said, "but I was wondering. Do you know who donated the GI Joe stuff?"

"Those are mine." She picked up a walkie-talkie and wrinkled her nose at it. "They were my ex-husband's when he was little. He said he was saving them in case we had a boy, but since he didn't bother to take them with him, I decided to get rid of it. Are you interested in any of it?"

For a moment, pure out-and-out greed struggled with my conscience. I knew darned well that if I could keep myself from drooling, I could offer her twenty or thirty bucks for the whole bunch and sell them for who knows how much via Aunt Maggie's connections. Heck, I tried to argue with myself, I could give her fifty, which would be fifty more than she'd get if she donated them to the white elephant sale.

Then I thought of the bare spots in Marlyn's house, and her daughter's dresses for homecoming festivities. Okay, selling four boxes of toys wasn't going to solve all of Marlyn's financial problems, but maybe she'd be able to get her daughter a new dress or two.

"Marlyn," I said, "do you know how much these things are worth?"

"What do you mean?"

"GI Joe collectibles go for big money these days. I've seen people at auctions bid on this stuff like it was gold."

"Really?" She looked at the walkie-talkie with more respect.

"If I were you, I'd keep them and do some research. There's probably GI Joe collectors' groups online."

"I had no idea." She smiled a wicked smile. "I'll have to tell my ex-husband. After I sell it all, of course. Would eBay handle things like this?"

"I'm sure they would, but if you want to save yourself the trouble of shipping it, you could see if my Aunt Maggie knows anybody local." I looked her right in the eye. "That is, if you don't mind working with a battle-ax."

She had the good grace to blush. "I actually don't know your aunt all that well. I'm sure she's charming."

"I don't know if I'd call her charming," I said, "but I'm sure she'd be glad to help you out."

Richard came out then to tell us the the signs were all finished, and the other ladies were cleaning up our mess. Marlyn carefully took the GI Joe boxes back into the house while Richard and I loaded the white elephant merchandise into the cars of two women who'd volunteered to take it to the carnival. Before we left, Marlyn thanked me profusely for my advice.

"Isn't helping a suspect solve her financial problems an unusual strategy?" Richard said once we were in the car and I'd told him what Marlyn had nearly given away.

"I know, I just felt sorry for her." Admittedly, Marlyn's idea of being broke was a long way from going hungry, but I remembered how I'd felt during college, when Paw hadn't been able to send me nearly as much spending money as my friends had. I'd never gone hungry, either, but I sure had felt poor. "Think of it this way: we want to catch the person trying to kill Big Bill, but it's a whole lot more important that we keep him alive. Well, if Marlyn is the one, we've helped to eliminate her motive."

"We could get Big Bill to pay off all the suspects," Richard said speculatively.

I stuck my tongue out at him, which was undoubtedly the answer he'd expected.

Chapter
Fifteen

It was almost noon, so we stopped at Hardee's for lunch and carried in the copies of Big Bill's letters to flip through while we ate.

"We've visited all of my leading candidates," Richard said. "Have you got anyone else?"

"There's still Molly Weston in Rocky Shoals," I said.

"Her letters are over a year old," Richard objected, "and there were just two letters, not five or six like some of the others."

"I know, but we're running out of possibilities."

"I don't even think those letters sounded all that threatening," Richard said, chewing on a french fry. "I bet Big Bill only included them in the file because she used the *L* word."

"The *L* word?"

"*Lawyer.*"

"I think she should talk to a lawyer. She has a much better case than some of the others." According to her letter, Molly Weston had worked at Walters Mill for many years and, after retirement, came down with breathing problems that were likely caused by inhaling cotton dust for all that time. But since she retired before she became seriously ill, Big Bill had refused to take any responsibility. "Let's go see her."

"But Laura . . ."

"Have you got any better ideas?"

From the look on his face, I knew that he didn't.

Unfortunately, the phone number on the letter was no longer in service, and when I called information, they didn't have a Molly Weston listed in Rocky Shoals or Byerly.

"Maybe she passed away," Richard said, "which would take her out of the competition."

"Not necessarily."

"A vengeful ghost?"

"I was thinking more of her kids. They might blame Big Bill for their mother's death."

"It's possible," Richard conceded. "Who would know about people in Rocky Shoals?"

"Aunt Nora," I said promptly.

"I thought she specialized in Byerly gossip."

"She used to, but she ran out of fresh gossip in Byerly a while back and had to diversify to the neighboring towns." I called her up, and sure enough, Aunt Nora had plenty to tell me about Molly Weston. Molly had no children of her own, but she did have a devoted niece who lived in Byerly. Since the niece had only recently moved to town, she wasn't in the phone book, but Aunt Nora found her address in the "New Members" section of the church bulletin. After I promised Aunt Nora that she'd get another shift with Alice later in the week, I hung up with her, and Richard and I finished our lunch.

"So tell me who we're going to see," Richard said on our way back to the car.

"Wynette Weston. Named for Tammy Wynette, in case

you didn't catch that. Apparently, Wynette's mother was a big country music fan. The other daughter is Lynn, for Loretta Lynn."

"Any Hank Williams Weston or George Jones Weston?"

"Nope. Bill for Bill Haley, and Roy for Roy Orbison. Mr. Weston preferred rock and roll."

"Of course. Why are we going to see Wynette and not one of the others?"

"Because Wynette was the one who took care of Molly when she got sick. And because Bill and Roy moved away, and Aunt Nora thinks Lynn is too busy with her three kids to do anything vengeful. And especially because Wynette only moved to Byerly two months ago."

"Leaving her just enough time to research Big Bill's habits and go after him?"

"It's possible, isn't it?" I said.

"What's our cover story going to be this time?"

"Why don't we just use the truth?"

"You mean, ask her if she's trying to kill Big Bill?"

"Not that much truth. How about something along the lines of telling her we want more information about her aunt's case? I don't know about you, but I'm getting tired of trying to remember our cover stories."

" 'The seeming truth which cunning times put on to entrap the wisest,' " Richard said. *The Merchant of Venice*, Act III, Scene 2." I took that as agreement.

Wynette's house was small, but the paint was fresh and the yard was neat as a pin. I rang the doorbell, but when Wynette Weston opened the door and I got a good look at her, I was all but ready to cross her off of our list. Wynette was redheaded, freckled, and extremely pregnant, so much so that I wondered if she'd have time to talk to us before going into labor.

While I was willing to admit that a pregnant woman could turn murderous, especially when a hormone attack hit, I couldn't see her managing the sneaking around that the attempts on Big Bill had required. Still, we were there, so I figured it couldn't hurt to ask her some questions. Maybe the father of that baby she was carrying was involved.

"Wynette Weston?" I said, just to be sure.

"Yes?"

"I'm Laura Fleming, and this is my husband, Richard. We've been helping Big Bill Walters go through some of his files, and we found some notes from your aunt that we'd like to ask you about." When she looked confused, I handed her the photocopies of the letters.

She quickly read them, then nodded. "I'd forgotten all about Aunt Molly writing these. Duke put her up to it, but nothing ever came of it."

"Duke?"

"Why don't y'all come inside and I'll explain." We followed her in, and she lowered herself gingerly onto a big armchair while Richard and I took the couch. "The doctor says I'm supposed to stay off my feet," she complained, "but I just can't sit around doing nothing all day long."

"My doctor told me the same thing," I said. "We've got a seven-month-old girl."

"Is that right? Did you ever imagine how hard it is to be pregnant?"

"Lord, no. I'd never have gone through with it if I had." We might have gone on to compare stretch marks and swollen feet if Richard hadn't cleared his throat. "About these letters . . . ?"

"Right. Aunt Molly did have problems with her lungs—that's what killed her—but the doctor didn't say for sure that it was brown lung. Aunt Molly smoked like a smokestack my whole life, and the doctor said that was more likely to be the problem."

"Then why the letters?" I asked.

Wynette looked exasperated. "Duke put her up to it. He figured Big Bill Walters might send her some money just to shut her up. Aunt Molly knew better—Walters wouldn't have any money left if he paid off everybody who asked for it. She just wrote the letters so Duke would quit pestering her."

"Duke is your brother?" I asked, wondering if Bill Haley or Roy Orbison hadn't appreciated their father's musical taste, and decided to use a nickname.

"My husband. My ex-husband now. But like I said, we never expected anything to come from it, and until now, we never heard anything from Walters. Which is just as well. If Walters had sent Aunt Molly any money, Duke would have found some way to get his hands on it." She shrugged. "Aunt Molly's gone now, so I guess it doesn't matter."

Richard said, "Then nobody in your family intends to pursue this any further?"

"What's the point?" Wynette said. "Not that a few dollars wouldn't come in handy with the new baby on the way." She rubbed her tummy, just like I had when pregnant.

She sure didn't sound bloodthirsty. Maybe her ex-husband had been hoping for some money, but killing Big Bill was hardly a way to line his pockets, especially since he and Wynette were divorced. I was still curious about Wynette's child's father—there was no wedding band on her finger, but she hadn't gotten pregnant by herself.

Wynette must have been thinking while I considered the possibilities, because she said, "Laura Fleming . . . Aren't you one of the Burnettes? The one from Boston?"

"I'm surprised you've heard of me; I thought you just moved to town."

"We did, but Belva hears all the gossip."

"Belva Tucker?" I asked.

"That's right. She said y'all were working with Chief Norton to see who tried to kill Big Bill Walters. Am I one of your suspects?"

I looked at Richard, but he looked as nonplussed as I felt. "Well, sort of, but—"

Wynette giggled. "I'm just trying to picture myself killing somebody while looking like this."

"We didn't know you were pregnant before we met you," I explained.

"Of course not," she said as another giggle escaped.

"We've just been going through some threatening letters sent to Big Bill—"

"From what I've heard about Big Bill Walters, he must have a stack of threatening letters, and I bet most of them are a lot nastier than anything Aunt Molly wrote." Then she sobered. "I'm sorry—I forgot that he's your uncle."

"Only by marriage," I said, "and to tell you the truth, you can't say anything about Big Bill that I haven't heard before." I looked at Richard, and he shrugged. It looked as if he'd been right and we'd been wasting our time. "I apologize for disturbing you. If I'd known you were a friend of Belva's, I wouldn't have come by like this."

"That's all right," she said, levering herself out of her chair to walk us to the door. "Not many people know about us, because Belva's still kind of shy about it."

"I beg your pardon?"

"About us. Me and Belva." She must have been able to tell from the look on my face that I wasn't following her. "Belva and I are partners. We're a couple."

"Oh. I hadn't realized that Belva was a—I mean, I didn't know that." I didn't mean to, but I looked at her swollen stomach.

"Sperm donor," Wynette said. "Belva and I both really wanted kids."

"Kids are great," I said, feeling like an idiot. I lived in Boston, for goodness' sake—I was supposed to be sophisticated about things like same-sex couples.

Wynette went on. "Belva had a hard time in Rocky Shoals when word got out about us, which is part of the reason we moved here."

"Is Byerly any better?" I said.

"Oh, the people react about the same. Some folks are rude, and some act funny, but most are okay. But the important thing is that Belva's so much better off at work here than she was in Rocky Shoals."

"Chief Monroe had problems with it?" I'd dealt with him in the past and had thought better of him.[8]

"He tried not to, but he couldn't seem to keep it from bothering him. The other officers were the real problem—they teased Belva something fierce, and I don't mean friendly teasing. She doesn't have to worry about that here. Chief Norton doesn't care, so Belva is a lot happier now."

"Junior's a class act," I said, proud of my friend.

"Belva thinks the world of her, especially after she went to the bat for her."

"Oh?"

"Some of those old farts on the city council weren't too happy with the situation. Of course, I hear they were happy with the previous deputy, and that didn't turn out too well."

"That's putting it mildly." I'd had a hand in the downfall of Junior's last deputy myself.[9]

"Junior called in some favors to get them to give

[8] *Trouble Looking for a Place to Happen*
[9] *Mad as the Dickens*

Belva a probationary period, and things have been going just fine."

"I'm glad to hear that. Give our best to Belva, and it's nice to have met you."

Wynette waved as we drove off, which I thought was awfully nice, considering that we'd suspected her of murder.

"I'll refrain from saying 'I told you so,' " Richard said.

"Don't be so smug. Didn't you hear what Wynette said about the Byerly City Council? Big Bill runs that council. If Big Bill was trying to keep Belva off the force, that makes a lovely motive."

"That still leaves us the problem of Wynette sneaking around in places where she'd hardly go unnoticed."

"That's true of Wynette, but not Belva. Might I remind you that Belva was at the party?"

"Outside, directing cars," Richard said.

"But nobody would have noticed if she'd come inside." I speculated for a minute. "Still, I sure hope it wasn't Belva."

"Why's that?"

"Because Junior will shoot me if I cost her another deputy."

Chapter
Sixteen

We were now definitely out of ideas, and were heading back to Aunt Nellie and Uncle Ruben's to pick up Alice when my cell phone rang. Since I was driving, I said, "Richard, can you get that?"

"Sure," he said, and pulled it from my purse. "Hello? . . . Hi, Aunt Maggie. . . . On our way to Aunt Nellie's to get Alice. . . . I suppose we could. Let me check with Laura." He held his hand over the phone and said, "Aunt Maggie wants to know if we can come by the mansion and tell Big Bill what we've been doing."

"We've been twiddling our thumbs," I said with more than a little irritation. "What does he think we've been doing?"

He didn't answer, just waited patiently.

I relented, as he'd known I would. "All right, tell her we're on our way."

He lifted the phone back up. "We'd be happy to. See you in a few minutes."

I groused as I turned down a side street to turn around and head toward the Walters mansion. "Are we going to have to report back to them all the time? Don't you think it's kind of insulting? Not to mention a waste of time."

"Neither of which you'd mind if you had any progress to report," he said blandly.

"I really hate it when you're right." As I pulled back onto the main road, I noticed that a tan Taurus had made the turn along with us. I slowed down, hoping to get a better look at the driver, but the other car slowed down, too. I sped up to a reasonable speed, and said, "Richard, I think that car is following us."

"Really?" he said, but was too smart to turn around to look. "Are you sure? What does it look like?"

"It's a tan or beige sedan. A Taurus, I think."

"You know, I saw a tan car parked near ours when we left Marlyn's house. I only noticed it because it's got the same rental company sticker on it as this one has."

"Interesting. I can't see the driver very well, but I don't think it's one of our suspects." I saw that the light at the intersection we were approaching had just gone to yellow. "Hang on," I said, and hit the brakes. There'd been plenty of time to get through, so the driver behind me was caught by surprise, and barely stopped his car in time. That meant he was right on our bumper, close enough for me to get a good look at him in my rearview mirror. He looked mighty peeved at my driving, but more important, he looked familiar.

"Richard, do you remember that man with the funny dent in his head?"

"The one we saw at Pigwick's?"

"That's the man who's following us. I bet he followed us to Pigwick's, too."

"Surely he knows that we've spotted him now," Richard said.

The light turned green, and when I drove off, the

Taurus was right behind me. "Apparently not. He's still behind us." If I'd been alone at night, I'd have called the police or driven to the station. Looking foolish didn't bother me nearly as much as the possible alternatives. But it was broad daylight, and if this guy wanted to try something, he'd had plenty of chances.

So when Richard asked, "What do we do now?" I answered, "Nothing. Let's see what he does."

Though the Taurus didn't tailgate, it stayed right with us until we got to the Walterses' driveway. The man drove on past, but I had a hunch he hadn't gone far.

"Now what?" Richard asked.

"Now we go inside," I said. "I've got an idea."

Miz Duffield must have been getting used to us, or at least resigned to our frequent appearances, because she let us in the door without making us wait for Aunt Maggie's say-so. She still had to lead us upstairs, of course, and I startled her when I said, "Can we go up to the third floor? I need to look out the window."

"I suppose it—" she started to say, and I broke in with, "Wonderful. We'll find our own way." I trotted up the stairs with Richard, leaving Miz Duffield squawking indignantly behind us.

I'd have opened closed doors if I'd had to, which probably would have given Miz Duffield a conniption, but fortunately the upstairs landing included a window facing the right way. I could see all the way down the block in both directions, and it only took a moment to spot the tan car, even though the driver had parked behind a large hedge. "There he is."

"Whoever it is," Richard said.

"I've got an idea about that, too, and if I'm right, I'm about to blister Big Bill's ears! Come on."

Miz Duffield was still standing on the stairs, but we breezed past her on our way to Big Bill's room. I knocked sharply on the door and just barely managed to hold on to my temper long enough for Vivian to let us in. Then she retreated to a corner of the room where she could read and we could pretend she wasn't there.

Aunt Maggie had an open magazine in her lap, and Big Bill was watching something on TV. I went in and stood right in front of the screen and said, "Big Bill, do you trust us?"

"Of course I do," he said.

"Do you really want us to find out who it is trying to kill you?"

"What kind of question is that? Haven't I answered all your questions, even those that can't possibly have anything to do with this business? Haven't I done everything you wanted me to do?"

"Yes, you have. I'm just wondering if you've done something else."

He turned to Aunt Maggie. "Do you know what she's talking about?"

"No, and I'm waiting for her to explain why she's acting this way," she said, not at all happy with me.

But I wasn't real happy myself right then. "A man has been following Richard and me all through Byerly."

"Who?" Aunt Maggie asked.

"That's what I want to know." I glared at Big Bill.

"What are you getting at, Laurie Anne?" he asked.

"Did you hire a private detective to keep an eye on us?"

"A private detective?" he said. "Why would I do that?"

"Because you don't think Richard and I are up to the job." Then I decided to add a more charitable interpretation. "Or maybe you're worried that we're in danger, and wanted to protect us."

But Big Bill was shaking his head. "I swear to you that I haven't hired anybody."

He sounded sincere, and besides, I didn't think he'd risk lying to me in front of Aunt Maggie. "Do you think Burt might have hired somebody? Or Dorcas?"

"Not without consulting me."

"Oh," I said, feeling more than a little foolish. "I'm sure this guy is following us. We've seen him all around town, and he's parked down the street right now. I even saw him at your party."

What does he look like?" Big Bill asked.

"Balding, but what hair he's got is gray. Older— maybe around y'all's age."

"Thanks a lot," Aunt Maggie said.

"Sorry. Not real tall, but not short, either." Being on the short side myself, I'm no good at estimating heights.

"About five foot eight or nine," Richard put in.

"He's tanned, like he works outside. Kind of a big nose, not huge, but sort of round."

"That's not ringing any bells for me," Big Bill said. "How about you, Maggie?"

She shook her head.

"What about his head?" Richard reminded me.

"Oh, right. Most of the time he's been wearing a ball cap, but we've seen him without it, and he's got the weirdest dent on his head. U-shaped, I think almost a quarter of an inch deep."

Aunt Maggie stiffened. "Like a horseshoe?"

"Sort of."

"What color are his eyes?" she demanded.

"I haven't been close enough to know for sure, but I think they're light."

"Light blue?"

"Maybe. Aunt Maggie, do you know this man?"

Big Bill looked as if he wanted to hear what she had to say, too.

Aunt Maggie didn't answer right away, and when she did, her voice sounded as if it came from a million miles away. "Could it be Pudd'nhead, after all this time?"

"Pudd'nhead?" Richard asked incredulously. "Like *Pudd'nhead Wilson?*"

"You say he's outside?" she said.

I said, "He was a minute ago, parked just out of sight of the front door."

Without hesitating, she started for the bedroom door.

"What are you doing, Maggie?" Big Bill called after her. "You don't know that the man they're talking about is Pudd'nhead Wilson. Maybe it's the man who's trying to kill me."

Aunt Maggie didn't even hesitate, and Bobbin eagerly trotted along beside her.

"Maggie Burnette, you come back here," Big Bill said in his most authoritative voice, but he might as well not have spoken.

Richard and I looked at each other, shrugged, and hurried after her. Catching up wasn't easy, because Aunt Maggie moves awfully quickly when she wants to, and this time she wanted to. She didn't seem to notice us walking behind her down the stairs, through the house, and out the front door, but as we followed her down the driveway, she said, "Which way?"

"Left," I answered.

She turned that way, and sure enough, the tan Taurus was still parked there. The man inside sat up straight when he saw us, no doubt alarmed at my aunt bearing down on him with such a forbidding expression. He reached for the key, and I figured he meant to drive away before we could get to him. Then the engine shut off, the door opened, and he stepped out and stood there, waiting for us. Or rather, waiting for Aunt Maggie, because he sure didn't have eyes for anybody but her. He yanked his cap off, revealing that horseshoe-shaped dent.

Aunt Maggie got right up to him and studied his face, and he seemed to be looking at her just as thoroughly. Then she reached up, pulled his face down to hers, and gave him one of the most passionate kisses I've ever seen. Their arms went around each other, not in a vulgar way, but there sure wasn't any space between them. My mouth fell open, and I probably should have turned away, but I just stood there gawking. Bobbin whined in confusion, not knowing if she should be protecting her mistress or not.

Finally, they pulled back and looked into each other's eyes. The man's were light blue, just as Aunt Maggie had said they were.

"Hey there, Troy," she said softly, using a tone of voice I'd never expected to hear from her.

"Hey, Maggie. Damn, you look good."

"Yes, I do. But I'm surprised you even remember what I look like, let alone my name!" Then she turned on her heel and strode past Richard and me on her way back to the house, with Bobbin beside her. The door slammed loud enough to be heard halfway across Byerly.

The expression on the face of the man Aunt Maggie had called Troy should have been funny, but instead it was sad. If ever I'd seen a man with his heart on his sleeve, it was him, and his love for my great-aunt was painfully obvious.

After one of the most awkward moments I'd ever endured, Richard said, "Hello. I'm Richard Fleming, and this is my wife, Laura." Richard offered his hand, and Troy took it automatically.

"Troy Wilson," he said, "but most folks call me Pudd'nhead."

That's when I remembered when I'd heard his name before. I'd been helping Aunt Maggie sort through a load of stuff she'd picked up at an auction, and at one point she'd pulled out a red felt baseball pennant for the Byerly Bobbins and whispered his name. The Bobbins had been part of the textile league, back when there was such a thing. At that point, professional ball players didn't have spring training. Instead, they'd played down South during the winter, supposedly working for the mills but in truth, playing as ringers on various mill teams. According to what Aunt Maggie had told me that day, Pudd'nhead Wilson had been Big Bill's ringer.

"You used to play for the Bobbins," I said to him.

"Yes, I did, and for plenty of other teams. I played catcher mostly."

"You knew Aunt Maggie then?"

"So she's your aunt? I figured you were related somehow."

"She's my great-aunt, actually. Her brother Ellis was my grandfather."

"Ellis Burnette," he said as if trying the words on for size. "I remember him. Small but tough. Is he still living?"

"No, sir. He's been gone for several years now."

"I'm sorry to hear that. I always liked Ellis—he didn't mind my being a Yankee the way some of the others did."

"Times have mellowed," Richard said. "Sometimes they even marry Yankees into the family now."

"Is that a fact?" Pudd'nhead said with a grin.

"I take it that you knew Aunt Maggie, too," I said pointedly.

"Oh yes, I knew Maggie." He shook his head. "Never met another woman to beat her. Strong as a horse, tough as nails, and she had a temper hot enough to burn right through you. I guess she still does."

Those weren't exactly the tender memories I'd expected from a long-ago romance.

"She and I worked in the same department at Walters Mill," he said. "I noticed her right off and tried to talk to her, but she wouldn't have anything to do with a carpetbagger like me. So I moved on to greener pastures."

Not exactly love at first sight, I thought.

Pudd'nhead went on. "She wasn't the only one who didn't care for me being there, what with my bringing down a bigger paycheck than anybody else just because I could play ball. And I didn't exactly help matters by slacking off on the job every chance I got. I was a ball player, not some mill hand, and I made sure nobody forgot it. So I can't blame anybody but myself for what happened."

"What did happen?" I asked.

"One day at the mill I was messing around, not paying attention to what I was supposed to be doing. I don't even remember the piece of machinery I was running, but something came loose. I found out later that any half-wit mill hand would have seen the problem coming and shut down the machine to fix it, but like I said, I was a ball player. This piece of metal came flying through the air and hit me on the head." Absently he rubbed the dent that had helped Aunt Maggie realize who he was. "The next thing I saw was Maggie—she had my head in her lap, with her smock held up against my head to stop the bleeding, and was yelling for somebody to get a doctor. She looked down at me and said, 'You dad-blamed idiot! I'll be surprised if you don't have pudding for brains after this.'"

"Hence the nickname," Richard said.

"That's right. I started liking it after a while. All the great ball players had nicknames, and maybe I couldn't be great, but I could have a nickname."

"And one heck of a dent," I added.

"It didn't show so bad until my hair started to go, but now . . ." He shrugged. "Anyway, I was in pretty bad shape for a good while after that, and the Burnettes— your family, that is—took me in and nursed me back to health. All the girls helped out, of course, but Maggie took the most interest in me. She said it was because she hated the idea of ruining her best smock if I was just going to up and die. How could I not fall in love with a woman like that?"

"'O tiger's heart wrapp'd in a woman's hide!' *King Henry VI, Part III,* Act I, Scene 4," Richard said in agreement.

"We were getting along pretty good, and I started thinking about settling down here in Byerly, maybe even becoming a mill hand for real. But then spring came, and my catching hand got that itch, and I decided that playing ball meant more to me than Maggie did. So I left."

I didn't know whether I should feel sympathy for the man or hit him upside the head for running out on my great-aunt. "You haven't been playing ball all this time, have you?" I said.

"I wish," he said with a grin. "I only played another seven, eight seasons after that. Then I went into coaching, managing, and a whole lot of other jobs. Anything that would keep me working at a ball park. But I got old, and the game changed, and it was time to retire."

"Then you came looking for Aunt Maggie?"

"Not right away, but eventually curiosity got the better of me. I'd always wondered what happened to her— we didn't exactly keep in touch after I left."

"You mean you didn't write her or call?"

He shook his head, looking ashamed.

"You're lucky she didn't set the dog on you," I said.

"Probably so. It looks like she's done a whole lot better for herself than I have." He nodded at the Walters mansion. "Big house like that, and a rich husband. I guess things worked out right for her."

It was petty of me, but I said, "Did you know they only got married a couple of weeks ago? If you'd come back sooner, you might still have had a chance."

"Yeah, I've been beating myself up over that. One of the first things I did when I hit town was pick up a newspaper, and I saw the story about them eloping."

"So why are you still in town?" I had to ask. "Why didn't you leave once you found out she was married?"

"Even a married woman might want to see an old friend," he said.

"Then why didn't you call her, or knock on the door?"

"I've been trying to get my courage up. I didn't know how she was going to react. And I sure didn't expect what I got. Maggie always did have a way of surprising a man."

"She gives as good as she gets," I said pointedly.

"Yeah, well, I never said I was smart. Leaving Maggie the way I did was probably the dumbest thing I ever did. I'm just glad she's happy. You can tell her that for me, if you don't mind."

"Does this mean you're leaving town now?"

"I'm not sure. I don't have anyplace I need to be, so maybe I'll stick around a few more days. If Maggie asks, tell her I'm staying at the Holiday Inn in Hickory."

"If she asks," I said noncommittally.

He nodded sadly, then climbed into the car. As he drove away, I saw him looking back at the Walters mansion.

"You were kind of hard on him, weren't you?" Richard said. "I thought it was quite romantic of him to look up his old flame after all these years."

"Richard, did you ever wonder why Aunt Maggie never married?"

"I assumed she never found a man that suited her."

"Or maybe it was because she found the right man, and he left her."

Richard looked doubtful. "I never noticed her pining away."

"By the time you knew her, Pudd'nhead was long gone. She must have given up hope of him ever coming back."

"Maybe, but I wouldn't exactly cast her as a spurned maiden. If she'd really wanted to spend her life with him, she could have gone after him."

"You think? What if I'd left Boston after graduation and never called or wrote you again? Would you have come looking for me?"

"In a heartbeat," he said promptly.

"Really? Your pride wouldn't have gotten in the way?"

"'He that is proud eats up himself.' *Troilus and Cressida*, Act II, Scene 3." He added, "Me, I'd pick happiness over pride any day. I wouldn't have turned stalker or anything like that, but I wouldn't have rested until I knew for sure that you didn't love me anymore."

Looking at Richard, I knew he was completely serious. So what could I do but put my arms around him and do my best to prove that I could kiss just as well as my great-aunt? From his response, I don't think he had any complaints.

When we'd both caught our breath, Richard added, "Of course, since you did love me, if you'd suddenly left me, I'd have known there was a good reason. Maybe Aunt

Maggie knew that Pudd'nhead loved baseball more than he did her."

I couldn't imagine myself wanting to play a game that much. "Now he can't play anymore, and as far as he knows, Aunt Maggie's taken, so he's got nothing. Unless . . ."

"You think Aunt Maggie will divorce Big Bill and go back to Pudd'nhead?"

"Who knows? Like Pudd'nhead says, Aunt Maggie has a way of surprising folks. But what I was thinking was that maybe Pudd'nhead came to town a little sooner than he claims."

"Why would he lie about that?"

"What if he came a couple of weeks back and found out Aunt Maggie and Big Bill were an item? None of us really thought the two of them would get married, but maybe Pudd'nhead did. I mean, it would be mighty hard for a retired ball player to compete with a rich, powerful man like Big Bill."

"You think he's the one trying to kill Big Bill? To level the playing field, as it were?"

"Maybe."

"So why has he stuck around now that Big Bill and Aunt Maggie are married?"

"Are you kidding? If he can kill Big Bill and then win over Aunt Maggie, not only has he reclaimed his lost love, but now she's a rich, powerful widow."

"He seemed more like a lover than a fighter to me."

"Love does strange things to folks."

"'If you remember'st not the slightest folly that ever love did make thee run into, thou hast not lov'd.' *As You Like It*, Act II, Scene 4."

I nodded absently, my mind partially occupied by the concept of Aunt Maggie as a femme fatale, and partially realizing that Pudd'nhead hadn't explained why he'd been following Richard and me.

It only took a moment to pull out my cell phone to call Belva at the police station and give her Pudd'nhead's name and the hotel where he was staying. I wanted to see what else I could find out about Aunt Maggie's former flame.

Chapter
Seventeen

Once I'd put Belva to work, we went back inside. I'd been so busy accusing Big Bill of hiring a private detective that I hadn't told him what we'd been doing, and under the circumstances, I thought I owed him that report.

Aunt Maggie was back in Big Bill's room, but she and he weren't talking. Not in the sense of not having anything to say right then, but in the sense of going out of their way not to speak one word to each other. Aunt Maggie was flipping through the pages of her magazine far too quickly to be reading, and Big Bill was flipping through channels on the TV just as quickly. Given that they were newlyweds, I thought it was a shame, but the last thing I wanted was to get involved in their quarrel.

Instead, I just told Big Bill what progress Richard and I had made, knowing that Aunt Maggie would be listening, too. Once I'd finished, Big Bill frowned and said, "Is that it? It doesn't sound to me that you know a bit more than you did when you left here last."

I counted to ten twice, then decided to tell him off

anyway, but before I could, Aunt Maggie said, "It seems to me that some people could show a little gratitude."

"Well, it seems to me that some people might stop keeping secrets when a man's life is at stake," Big Bill shot back.

"A real man wouldn't assume that every little thing has something to do with him."

"Oh, cut it out!" I said in disgust. "If y'all want to fight, go right ahead, but I'll be darned if I'm going to sit here and listen to you."

That got them to stop glaring at each other and to start glaring at me.

"Big Bill, if you don't like what Richard and I are doing, that's too bad. We're doing this our way, and don't keep calling us for status reports—we're not coming back over until we want to." Aunt Maggie looked smug until I turned to her. "As for you, Aunt Maggie, I want you to think long and hard about Pudd'nhead Wilson. Big Bill's right about one thing—this is no time to be keeping secrets."

Neither of them could decide whom they wanted to glare at after that, so I decided to make it easier on them.

"Now, if you two lovebirds will excuse us, we have work to do." I stomped out of the room, with Richard right at my heels, and there wasn't a peep out of either of them.

I paused outside the door, listening to hear if either Aunt Maggie or Big Bill yelled for me to come back. When neither of them did, I took a deep breath and relaxed.

"My, my, my," Richard said.

"Was I awful?" I asked. "I know they're worried, but—"

"No, don't say a word. I want to remember you just

the way you were, eyes blazing and nostrils flaring." He sighed. "What a woman!"

"Now you cut it out!" I said, but I couldn't help grinning.

"Anything you say, ma'am," he said with a mock quaver in his voice. "I am yours to command."

"Really?" I said. "This has possibilities." I put my arms around his neck, pulled his face closer to mine, and started to take advantage of one of those possibilities. Then I heard someone clearing his throat and jerked away.

Burt Walters was standing on the top stair, very carefully not looking in our direction.

"Hi, Burt," I said. I couldn't very well be angry at him for being in his own house.

"Sorry to interrupt," he said. "I was just going to check on Daddy."

"You might want to wait until later," Richard said.

"Is Daddy all right?" Burt asked in alarm.

"He's fine," Richard said, "but he and Aunt Maggie are having a disagreement."

Burt moved closer to Big Bill's door. "I don't hear anything."

"Well, Laura and I haven't been married as long as you have, but in my experience, the quiet arguments are more deadly than the noisy ones."

"I see your point. Perhaps I will wait until later." He started to go past Big Bill's room and on down the hall.

"As a matter of fact, Burt, if you've got a few minutes, we'd like to talk with you." It occurred to me that while I didn't consider Burt a leading contender, he was still a suspect, and we hadn't had a chance to speak to him alone.

"Of course," Burt said. "Why don't we go down to the

study?" He led the way to the same room that Dorcas had used to talk to me the day before. "Would either of you care for something to drink? I could ring for Irene."

"Nothing for me," I said, and Richard shook his head.

"Then what can I do for you? This is about the attempts on Daddy's life, isn't it?"

"Yes, it is," I said, wondering if I could program an e-mail system that would work as quickly as Byerly's grapevine. It was a good thing that Richard and I weren't trying to be covert. "What with being Big Bill's son and working with him the way you do, it seems to me that you're in the best position of anyone to know who would want him hurt. Do you have any ideas—anybody you're suspicious of?" If Burt was guilty, that would be his chance to list a dozen or more names, just to throw us off the track.

But Burt shook his head. "I wish I did, but I just don't. I'm not saying that Daddy is the easiest man in the world to get along with; we all know better than that. But that's not the same thing as wanting to kill him. What would be the point?"

"The classic ones are money, sex, and revenge," I said.

"Money?" he said. "I guess that would mean me. Nobody else is getting enough out of the will to be worth killing over. Only I suppose now all Daddy's money goes to Aunt Maggie, anyway." He was either being totally frank or wanted to sound that way.

"Sex?" Richard suggested.

Burt looked distinctly uncomfortable. "That's one thing Daddy and I don't talk about. He was devoted to Mama. At least, he seemed to be, and neither he or Mama ever said anything to make me think different. Now he's got Aunt Maggie. If there was anybody in between, other than somebody to dance with at a party, I never heard about it."

"Revenge?" I suggested. "It could be from something a long time ago."

"There were some unpleasant incidents when the union moved in." He very carefully didn't look at me, no doubt remembering that many of my relatives had been on the opposite side of Big Bill during that time. "Plenty of people wanted his hide then, and they weren't shy about letting him know it. Carrying sticks, throwing rocks, and worse. That's when Daddy had this house built, to make sure he had someplace he could defend."

"Didn't one man break in?" I said, suddenly curious about a tale I'd heard repeated over the years. "Only he couldn't find Big Bill, and then the police came and got him. The story was that Big Bill had a bolt-hole."

"You hear all kinds of stories," Burt said, but he still wasn't looking me in the eyes. "Anyway, I can't picture any of those men waiting all these years to come after Daddy."

"Did anybody go to prison over the strikes?" Richard asked. "Perhaps there was someone who was only recently released."

"Not that I know of," Burt said. "Most of the folks, even the ones who were the angriest, ended up back at the mill once it was all said and done."

"The mill," I said. "That's an idea. Richard and I should go visit to scout out the gossip."

"No, that'd be a waste of your time," Burt said quickly, and when I looked at him in surprise, he added, "I mean, most of those people were old-timers. They've all retired by now."

"True," I said, noting how relieved he seemed. Just to see how he'd react, I added, "Of course, some of those people still have family working at the mill. Sometimes it's the next generation that really gets hot for revenge. It might be worth a trip out there. If you don't mind, that is."

Burt was literally sweating. "Of course I don't mind. I'll take you around myself. How about tomorrow?" He pulled a dark-blue date book out of his pocket. "I've got a meeting in Hickory in the morning. How about tomorrow afternoon?"

"That would be great," I said. "We've got plans for tomorrow morning, anyway."

"Great, great," he said, scribbling in his book. "Maybe I'll have some ideas for you by then."

Burt excused himself, and after he was out of earshot, Richard asked, "What plans do we have for tomorrow morning?"

"What do you think? We're spending the morning at the mill."

"Burt did seem nervous, didn't he? Do you think he's hiding something?"

"Lord, he couldn't have been more obvious if he'd gotten Tattoo Bob Tyndall to tattoo *I've got a secret!* across his forehead. Whatever Burt's hiding out there, we're going to find out what it is."

"Maybe there is something to the rumors about that young protégé."

"If so, then that's exactly who I want to meet."

Chapter Eighteen

Richard and I were planning to leave then, but Miz Duffield came panting into the room.

"Thank goodness y'all are still here," she said. "Mr. Big Bill needs to see you right away."

"I told him . . ." I started to say, but stopped. Miz Duffield was only the messenger—there was no reason to fuss at her. "All right, we'll go see what he wants." But I was fussing under my breath all the way up the stairs. I quit when I got to the top, but not because I was worried about Big Bill hearing me—there was so much commotion coming from Big Bill's room that I couldn't even hear myself.

I knocked, but when nobody answered, Richard and I let ourselves in. Aunt Maggie was standing in front of Big Bill's bed, hands on her hips and a fierce look on her face. Big Bill was glaring right back at her. Vivian was hiding behind a magazine, which I didn't blame her for, and Tavis Montgomery was standing next to Big Bill's bed, looking as if he wished he were just about anyplace else.

Aunt Maggie saw us and said, "Laurie Anne, talk some sense into this old man."

"Who are you calling old?" he snapped back at her. "Laurie Anne, kindly remind your aunt that I'm not really . . ." I was sure he was about to blurt out that he wasn't really sick, right in front of Tavis, but he stopped himself. "Remind her that I'm getting better, so there's no reason I can't go to the Halloween carnival."

"How about the fact that you were at death's door two days ago?" she said.

"If I'm so bad off, then why are you going?"

"Because I'm in charge of the white elephant sale. I've got to go."

"If it's a problem . . ." Tavis started to say, but shut up when Aunt Maggie flashed him a look.

"If you're going, I'm going," Big Bill nearly yelled.

"No, you're not," Aunt Maggie said just as loudly.

Tavis broke in with, "I'm sorry, it's my fault. I stopped in to check on Big Bill, and mentioned that we'd miss him at the carnival. That's when—"

"That's when I told him that I'm going to that carnival," Big Bill said. "I've already got my costume prepared."

"Well whoop-de-doo," Aunt Maggie said. "You've been wearing the same costume for the past twenty years."

Big Bill always dressed up as a Confederate general. He added an accessory every year or so, or replaced a moth-eaten hat, but otherwise, the costume stayed the same.

"Are you saying there's something wrong with my costume?" Big Bill said icily.

"I give up!" Aunt Maggie said, throwing her hands up in disgust. "There's no talking to you. I'm going to take Bobbin for a walk." Upon hearing her name, the dog scrambled out from under the chair where she'd taken cover, and followed Aunt Maggie out of the room.

"That's right," Big Bill called after her. "Cut and run. Again!"

Both Tavis and I started to speak, but Richard interrupted us. "If you two don't mind, I think I should talk to Big Bill alone."

I blinked at him in surprise.

"Please," he added.

"Okay," I said, and went out the door, with Tavis at my heels. A few seconds later, Vivian stepped out, too. I was dying to stick my ear to that closed door in hopes that I'd be able to hear something, but I wasn't willing to do it in front of the others.

Tavis said, "I didn't mean to cause such a ruckus. I just wanted Big Bill's advice on who should judge the costume contest in his place."

"It's not your fault," I told him. "This isn't the first time they've been riled up today."

"Oh?" Tavis said, looking concerned. "Big Bill is doing better, isn't he?"

"He'll be fine." I wasn't sure if I should mention Pudd'nhead or not, so I settled for, "They're just worried about the poisoning attempt and all."

"Has there been any progress on that? I'd heard that you and your husband are investigating."

Since Tavis was a suspect of sorts himself, I didn't want to say much about that, either. "We're still working on it, but we'll get to the bottom of it sooner or later." Though it was likely to be later if we had to keep playing referee for Aunt Maggie and Big Bill.

Conversation petered out after that, though I did think about asking Tavis if he had anything going with Dorcas. Somehow, it just didn't seem like the right time.

After a long spell of awkwardness, Aunt Maggie trooped up the stairs with Bobbin. "What are y'all doing out here?"

"Richard wanted to talk to Big Bill," I explained, "so he chased all of us out."

"Richard did that?" she said, surprised.

I shrugged. It wasn't my husband's usual style, but since my approach hadn't worked, I was in no position to complain.

I halfway expected Aunt Maggie to burst in on Richard and Big Bill, but she seemed content to wait with the rest of us. At least she had something to say to break the silence: she started quizzing Tavis about arrangements for the white elephant sale. Listening in gave me something to do to pass the time until the door finally opened and Richard stepped out. He looked intact, and I peeked around him to make sure Big Bill was okay, too.

"Ready to go?" Richard asked, as if nothing were wrong.

"I guess so."

"Good. Tavis, Big Bill asked me to tell you that he regrets that he'll have to miss judging the costume party this year, but that he's sure Burt will do an excellent job. Vivian, Big Bill says he'd like something to drink. Aunt Maggie, Big Bill would very much like to speak with you." He headed down the stairs, not waiting to see if people did what he wanted them to, and I had to scoot to catch up with him at the front door.

"Richard?"

"We'll talk in the car."

I restrained myself that long, but just barely. I was driving so he'd have no excuses to keep him from explaining. "Talk," I said.

"That's just what Big Bill and I did. You see, I realized that what Big Bill really needed was a man-to-man talk. Though I'm not the first man he'd have picked, I was available, so I stepped in. Now, of course you realize that Big Bill wasn't really upset about the Halloween carnival."

"He sure sounded upset to me."

"He was upset, but not about the carnival. It was Aunt Maggie's encounter with Pudd'nhead Wilson that was bothering him, especially because she refused to talk about it. So I told him what happened."

"All of it?" I said, aghast.

"I did leave out the kiss. No man newly married needs to hear about something like that. What he did need to hear was that Aunt Maggie was furious at Pudd'nhead for deserting her all those years ago, and that she did not seem inclined to forgive him."

Realization dawned. "Big Bill was jealous?"

"Of course. Why wouldn't he be?"

"Because . . . because he's Big Bill. The man is self-confidence personified."

"Not where Aunt Maggie is concerned. He really loves her, you know."

"I figured that, since he married her."

"People marry for lots of reasons other than love. Companionship, possession—in this case, fear. But Big Bill honestly loves her and doesn't want to lose her."

"Do you think Aunt Maggie loves him that way?"

"This was a man-to-man talk—you'll have to handle the woman-to-woman talks."

"Sorry. What else did y'all say?"

"After I reassured him about Pudd'nhead, I told him why Aunt Maggie was so adamant about going to the carnival while he stayed home."

"That's obvious. She wants him safe but doesn't want to miss out on running the white elephant sale."

"Maybe that was obvious to you, but not to a man grappling with jealousy."

"Did he think she was going to meet Pudd'nhead there?"

Richard nodded.

"Poor Big Bill," I said, which was not something I'd said often. "What did you tell him?"

"I told him that Aunt Maggie is having trouble dealing with the changes their sudden marriage has caused. She's used to doing what she wants, when she wants, and not answering to anybody. It's going to take her some time to adjust, and if he doesn't want to frighten her off, he'll have to give her some space. Eventually, he realized I was right."

"Big Bill said he was going to give Aunt Maggie some space," I said skeptically.

"To be accurate, he used a horse-training metaphor, but the meaning was close enough."

"Well, bless his heart. I'm impressed you figured it all out and came up with a way to explain it to him."

"I do have some experience with Burnette women," Richard said dryly.

"Are you saying I . . . ?" Then I remembered a couple of incidents from our first year of marriage. "Okay, I see your point." Then I carefully asked, "That's not a problem anymore, is it?"

"Oh, no," he said. "You're thoroughly broken to the saddle, now."

"I'm going to break something upside your head in a minute!" I said.

He just grinned.

When we picked up Alice, Aunt Nellie and Uncle Ruben insisted on our staying for dinner with them and the triplets, and we spent an interesting evening hearing about their latest scheme to make money. Since their idea of sending spam to computers all over the world had been a bust, Aunt Nellie and Uncle Ruben were now trying to decide between opening a cyber-café in downtown Byerly or starting a web site for selling collectible ball caps. I figured either idea was bound to fail, at least with those two in charge, but I leaned toward the ball caps, figuring they'd lose less money that way.

I'd hoped to ask Idelle, Odelle, and Carlelle about useful gossip from the mill, but Alice got cranky and I never got a chance, so I told them I'd catch up with them at work the next day.

Chapter Nineteen

Visiting Walters Mill always arouses mixed emotions in me. On one hand, more family and friends than I can keep track of had worked there over the years, and a slew were still working there. Heck, looking at the dusty framed company photos was almost as good as going through one of the Burnette family photo albums.

On the other hand, work there hadn't always been pleasant. Even if I didn't count the brown lung that had hurt so many workers, I couldn't forget that most of the workers were considered more easily replaced than the machinery, with only a handful escaping the hard work to make decent money in the upstairs offices.

Most of all, I remembered how desperate I'd been never to work in that mud-brown building, which had been a large part of my decision to go to school up north. Of course, that had led to my meeting Richard and having Alice, so maybe I should be grateful to the mill for giving me a place to run away from.

Richard and I got to the mill the next day, several hours before Burt was expecting us. This time, we had

Alice with us, both as an excuse to visit with folks and as camouflage. The sailor dress she was wearing had a matching hat, and if that wouldn't disarm people, I didn't know what would. As Burt's secretary, Michelle was in an excellent place to know where the bodies were buried, so we called her from the reception desk at the front door and asked if we could come up. She was waiting for us when we got off the elevator.

"What are you guys doing here?" she asked. "Burt said you wouldn't be coming until after lunch."

"Are we early?" I asked innocently. "I must have misheard Burt."

Michelle grinned. "I get it. You guys wanted to snoop around some before he gets back. Am I right?"

"Our being here won't get you in trouble, will it?" Richard asked.

Michelle made an Italian gesture of unconcern. "How am I to blame if you got the time wrong? Now give me that baby! As long as you're here, I'm going to show off this little cutie patootie to everybody in the building."

"That sounds fine," I said nonchalantly. "So does the new guy like babies? I think you said his name was Mike."

"He does, and it's a good thing you're here now. Mike told me that Burt is sending him to take care of some business out of the office this afternoon. If you'd come later, you'd have missed him."

"Aren't we lucky?" I said. I'd had a hunch that Burt was going to try something like that. Not wanting to be too obvious, we let Michelle show us around some of the other offices first, not bothering to remind her that I probably knew the building as well as she did. Besides, I knew most of the people who worked there, at least to say howdy to, and it was fun to let them meet Alice. Eventually, we got to the person we really wanted to see.

"And this is Mike Cooper's office," Michelle announced, tapping on the door before going inside.

"Mike *Cooper?*" I said. It was the first time I'd heard the man's last name, and it sounded familiar. Michelle stepped out of the way to let us inside the office, and that's when I saw him.

"Laura, Richard," Michelle was saying, "this is Mike Cooper. Mike, this is Laura and Richard Fleming, and their baby, Alice. Laura is one of Thaddeous's cousins."

"Another one of the Burnettes?" he said with a smile, standing up and holding out his hand to Richard. "And I thought my mother had a lot of relatives."

Richard shook his hand, then turned to me. We'd agreed before that I would take the lead in the conversation, with Michelle taking Alice out as soon as it started to get heavy. But I couldn't say a word. I just stared at Mike.

Realizing that something was wrong, Richard made small talk while Michelle looked confused. Finally, I managed to choke out, "Michelle, where did you say the ladies' room is?"

"I'll take you." She handed over Alice and said, "Richard, you keep this little girl busy."

Michelle waited until we were safely locked in the ladies' room before saying, "Laura? What's with you? You look like you've seen a ghost."

"Not a ghost," I said shakily. "A ghost's son."

"What are you talking about?"

"That man. Mike Cooper. I've met him before. He was going by Michael when I talked to him, but it's him."[10]

"How do you know him? He's not from around here."

"No, but his father was."

[10] *Dead Ringer*

"So? He said his father was dead."

"Yeah, he's dead, all right. I'm one of the people who found his body. I'm surprised nobody's made the connection, but Cooper is a pretty common name."

"Okay, Laura, start explaining. From the beginning."

"I can't," I said, and when she opened her mouth to argue, I said, "I would if I could, Michelle, but I can't. I promised."

She didn't look happy, but I couldn't help it. "I'm sorry—"

"I know, I know. I'm not officially in the family yet."

"That has nothing to do with it," I said. "There aren't many Burnettes who know about this, either. Just Richard and I, and Aunt Maggie, and—and one other aunt."

"You can't even tell me which aunt?"

I shook my head. "I can tell you one thing. Burt is not Mike Cooper's lover."

"How do you know?"

"Trust me. I'd be willing to bet that Burt honestly wants him to take over here at the mill, and I know why."

She looked very dubious, but I knew doggoned well Burt wasn't sleeping with Mike Cooper. Maybe Burt or Mike was gay, though I doubted that as well, but even if they were, there was no way Burt Walters would have slept with his own nephew.

Chapter
Twenty

Richard and Alice were waiting for us outside the bathroom.

"Did he recognize you?" I asked Richard.

"I don't think so. I used Alice to distract him as best I could. Then Tavis Montgomery came in to give Mike an assignment, and I beat a hasty retreat."

"Good," I said. "We have to talk to Burt. Michelle, when did you say he'll be back?"

"Not until after lunch."

"Rats!" I said, even though we'd come early for the sole purpose of avoiding him.

"Since we're here, why don't we go ahead and talk to some other people?" Richard suggested.

"I suppose it beats sitting around and waiting," I said.

"You want me to show you around?" Michelle asked.

"That's okay, you've got work to do. Richard and I know our way."

We spent the next couple of hours visiting with people around the mill. Uncle Buddy, Thaddeous, Linwood, and the triplets were all on duty, so we got to see them; and I had some old friends working there, too. At noon, we got sandwiches out of the machines so we could chat while eating. It was nice catching up with people, but nobody knew anything that would help us find the person trying to kill Big Bill. Oh, we heard the rumors about Burt and Mike Cooper repeated a number of times, and the latest speculations about office politics, and complaints about quotas, but nothing useful.

Once the lunch bell rang, we headed back upstairs.

"Burt's not back yet," Michelle said when she saw us. "Why don't you wait for him in his office?"

Burt's office was nearly as plush as Big Bill's at the mansion, but had the added glory of a full-length portrait of Big Bill on the wall behind the desk. Personally, a painted face looking over my shoulder all day would have made me nervous, but I guess Burt was used to it.

By then, Alice was ready for a snack and a nap, and managed to combine the two by falling asleep while nursing. Once she was thoroughly out, Richard and I put her in her carrier and left her by the couch, and then moved chairs to a corner of the office so we could talk without disturbing her.

"That really was Michael Cooper, wasn't it?" I asked him, but didn't wait for an answer. "I can't believe Burt brought him here. Do you suppose Mike knows who he really is?"

"I assume that's what you wanted to ask Burt."

"That's one thing." Before I could tell him what else I wanted to ask about, the door opened and Burt came in.

He stopped when he saw Alice in her carrier, and whispered, "Is she asleep?"

"Soundly," I said in a normal voice. "Don't worry—it takes a lot to wake her up."

"Okay," he said, still whispering, and tiptoed toward

us, stopping just for a second to smile at the sleeping baby. Then he took the chair we'd left for him.

"Michelle tells me you've been visiting the employees," he said tentatively.

"We saw Mike Cooper, if that's what you were wondering."

He sighed. "I should have known that I couldn't keep him away from you forever."

"Yes, you should have," I said bluntly. "As small as Byerly is, we were bound to see him sooner or later."

"Later would have been fine," he said with a tiny grin. "Are you going to tell Daddy?"

"Of course not. We promised not to. Michael—Mike being here doesn't change that."

He exhaled deeply. "That's a relief. Daddy doesn't need any more shocks, not with what's going on right now."

"You are planning to tell him someday, aren't you?" I asked.

"I don't know, Laurie Anne, I just can't decide."

"Why did you bring Mike here if you didn't want Big Bill to know?"

"I didn't plan to bring him here," he said plaintively. "I ran into him by accident."

"I thought he was in school in Raleigh."

"He was, but he graduated and got a good job in the Research Triangle. Then he got downsized a few months back—you must know high-tech's been hit pretty hard. I didn't know about any of that beforehand, mind you. I was just looking for a new manager trainee and went to meet with folks at the NC State placement office. They'd set up some appointments for me to meet with graduates and alumni, but it never occurred to me that one of the candidates would be Mike."

"Had you seen him before?" I asked.

"Only from a distance, but I knew it was him right away. Once I got over the shock of seeing him again, I was glad for the opportunity to talk. It turned out he really was qualified for the job—shoot, he'll be ready to replace me in a few years. I just had to hire him." At my quizzical look, he added, "I couldn't leave my own nephew to walk the streets, could I?"

"I seem to recall that he's got family to help him out," I said.

"*I'm* his family," Burt said.

"Does Michael know that?"

When Richard and I had met Michael before, he'd had no idea he was a Walters. In fact, he didn't even know that the Walters family existed. Michael's father started calling himself Leonard Cooper long before Michael was born, but the name everybody in Byerly had known him by was Small Bill Walters—Big Bill's older son, and Burt's big brother.

I'd never known the man as Small Bill or Leonard, but I could understand why he hadn't been happy in Byerly. As the elder brother, he'd been destined to step into his father's footsteps, or at least to follow along after them. But Small Bill hadn't wanted to spend the rest of his life with his father's portrait watching over him, and during a tour in Vietnam, he'd gotten his chance to escape.

His best buddy, the real Leonard Cooper, was killed, and Small Bill had switched dog tags with him. Leonard was shipped back to Byerly in a sealed coffin and buried as Small Bill, while Small Bill moved to Tennessee to become Leonard Cooper. Eventually he got married and had a son. Michael Cooper, who was calling himself Mike, was that son.

Many years later, Small Bill had come back to Byerly

because of one of the secrets I hadn't been able to tell Michelle about, and he'd been murdered. With a shiver, I remembered that he'd died in the very room where I was sitting, and I had an irrational urge to snatch up Alice and get her out of there.

Though Richard and I had figured out who killed Small Bill, the killer had committed suicide before being arrested. So Junior had officially closed the case, even though she knew that there were secrets left untold, including Leonard Cooper's real identity and the existence of Mike.

Burt had known but couldn't stand the idea of his father finding out that his favorite son had pretended to be dead rather than come home. For reasons dealing with secrets in my own family, Richard and I had promised to keep Burt's secrets.

"Does Mike know?" I asked again. "About his father, I mean."

"No."

"Are you sure?"

"Of course I'm sure. I haven't told him—how else would he find out?"

"He does know his father died in Byerly, right? Wasn't he suspicious when you brought him to work here? Didn't he have questions?"

"I told him what I thought Small Bill would want him to know. That his daddy came back here to settle a debt of honor from Vietnam, and that he was killed for it. Which is the truth, after all."

"He was satisfied with that?"

Burt shrugged. "He seemed to be."

"Really? Personally, I'd want to know a whole lot more details if my father had been murdered."

"Most people aren't as nos—as inquisitive as you are, Laurie Anne."

I heard Richard stifle a chuckle, but ignored him. "Hasn't anybody noticed how much Mike looks like a Walters? His chin alone is a dead giveaway."

"Not everybody is as observant as you are, either," Burt said. "And I've kept Mike away from Daddy so far."

"How long can you keep that up? You're sitting on a powder keg here."

"I know, I know," he said with a sigh. "I should never have let it happen, but when I met Mike . . . I'd missed him growing up already; I didn't want to miss the rest of his life. Maybe it's because I never had any children of my own, but I couldn't stand to lose a chance to get to know my nephew." He glanced over at Alice, snoring softly in her carrier. "Surely you can understand why."

There was nothing I could say to argue with that. "I have one question. Was Mike at the party?"

"He was invited, but I told him it was going to be a bunch of boring old folks and that he'd have a better time somewhere else."

"You'd better hope that Aunt Maggie never hears you say that," Richard warned.

"I'm not that reckless," Burt said. "Anyway, I didn't see him there, so he must have believed me. Why?"

"Just curious," I said, which was only partially true. To change the subject, I said, "By the way, do you know what folks are saying about you and Mike?"

"No. Why?"

When I told him, his reply promptly woke Alice up, and Aunt Maggie would have been mighty peeved if she'd heard the words he used in front of that baby.

Chapter
Twenty-one

As soon as we got back in the car, Richard said, "At least we can write off the idea of Burt trying to kill Big Bill to hide his homosexuality. Unless he's a better actor than Kenneth Branagh, he had no idea what people thought about his relationship with Mike."

"True, but we have to add him back to the list in case he wanted to kill Big Bill to secure Mike's inheritance. Burt's out of the will now, anyway, but before, he was the main heir. If Big Bill had found out about Mike and realized that Burt knew about him all along, there's no telling what he would have done. He might have rewritten his will to make sure neither of them got any of the money."

"Would Burt kill for money?"

"Maybe not for money, but for his surrogate son's future? You're a daddy—what would you do for Alice?"

He considered it. "If she were starving, I might kill to feed her, but Mike isn't anywhere close to that."

"I don't think it's a strong possibility," I said, "but I've got another angle, which is much ickier. What if Mike does know who he is?"

"Meaning?"

"Meaning that if he knows he's a Walters, then he probably realizes that he'll be Burt's heir. Maybe he wanted to get rid of Big Bill before Big Bill could rewrite the will. Or maybe he just wanted Burt to get the money sooner, so he could get to it himself."

"How could he have found out?"

"Small Bill could have left a journal, or something in his things for Mike to find. For all we know, Mike arranged to 'accidentally' run into Burt. I'll lay odds Burt didn't check into his references the way he would have for anybody else."

"But Burt said Mike wasn't at the party, so he couldn't have poisoned the champagne."

"Burt says he didn't see Mike there. It was an awfully big party; if somebody had been trying to stay in the background, it wouldn't have been too hard."

"Would Mike kill his own grandfather?"

"He barely knows Big Bill. Maybe he's a grandfather by blood, but I don't know that that's enough to stop somebody who's willing to kill in the first place."

"I suppose not."

"Anyway, he's worth checking out, and I'm sure Junior would be happy to have another name to investigate."

"What are we going to tell her about Mike's motive?"

"Let her think he and Burt are lovers, like everybody else. If Junior's okay with Belva and Wynette, the idea of Burt being gay won't freak her out."

For once, Junior was in the office with Belva, though Junior was on the phone and waved us over toward her deputy.

"Hey there, Laurie Anne, Richard," Belva said. "This must be Alice—I didn't get a chance to see her the other other night." She reached for her. "May I?"

"Sure," Richard said, and handed her over.

"I figure I need the practice," she said with a cute smile.

"I don't know," I said, "it looks like you've already had practice." Though I would have thought a baby in Belva's arms would look incongruous, especially when she was wearing her uniform, she did look pretty comfortable. Though she was going to have to quit wearing that gun all the time.

Belva said, "My, uh—Wynette told me you and your husband stopped by yesterday."

"Yes, we did," I said sheepishly. "You remember we told you that we'd been tracking down people who wrote threatening letters to Big Bill Walters? Well, Wynette's late aunt sent a couple. We wouldn't have bothered checking them out if we'd known about you two."

"That's all right. I understand you've got to go where the trail leads; it's one of the things a cop learns."

"Good," I said, relieved.

"It's just that—not everybody knows . . ."

"About y'all being together?"

She nodded. "It's not that I'm ashamed of it or anything, but . . ."

"I understand. Folks had a hard time accepting Richard at first, too. Him being a Yankee and all."

Belva chuckled. "Yeah, at least Wynette is a Southerner."

"So, are you looking forward to being a mama?" I asked.

"Oh yeah, it's just that babies are a lot of work, aren't they?" she said, concerned again. "Wynette is going to be staying home with her—we know she's having a girl—but I'm still worried about how we're going to handle it. Me working crazy hours, and all."

"I wish I could tell you it's going to be easy," I said

with a sigh, "but it is hard to get everything done. Heck, some days it's hard to get *anything* done. People swear to me that it gets better, but I don't know if I believe them or not." I stopped; I wasn't helping Belva a bit. "Fortunately, it's worth it. The first time you hold those little hands . . ." I realized I was echoing something Aunt Nora had said at my baby shower. It had irritated me when Aunt Nora said it, but darned if she hadn't been right on the money. "Having Alice around has been so much fun, Belva. You'll see. Forget about the house-work and laundry and all that junk—just enjoy that baby."

She looked a little more cheerful.

"Have you two picked out names?" Richard asked.

"We've narrowed it down to four: Charlaine, Aurora, Lily, and Sookie."

"An interesting range of choices," he said diplomati-cally.

"Family names," Belva said, and Richard and I nodded in understanding. Both Southerners and New Englanders are frequently afflicted with family names.

We talked about vaccinations and disposable diapers until Junior got off the phone and announced, "I don't want to hear one word about potty training—I've been through it with my sisters' kids, and that's enough for anybody."

"Don't worry, Chief, Alice is too young for potty train-ing," Belva said.

"Not according to my aunts," I said glumly. "Aunt Ruby Lee said she had Clifford trained by the time he was—"

Junior cleared her throat loudly. "I just said that we aren't having this discussion, Laurie Anne."

"Sorry. I get carried away."

"So what do y'all have for me?" Junior said.

"I was going to ask you the same question."

She looked disgusted. "All I've got is a big helping of nothing. Only a couple of people have enough of an alibi to help us."

"We can't eliminate anybody?" I said.

"Just a couple." She pulled out a pad covered with notes. "Now, leaving out the party, because everybody and his kid brother were there, we've got three events to track. The attempted shooting, the attempted hit-and-run, and the attempted electrocution. Are you following?"

We all nodded, except Alice, who cooed.

"Our first suspect is Burt Walters. He was home the nights of the shooting and the hit-and-run, but nobody can verify he was there the whole time, because Dorcas was at committee meetings both nights. He was out of town on business the day of the electrocution, but since that was set up ahead of time, that's no help.

"Next is Dorcas Walters. She was at the aforementioned committee meetings, but the timing is loose enough that she could have skipped out, and she was in town during the electrocution."

"What if the two of them were in it together?" I asked.

Junior made a face. "I thought of that. If they were in it together, I don't know that I'll ever catch them."

It wasn't what I wanted to hear, but I don't imagine she liked saying it, either.

"Then we've got Irene Duffield. Off duty the two nights in question, and could easily have gotten away to set up the electrocution. Maggie Burnette Walters—"

"Hey!" I said indignantly.

"Everybody involved is a suspect until proven otherwise," Junior said.

"You talked to Wynette," Belva reminded me.

"They're right," Richard said, and I reluctantly nodded.

"Fortunately for our working relationship," Junior said, "the new Mrs. Walters has a good alibi. She was with a man named Red Clark at the very moment when somebody tried to run down Big Bill. So she's in the clear."

"Glad to hear it," I said stiffly.

Junior grinned. "Come on, Laurie Anne. You know I never thought it was her, but I've got to cover all the bases. Speaking of bases, we've got your friend Troy Wilson, a.k.a. Pudd'nhead. He's got no criminal record to speak of, unless you want to count a drunk-and-disorderly from thirty years ago. He didn't check into the Holiday Inn in Hickory until after the first three attempts, so he looks clean."

"What if he was staying at a different hotel before then?" I asked.

"We thought of that," Junior said, "so poor Belva called every hotel in the area to check, using the name and the description, but nobody remembered him. I'm keeping him as a long shot, mostly because of the way he was following you two around."

"He's stopped that," I said, "at least, as far as we can tell."

"Then we've got your threatening letters," Junior said. "Sandie Herron." She shook her head. "Not the first hint of an alibi, and he wouldn't talk to me or Belva. He's a strange one, but even though he had some wild times when he was younger, he's been pretty quiet for a long time. Another long shot.

"Marlyn Roberts is the only other person I've eliminated with any degree of certainty. She was working at a fund-raiser at the high school the night of the hit-and-run."

"Those things can be awfully disorganized," I objected. "How can anybody be sure she didn't sneak out."

"Because the fund-raiser was a fashion show, and Marlyn was the announcer."

"Good enough," I said, glad to be able to cross somebody off our list.

"Last but not least," Junior said, "we've got Belva here."

I'd been kind of wondering about Belva's alibi myself, but hadn't thought it would be polite to say so, especially not when she was holding my baby.

"The hell you say!" Belva said, but lowered her voice when Alice whimpered. "Why am I a suspect?"

"Because Big Bill almost prevented you from being hired, and is still making me keep you on probation," Junior said matter-of-factly. "No offense, Belva, but after what happened with my old deputy, I'm not taking anything for granted."

"I guess I can understand that," Belva said.

"Fortunately for my piece of mind, you've got solid alibis for two of the attempts. On the night of the shooting, you and Wynette were eating dinner with Wynette's sister. Not only does the sister vouch for you, but her neighbor saw you, too. The night of the hit-and-run, you were working security for that fashion show at the high school, and Marlyn Roberts would surely have squawked if you'd left early."

"So I'm in the clear, right, Chief?"

"That's right." Junior turned to Richard and me. "Can you add anything useful?"

"I wish I could," I said, "but all I've got is another possibility."

"Who?"

"Mike Cooper."

"Burt's new employee?" Junior said. "Does this mean that you've confirmed that he and Burt are an item?"

"Not necessarily," I said, "but there might be more to him than meets the eye." I was going to leave it at that, but I should have known better.

"I remember who Mike Cooper is, Laurie Anne," Junior said.

"Who's Mike Cooper?" Belva asked.

"I'll brief you later. Or at least I'll tell you what I know. I've always thought that I might have missed something about that case." She gave me a long, hard look.

I looked right back at her. "Junior, if I really believed that there was a connection with this case, I'd tell you right now, but I don't think there is. If I find out something that convinces me otherwise, you'll be the first to know."

"That's good enough for me," she said, which I took as quite a compliment. "Belva and I will go ahead and check on Cooper's background and his alibis, and we'll go from there."

Then I gave Junior a rundown of our various interviews, except the one with Burt, but we really didn't have anything concrete for her, and she didn't have anything else for us.

Finally I said, "I'm lost, Junior. What about you? Have you had one of your hunches?" Junior's hunches were both well known and well regarded.

"I'm a police officer," Junior said sternly, "not some carnival fortune teller. I rely on facts, not hunches." That might have worked if she'd been able to keep a straight face, but her grin gave her away. "Sorry, no hunches this time. I wouldn't bet on any of these folks, but then again, I wouldn't bet against any of them, either."

"Great. Here we are, all working together, and we're

still lost," I said. "Maybe we should go back to working against one another."

"No," Richard and Junior said in unison. We all laughed, and Belva plopped Alice back into my arms, saying, "Let's see you try to be grumpy with this little doll looking at you."

I tried; I really did, but babies have a way of cheering you up, whether you want to be cheered or not. That must be one of the reasons why parents put up with two A.M. feedings.

Chapter
Twenty-two

Even with the dose of baby-induced euphoria, Richard and I were tired, and we headed back to the house after that. I really didn't know where to go next, other than for a talk with Mike Cooper, and we were giving Junior a chance to do her stuff first.

"I guess we could go back through Big Bill's threatening letters," I said halfheartedly. "We might have missed something. Or we could go visiting and see if we can scrape up some more gossip."

"I've got a better idea," Richard said.

"Good," I said. "Let's hear it."

"We're taking tomorrow off."

"We can't—"

"All work and no play makes Jack a dull boy," Richard said in a tone that brooked no argument.

"That's not Shakespeare."

"No, but it's true. Listen, Laura, we've got Big Bill as safe as we can get him, and we've followed up on every lead we've got. Not to mention the fact that we're taking care of a baby."

"My aunts have been taking care of Alice," I said.

"They're not covering the two o'clock feedings, are they? Or nursing her first thing in the morning and last thing at night?"

"No, but—"

"Then no *but*s. We're taking tomorrow off, and tomorrow night we're going to the Halloween carnival."

"I'd forgotten the carnival was tomorrow," I said. "I would like to take Alice."

"And you promised me a chance to dress up. So here's my plan. Tonight, we're calling out for pizza and getting to bed early. Tomorrow, Alice is going to visit Aunt Edna and I'm going to hunt up some costumes for the three of us."

"What about me?"

"You're going to lounge about."

I opened my mouth to object, but Richard's plan sounded too good to resist. After all, who was I to argue with the world's most thoughtful husband? So what I said was, "You're not going to make me dress up in anything ridiculous, are you?"

"You'll just have to trust me," was his airy reply.

We stuck to Richard's plan for the rest of the evening, with one slight modification. Though we did indeed get to bed early, we didn't get to sleep right away. Since that kind of activity can ultimately be even more relaxing than sleep, Richard was willing to let me get away with it. In fact, he cooperated quite enthusiastically.

Though I did take care of the two o'clock feeding, that was the last bit of child care I did for the day. Richard was the one to go get Alice when she woke up in the morning, and he brought her over for me to nurse. Then he pushed me back into bed, got himself and Alice ready, and took her to Aunt Edna's before disappearing himself. I slept until ten, then got up to find a note reminding me to lounge and announcing that I would have company for lunch.

When Aunt Daphine showed up at twelve, not only did she come bearing takeout from Pigwick's, she had a box full of supplies for cutting my hair, doing my nails, and giving me a facial. I'd never been one to mess with a beauty regimen, but there's something about having a baby that had made me crave pampering, and Aunt Daphine was happy to oblige. While she worked me over, we talked about everything under the sun except for Big Bill Walters's situation, and I continued to lounge, in accordance with Richard's stern instructions.

After Aunt Daphine left, I lay down and took a nap on the couch even though I wasn't worn out from sitting up with Alice all night. By the time Richard arrived with an armload of intriguing bundles, I was bright-eyed and bushy-tailed, and only a little apprehensive about the Halloween costume he'd picked out for me.

"Stay down there," he ordered as he lugged it all upstairs. "I want to arrange things first." I waited more or less patiently until he called, "Okay, now you can come up."

When I got to our bedroom, I saw that he'd laid my costume out on the bed: an Inverness cape, a deerstalker cap, a meerschaum pipe, and the biggest magnifying glass I'd ever seen.

I burst out laughing. "Sherlock Holmes?"

"What better way to remind you that you're the world's greatest detective? Or at least Byerly's. Do you like it?"

"I love it." I wrapped my arms around him in a way that Sherlock himself would never have done, and gave him the world's greatest kiss. "Are you going to be Dr. Watson?"

He shook his head. "Though I admire the good doctor, his style of dress isn't nearly flamboyant enough for my taste. Feast your eyes on this!"

The outfit that Richard pulled out of the closet with a flourish was indeed a feast for the eyes. Purple leggings, gold sandals that would lace up his legs, a tunic with gold and purple diamond shapes and a slew of sequins, a shiny crown with purple fur trim, and if that weren't enough, a pair of wings lavishly feathered in purple, and of course, more sequins.

"Behold, Oberon, King of the Fey!" he announced triumphantly.

"Where on earth did you find that?" I said. "I'm going to need sunglasses just to look at you."

"A group in Rocky Shoals put on a production of *A Midsummer Night's Dream* last week," he said. "I saw a poster still up, which included a picture of their Oberon. So I asked around until I could arrange to borrow the costume. Having Dorcas make the request for me didn't hurt."

"What about the ears?" I said, but I should have known better.

He pulled a pair of rubber pointed ears from a bag on the bed, looking more than a little pleased with himself.

"I don't think I need to bother getting dressed up at all," I said in mock exasperation. "Nobody's even going to see me with you around."

"The costume for Titania is available," Richard said.

"No, thanks," I said quickly. "I'll stick with Sherlock. What about Alice?"

"She was the tough one," he said. "For some reason, there aren't a lot of choices for seven-month-olds."

"Imagine that."

"But I did find this," he said with a grin. He reached

back into the closet to produce a blue dress with a white pinafore, blue-and-white-striped tights, and a headband with a white bow on top. "Alice in Wonderland." There was even a plastic Cheshire cat for her to chew on.

"Perfect," I said, and smooched him again. I might have done even more to reward his mighty efforts, but Aunt Edna was going to be bringing Alice back in an hour, and I figured it would take every bit of that time for Richard to get himself fixed up. I hurried through my own preparations, both because they were so much simpler and because I couldn't wait to watch him try to get his ears straight.

Alice looked a little confused when she saw Richard dressed like a fairy king—especially when Aunt Edna nearly fell over laughing—but eventually accepted Richard as her daddy. She had no problem with me dressed as a man, and I wasn't sure if I found that comforting or not. We took charge of her while Aunt Edna rushed home to get into her own Halloween getup.

Alice looked adorable in her Wonderland costume, of course, and after we took a ridiculous number of pictures of her and ourselves, we headed for the carnival.

Chapter
Twenty-three

I'm always a little nervous when approaching someplace or something I loved as a child, not knowing if it will still appeal to me as an adult, but after ten minutes at the Byerly Halloween Carnival, I knew it was exactly as much fun as I remembered. The decorations were just as cheesy, and I could smell cotton candy, and everybody was in costume, and almost everybody was cheerful, even the vampire trying to lure people over to the haunted house. Alice looked as happy as a clam to be surrounded by so much noise and so many people as we pushed her stroller through the throng.

Byerly High School was built in the shape of a U, with the grassy quadrangle in the middle crisscrossed with sidewalks for students going from one wing to another. Most of the carnival booths were set up in the quad, with more spilling out onto the football field. The cafeteria, library, and auditorium were in the center of the U and, since they were open to the quad, were being used for the snack bar, white elephant sale, and costume contest.

"Where to first?" Richard asked.

"I want to take Alice on her first pony ride," I said.

"Laura, she can't even sit up by herself."

"They'll let you walk next to her to hold her up."

Richard looked unhappily at his pretty sandals.

"It's a great photo op," I wheedled.

"Let's go!"

Having helped with the signs, we had no problem finding the area where two dozen kids and their parents were already waiting for their chance to ride one of the sturdy little ponies around the cross-country track. "You go ahead and get in line. I'll get tickets."

I was standing in front of the ticket booth, trying to figure out how many we'd need, when a voice said, "Nice costume."

"Thanks." I turned to see Mike Cooper smiling at me, dressed as Luke Skywalker. Since Richard had forbidden me from calling Junior on our day off, I didn't know if he was still a suspect or not, so I felt a little awkward. "You, too."

"Thanks. I'm glad I ran into you. You and your husband must think I'm a major flake for not remembering y'all the other day. You two are the ones who came to talk to me after my father died, aren't you?"

"That was us. We didn't place you right away, either." That was mostly a lie. I'd known him as soon as I saw him; I just hadn't recognized his name right away. "It was kind of a surprise, finding you in Byerly."

"Just one of those crazy coincidences. I met Mr. Walters at the placement office at State, and we really hit it off, so when he offered me a job, I jumped at it. I'm really enjoying the work, and Byerly is a great place to live. I know this is where Dad . . ." He paused for a second. "I know this is where Dad got hurt, but I also know it was just some crazy person. Every place has those."

"I'm afraid you're right."

He looked away for a minute. "Chief Norton said you had a lot to do with finding the person who shot Dad. I wanted to thank you."

"You're welcome" just didn't seem like an appropriate response, so instead I said, "I was glad to be able to do that much for him. I never met your father, but I understand he was a good man."

"Yeah, he was." He looked around the carnival. "He'd have loved this for sure. Dad was crazy about dressing up."

"Is that right?" I said, thinking that Mike had no idea how true that was. Or did he? I couldn't picture the young man in front of me prowling with murder on his mind and then acting so normal. Still, his father had deceived his own family, as well as the town where he'd grown up. Maybe Mike had learned how from him.

Mike looked behind me. "Excuse me, but I think that fairy wants to get your attention."

I turned around and saw Richard waving wildly. He and Alice were nearly at the head of the line. "Tickets!" I yelped. "Excuse me, but I've got to get tickets for Alice to ride a pony."

"Hey, I wouldn't want her to miss that. I used to love pony rides."

I hurriedly bought far more tickets than I should have and ran back to get to Richard just in time.

Alice giggled the whole time she was on the pony, and as I marched around the cakewalk with her, and while all three of us took the hay ride. Then, with the suddenness only an infant can attain, she fell sound asleep, and we loaded her back into the stroller.

"What next?" I asked Richard.

"Does this carnival have games?"

"Of course. Milk bottles, darts, water pistols, ring toss, all the usual suspects."

Richard got a gleam in his eye I usually only saw when Shakespeare was being discussed. "Then let us hie ourselves thither."

"Which one?" I asked as we approached Game Row.

"All of them," he said eagerly. "I want to win something for Alice to take home."

With some trepidation, I handed over the rest of our tickets. "You go ahead. I think I'll go see how Aunt Maggie is doing at the white elephant sale."

"Don't you want to try out some games?"

"Not right now." I didn't want to tell him how bad I was at carnival games. I'd never forget the time when I played the one where all you have to do is pick up a plastic duck and look at the number written on its bottom, and I managed to find the only duck in the pond without a number.

Aunt Maggie had done her usual outstanding job getting merchandise for the white elephant, and the library was filled with people hoping to replace the unneeded items they'd donated with different unneeded items. My cousin Augustus, who regularly worked the flea market and auctions with Aunt Maggie, was helping her out, so I didn't feel guilty in pulling her aside for a minute.

Though Augustus made a very dashing pirate, the only concession Aunt Maggie had made to the holiday was a T-shirt with a pumpkin on it and a witch's hat. Even then, the hat had a price tag on it.

"Is everything all right at the house?" I asked her.

"Just fine, other than Bill not having a nurse with him. Vivian got sick, and we couldn't get a hold of Anne or Jan."

"He's alone?" I said, alarmed.

"No, Irene said she didn't care anything about the carnival so she'd stay with him."

"That was nice of her."

"Not really. She only did it so she could make me look bad for abandoning my ailing husband. But Bill told me it was all right for me to come."

"Good for him." I shouldn't have asked the next question, but I couldn't resist. "Have you and he made up?"

"None of your business," she retorted, but she was grinning like Alice's Cheshire cat when she said it. The grin faded when she looked toward the door. "Lord almighty, can't that man find a spot and roost?"

Tavis Montgomery, dressed in his volunteer fireman uniform, had just come in. Spotting Aunt Maggie, he came over and asked, "How is everything going, Mrs. Walters?"

"Everything's fine, Tavis, just like it was the last time you asked."

"Do you want a cup of cider or a bathroom break?"

"I've been going to the bathroom by myself for a long time, Tavis."

"Good, good." He started to lift the lid of the cash box, but Aunt Maggie slapped his hand away. "Don't you mess with my money."

"Just checking to see if you needed more change," he said, but he must have been used to Aunt Maggie, because he didn't sound offended.

She heaved a mighty sigh and went to help somebody sort through the piles of used clothing.

"You've done a great job with the carnival," I said to Tavis.

"Thank you, Laurie Anne. It's been a lot of work, but when I see happy children like yours, I know it's worth it."

Since Alice was still sound asleep, I'm not sure how he knew she was all that happy, but I was willing to concede the point. "Nice costume," I said.

"Yours, too. Very appropriate." He glanced at his watch. "If you'll excuse me, I need to make sure everything is running smoothly." He slipped out the door, smiling and nodding like a politician trolling for votes.

Aunt Maggie was still busy with her customer, so I waved at her and Augustus and went to find Richard. He was at the dart booth, and in the short time since I'd left him, he'd collected a bundle of stuffed toys that included a mouse, a cat, two unicorns, and one thing that looked like a carrot. "What are you doing?"

"I told you," he said as he took aim, then let the dart fly. It burst a balloon to reveal a gold star. "Winning souvenirs for Alice." The man tending the booth handed him a stuffed Scooby-Doo. "She'll love this."

"Richard, she's seven months old. If she can't chew on it, she's not interested." But when he looked disappointed, I quickly added, "So we'll have to put it all up until she's older." How we were going to get it all home, or where we'd store it when we got there, were questions I didn't want to think about.

"Good idea," he said. "Wait until you see what they're giving away at the ring toss." He started to gather up his prizes but ran out of hands. "Maybe I should take a load out to the car."

"Here, we can put some of it under the stroller." I shoved as much as I could in the basket, leaving the rest for Richard to keep up with. "How much longer are you going to be?"

"Just the ring toss, and the milk bottles. And maybe the—"

"Never mind. I'm going to wander. Don't forget the costume contest."

I left Richard to continue proving his manhood, and pushed the still-snoozing Alice on down Game Row, graciously accepting compliments on her behalf. There was a crowd of kids gathered around the milk bottle toss, and I pushed in just far enough to see what the fuss was about.

"Did you see that?" a little boy was saying to another. "That's seven times in a row." There was a loud crash. "Eight!"

I peeked over the boy's head and saw Pudd'nhead Wilson, his feet surrounded by stuffed bears wearing baseball uniforms, and wearing an old-fashioned baseball costume himself. He threw a softball at the only pyramid of metal milk bottles still standing and knocked over every bottle.

"Nine!" the boy said in awe.

Pudd'nhead accepted another bear, then turned around to the kids, counting silently. "That'll do," he said to the woman in charge of the booth. Then he started tossing bears to the assembled kids, smiling at their surprised delight. As they ran off to tell their parents, Pudd'nhead caught sight of Alice and me.

"I didn't see you there. Hold on, and I'll win that little lady a bear, too." He started to reach into his pocket.

"Please don't," I said. "Richard's already won enough critters to fill a suitcase, and Alice won't be able to play with most of them for years."

"All right, if you're sure." He stepped out of the way for a teenage boy waiting to show off his pitching arm to the girl with him.

"That was some throwing," I said.

"I don't have the speed or strength I used to," he said, "but I've still got the aim. I'd have done even better if I'd used my lucky ball." He pulled a battered baseball out of his pocket.

"You carry your own ball?"

"Not all the time, but I figured it went with the costume." He tossed it up and down a couple of times, then put it back in his pocket. "If I can't win you a bear, can I at least buy you a drink?"

Since I was still awfully curious about Aunt Maggie's old flame, I said, "That would be very nice," and we strolled toward the cafeteria, where refreshments were being served. I knew that having a drink with a suspected poisoner might not have been the brightest move, so I watched very carefully as he got two cups of cider and brought them over, along with a couple of homemade chocolate cupcakes. "I thought you might like something to nibble on, too," he said. "Do you want the one with the black cat or the pumpkin?"

"Aren't you sweet? I'll take the pumpkin." He handed it over, and I took a bite. "Wonderful."

"This cider is good, too. Byerly sure knows how to throw a carnival."

"It's one of the best things about the town," I agreed. "How did you find out about it?"

"Are you kidding? There's a poster for it on every light pole in town."

"That's right; my cousin Vasti was in charge of advertising this year. She does things thoroughly."

"I saw it in the paper, too. When I used to be on the road all season, I picked up the habit of reading the local paper wherever I went. It's the best way to get to know a town. If I've got time, I even go to the library to check out back issues."

"What did the paper tell you about Byerly?" I said.

"That it's a not a bad little town. Maybe a little behind the times, and not the best place to be a stranger, but it's got a good heart."

"That sounds fair. It was a nice place to grow up."

"Do you want another cupcake?" he asked as I finished mine.

"No, thanks," I said, wiping the icing off my mouth.

"You aren't trying to get to Aunt Maggie through me, are you?"

"I'd do it in a heartbeat if I thought it would work," Pudd'nhead said without a trace of embarrassment, "but I know I struck out there." He shook his head sadly. "Fact is, I never even made it to bat, and I've got nobody to blame but myself."

"It must have been quite a shock," I said, "coming here and finding out Aunt Maggie was already married."

"Not really. I never thought a woman like her would end up alone."

"Still, the timing was bad."

"You mean her just being married? That did give me pause. I mean, what brand-new husband would want his wife's old boyfriend to come calling?"

"Is that why you didn't go see her? So you wouldn't intrude on the happy couple?"

"That's part of it."

I didn't say anything else, just drank cider while he made up his mind.

Finally, he said, "All I really had in mind was visiting her, seeing how things had turned out for her. Then I saw in the paper that she'd just married Big Bill Walters, and how there was going to be a big party, so I went and bought me a suit so I could sneak in. I was planning to ask Maggie to dance or something, just to surprise her. But then I saw her . . ." His voice trailed off.

"And?"

"And I realized I was just as in love with her as I ever was, and that I was an idiot for leaving her all those years ago, and that there was no way I could go up to her and make small talk when what I really wanted was to convince her to leave her husband and run away with me." He swigged down his cider as if he wished it were something a lot more potent.

I felt so bad for him, but there wasn't a darned thing I could say to comfort him. Especially not when I'd been feeling sorry for Big Bill being jealous just two days before. "I've always known that Aunt Maggie was a remarkable woman, but for her to have two amazing men in love with her just proves it."

"Thank you, Laurie Anne." He took a deep breath and said, "Anyway, that's why I didn't talk to her at the party. I might eventually have drummed up enough courage if I'd gotten another couple of beers in me, but then Walters got sick, and what with my being a gate-crasher, I thought it would be best if I took off." He looked sheepish. "I guess that looked kind of suspicious."

"A bit. You might want to explain that to the police."

"Probably, but I'm guessing you already told them about me."

"Why would you think that?" I said carefully.

"Because of what I found in the back issues of the *Byerly Gazette*. I went all the way back to the end of last year and read about you and your husband solving the killing at the Christmas pageant. The article said you two had done that kind of thing before. 'Byerly's Leading Sleuths,' the reporter called you."

"That sounds like Hank Parker." My aunts made a point of sending us all our clippings, but Hank was so effusive that I felt odd reading them, so I mostly just stored them away.

"After I realized that somebody had tried to kill Maggie and Walters, I guessed you'd be going after the guy, and decided to tag along in case you got into trouble. I might be old, but that doesn't mean I couldn't help if the need arose."

"And wouldn't Aunt Maggie have been impressed," I speculated.

He grinned. "That thought did cross my mind."

I should have been taking note of the fact that Pudd'nhead was still avoiding the police, but all I could think of was how lonely he must be. "Why don't you just talk to her? She won't bite you—she might bark, but she almost never bites."

"I want to. That's the only reason I'm still hanging around Byerly."

"She's here at the carnival, you know. Over at the white elephant sale."

"I was there when she opened up shop."

"And?"

"And she tried to sell me an old suitcase, said it might come in handy if I wanted to leave town."

"Ouch."

He shrugged. "I don't blame her. She's made a life for herself, and she doesn't need me around. It's just that . . . I just can't seem to leave town until I get a chance to explain. And once you caught me following you, I've been kind of at loose ends."

Like the ghost at the feast, I thought to myself.

"Laurie Anne, can I ask you a question?" Pudd'nhead said.

"Sure."

"Does Walters love her?"

"Yes, he does," I said without hesitation.

"And she loves him?" He shook his head. "No, don't bother to answer. Maggie would never marry a man she didn't love."

A voice came over the loudspeaker to announce that the costume contest was going to start in a moment. "Shoot, I better get over there. Richard is in the contest."

"You go on. I sure appreciate you talking to me."

"And I appreciate the cupcake."

Pudd'nhead was smiling when I pushed Alice out of the cafeteria, but he was still alone.

Tavis and the other carnival organizers had wisely divided the costume contest into divisions. First came the little kids, all of whom got some sort of award, whether they were wearing a ragged bed sheet, an expensive Cinderella dress from the Disney Store, or a robot costume clearly built by the proud papa standing in the wings. Once those awards were given out, the kids could return to the rides and games or, in the case of the real young ones, go home to bed.

Next were the older kids, and there were still lots of ribbons given out, but with a distinction between home-made and store-bought costumes. The clear preference was for costumes the kids made themselves.

Finally, the adults got their turn, and it was a treat to see grownups strutting across the stage. The triplets brought the house down with three famous witches: the evil queen from *Snow White,* Maleficent from *Sleeping Beauty,* and the Wicked Witch of the West from *The Wizard of Oz.* Uncle Roger and Aunt Ruby Lee were bedecked in sequined appliqués as Porter Waggoner and Dolly Parton, though I thought I recognized the song Roger was strumming as a Hawaiian tune from Brother Iz.

Finally, Richard came out in all his glory, with a spotlight enhancing the effect of the costume and his lordly demeanor. There were plenty of Burnettes in the auditorium to provide encouragement, but we weren't the only ones clapping, not by a long shot. He was a clear choice for first place, but we didn't find out until much later that he'd won, because my cell phone went off just as he was coming off the stage.

I'd set it on "vibrate," to make sure I wouldn't miss it, and had to put a hand over one ear to hear the voice on the phone.

"Hello?"

"Laurie Anne?"

"Big Bill? What's wrong?"

"Somebody's after me, Laurie Anne. Somebody's in the house."

"Have you called Junior?" I demanded.

There was no answer—the phone had gone dead.

Chapter
Twenty-four

I immediately dialed the Byerly police department.
"Junior Norton here."

"Junior, something's wrong over the Walters—"

"I'm already on the way." Only then did I hear the siren and other background noises that told me Junior was in the car. "I'll call when I know something."

"But—" The line went dead again.

I looked up. Richard was nearly to my seat, having been delayed by people congratulating him. When he saw my face, he ignored the high fives being offered to get to me faster.

"What's wrong?" he asked.

"Big Bill called. He said somebody's after him. We've got to get Aunt Maggie and get over there." Then I looked down at Alice, who'd finally woken up and was playing with her feet, oblivious to us.

"I've got Alice," Richard said. "Go!"

I stayed just long enough to kiss him before running down the aisle, dodging witches and genies. A small part of my brain took in the fact that Burt was on stage, meaning he wasn't the one trying to kill Big Bill, and as I passed through the crowd, I saw Dorcas, too.

I don't know how I made it to the school library without falling flat on my face or bowling over little children, but I did it. Aunt Maggie was making change for a gypsy when I got there.

"Aunt Maggie, Big Bill's in trouble," I said.

She asked no questions, just dropped the change she was counting out and went with me, Bobbin following along. Augustus looked curious but stepped in to take her place at the cash drawer.

"What's happening?" Aunt Maggie asked as we wove our way through the Halloween revelers.

"I don't know. He just said that somebody was after him. Then the phone hung up. I called Junior, but she was already on the way."

"At least he had enough sense to call her first."

By then we were at the parking lot.

"My car's closer," Aunt Maggie said, and tossed me the keys.

It was a good thing, because in the state I was in, I don't know that I would even have remembered what Richard's and my rental car looked like.

We threw ourselves into the front seat and shot out of the parking lot. I thanked God that it wasn't actually Halloween night, so I didn't have to worry about trick-or-treaters as I drove through Byerly's streets like a Boston cab driver who'd been offered a wicked big tip. I barely slowed down at stop signs and paused only briefly at the red light I passed under. At one point, I glanced at Aunt Maggie. Her face was a study in determination, and I knew that if Big Bill was dead, it was going to take Junior and me both to keep her away from his killer.

I was vaguely aware of sirens blaring through the

night, but it wasn't until I made it up the Walterses' driveway and slammed on the brakes that I realized that more cops than Byerly had were involved. I recognized squad cars from Rocky Shoals and Hickory, and it was a state trooper who came to the door of the car.

"You're going to have to move that car out of here," he said.

"Her husband is in there," I said. "She's Big Bill's wife."

"I don't care who . . ." he started to say, but amended it to, "I'm sorry, but the house isn't secure." As if to prove his point, we heard gunshots thundering. "You've got to get back!"

"Move the car, Laurie Anne," Aunt Maggie said in a deadly calm voice. "There's nothing else we can do now."

I backed the car down the driveway and parked on the street. As we watched, another state police cruiser raced up the driveway.

"Should we call anybody?" I asked.

"Not until we know something," she answered in that same awful voice.

"Aunt Maggie, are you . . . ?"

"I'm waiting, Laurie Anne. That's all I can stand to do right now." Bobbin, sitting on the floor at her feet, whined softly and licked her hands, and though Aunt Maggie scratched the dog's ears in response, she didn't look down at her. Instead, she stared at the little bit of the house we could see, as police with flashlights swarmed all over. There was nothing I could say, but I reached over and took her hand.

We didn't hear any more gunshots, and I honestly didn't know if that was a good sign or not. After maybe ten minutes, an ambulance pulled into the driveway, and Aunt Maggie's grip on my hand tightened enough to hurt. I was about to ask her if she thought we should try to go to the house, when my cell phone rang, making both of us jerk.

"Hello?"

"Laurie Anne, where are you?" It was Junior.

"We're at the house, at the end of the driveway. They wouldn't let us come any farther."

"Sorry about that. Nobody told me you were here. I'll come meet you at the front door."

"Is Big Bill . . . ?"

"Just come on up and I'll tell you what I can."

I hung up and stuffed the phone into my pocket. "Junior wants us to meet her."

"Stay," Aunt Maggie ordered Bobbin, and the two of us got out of the car and walked toward the house.

Even though the cops we saw were all still moving around, they didn't have the same edge, and I knew that whatever had happened was over. Junior was on the front porch, but before we could get to her, she stepped aside for the ambulance attendants to carry a stretcher past her. Even as far away as I was, I could see the blood on the figure on the stretcher, and I stopped, not wanting to see any more.

"That's not Bill," Aunt Maggie said calmly, and kept going, so I followed her. As we got closer, I saw she was right. There was an oxygen mask over the man's face, but I could still see enough to recognize him.

"It's Crazy Sandie," I said, then regretted calling him that. "Sandie Herron." His eyes were closed, and the green camouflage T-shirt he was wearing was in tatters from where it had been cut off for the attendants to work on him. In addition to the mask, he had an IV in one arm and a blood-pressure cuff on the other, and the bandages pressed onto his chest were saturated with blood. Just as they passed us, I noticed the tattoo on one arm. It was mostly covered by the cuff, but I saw part of the first letter and the surrounding heart, enough to realize what it was. Sandie had *Mother* needled into his skin.

"Y'all can come in now, but you're going to have to watch where you step," Junior said. There was blood on her crisp uniform and black boots, but I was pretty sure it wasn't hers.

We followed her inside, and my stomach clenched when I saw another body on the floor just in front of the staircase. This one was covered by a sheet, with more blood seeping through the cloth. It's not that blood smells bad, exactly, but because some part of my brain knew there should never be that much spilled, I didn't even want to breathe.

Aunt Maggie was staring at the body, looking as pale as the unstained parts of the sheet.

"Aunt Maggie?" I said, gently touching her back.

She looked at me, tears running down her face. "This wasn't supposed to happen. Bill said the house was safe. I wouldn't have gone to the carnival if I hadn't thought he'd be safe." She turned back to the body. "It's not Bill, is it, Junior?"

"No, ma'am, it's not," Junior told her. "It's Irene Duffield. I'm guessing Herron shot her to get to Big Bill."

My first reaction was relief, then guilt at feeling even momentarily glad that it was Miz Duffield. I hadn't much liked the woman, but she'd done nothing to deserve this.

"Where's Bill?" Aunt Maggie demanded.

"I don't know," Junior said. "We haven't found him yet. He's not in his bedroom, or the office. Are you sure he was here at the house?"

"Of course I'm sure. I left him in his bed." She started for the stairs.

"Miz Burnette—Miz Walters—whoever you are, you might better let me go first."

Aunt Maggie ignored her, and I knew that short of tackling her, there was no way Junior could stop her. Junior sighed and followed, and I went along behind them.

Aunt Maggie was calling out the whole way. "Bill? Bill? BILL! Where are you?"

There was no answer, and Aunt Maggie burst into Big Bill's bedroom. The place was a mess—the mattress had been pulled from the bed frame, and the sheets left tangled on the floor. The pulse oximeter Big Bill had been so proud of was lying in pieces on the floor.

"Herron must have come in here looking for Big Bill," Junior said, "but he didn't find him."

"Where can he be?" Aunt Maggie said, as much to herself as to us. "Bill!"

She pushed past Junior and me to get to the hall, then threw open the door to Big Bill's office. There was more chaos there: drawers dumped out, the desk chair turned over, slices in the leather upholstery with stuffing spilling out onto the floor. Herron must have gone crazy looking for Big Bill, and I could only imagine what he would have done to the man himself. But had he found him? Could he have hid the body? If not, where was Big Bill?

Aunt Maggie went back into the hallway, looking around wildly. "Bill! It's Maggie! Where are you?"

Finally, there was an answer, though the voice calling for Aunt Maggie was so muted, I'd have thought I was hearing things if it hadn't been plain from their reactions that Aunt Maggie and Junior had heard it, too.

"Bill?" Aunt Maggie said, trying to figure out where the voice was coming from.

"In the office," Junior said, and the three of us went back in.

At first I didn't see anything different. Then I realized a piece of the wall was jutting out behind Big Bill's desk. The chunk of paneling moved further forward, hitting on the overturned desk chair. A secret panel? I realized that it was the bolt-hole that people had been talking about for all those years.

"I'm in here," Big Bill's voice said.

Aunt Maggie was there in a second, shoving the heavy chair out of the way as if it were made of cardboard. The panel came out farther, and Big Bill squirmed out from a gap about the size of a closet. Aunt Maggie grabbed hold of him and hugged him so hard, I was afraid she'd crack his ribs.

"I'm all right, Maggie," he said softly. "He didn't find me. I'm all right."

Aunt Maggie pulled back and looked at him, almost as if she didn't believe him. "I thought you were—"

"I'm all right," he said again. Then he asked Junior, "Did you get him? It was Herron, wasn't it?"

She nodded.

"Is he dead?"

"No, but he might be by this time tomorrow. Live or die, he won't be coming after you again."

"Good work, Junior."

"It was good work, but it wasn't mine," she said. "Belva got him." I found out later that Junior, Belva, and some of the reinforcements had been making their way through the house when Sandie panicked and ran for the kitchen door. A Rocky Shoals cop had been between him and that door, but Sandie didn't stop until Belva fired on him, saving the other cop and bringing Herron down. Junior gave Big Bill a pointed look. "We might want to put an end to that probation period about now."

"I guess we should," Big Bill said.

"What happened?" Aunt Maggie said. "Why didn't you come when I called?"

"I didn't know it was you at first," he said, which was reasonable enough. "I was in bed when I heard shooting from downstairs. I grabbed the phone to call Junior and Laurie Anne, but then the line went dead. I could tell from the shots that whoever it was had more firepower than I did, so I ducked into my hidey hole here. I figured out it was Herron when he came in and started yelling and throwing things." He looked around the room. "Looks like I'm going to need some new furniture."

"Furniture? Is that all you can think of?" Aunt Maggie said.

"I know you're upset, Maggie," Big Bill said, patting her arm, "but everything is all right. I'm not hurt."

"Irene Duffield is dead," Aunt Maggie said flatly.

"What?"

"I guess she didn't have herself a hiding place like you did."

"I didn't know," Big Bill stammered.

"You didn't ask, either!" she snapped.

"He's still in shock, Aunt Maggie," I said. "So are you. Neither of y'all are thinking straight right now."

"I don't know what to think," Aunt Maggie said, looking at Big Bill as if she'd never really seen him before.

"Why would Herron kill Irene?" Big Bill asked. "She never did anything to him."

Junior said, "It appears that he shot Miz Duffield as soon as he came in the door. There's nothing you could have done to save her. If you hadn't hidden the way you did, you'd be dead, too."

Big Bill looked at Aunt Maggie beseechingly, and I think she relented, at least a little. But when she spoke, it was to say, "I want to go home now."

"But Maggie . . ." Big Bill said.

"It's over, Bill. Nobody's trying to kill you anymore, and it's time for me to go home. Give me the car keys, Laurie Anne."

"Y'all are breaking up?" I said as I automatically obeyed. Even though they'd told us they only got married to keep Big Bill safe, I hadn't expected them to divorce afterward. Aunt Maggie's next words explained that.

"We're not married, Laurie Anne—never have been. It was just a trick."

"You're not married," I said stupidly.

"That's right; we lied. Bill wanted to go through with the ceremony, but I wouldn't do it, so we just told everybody we were married. We're not, and I want to go back to my house now. I'll get my things later."

Big Bill tried to talk her out of it, but she just kept saying that she didn't want to spend another night in his house. Eventually, he stopped arguing, and she left the room. Not knowing what else to do, I followed her.

Burt and Dorcas were downstairs by then, but Aunt Maggie didn't stop long enough to answer any of their questions. She just said, "Bill's upstairs," and walked out the door. All she said to me was, "I'll see y'all at the house." Then she went to her car, ignoring everybody and everything around her, and drove away.

Richard was waiting for me in the driveway, cradling Alice in his arms, and I went to put my arms around them.

"Are you all right?" Richard asked.

"It was bad, Richard." I told him about Miz Duffield's death, and how Belva had shot Sandie Herron, and Big Bill's hiding place, and finally, how Aunt Maggie and Big Bill had deceived everybody. As I spoke, Richard handed Alice to me, and by the time I got to the end, my face was buried in her shoulder, where I could inhale that baby smell. Funny, I'd always thought that a mother's job was to comfort her children, and here Alice was already comforting me when she was still a baby.

Once I'd gotten it all out, Richard said, "We should go."

I nodded, and though I was tempted to keep Alice in my arms so I could cuddle her, I put her in her car seat and let Richard drive us back to Aunt Maggie's.

"It's not your fault," Richard said when we were in the car. "None of it."

"I know it's not."

"It's *not* your fault," he said again.

I nodded, but that wasn't how I felt, and Richard knew it. Here I'd insisted on taking over from Aunt Maggie and Big Bill, sure that I could find the one who was trying to kill him, and I'd never even come close. Heck, our talking to Sandie could well have been the thing that tipped him over the edge, from stealth to all-out assault. Not only had I been unable to protect Big Bill, but I'd gotten Miz Duffield caught in the crossfire. I realized then that I was still wearing my Halloween costume, and I pulled the deerstalker cap from my head. The world's greatest detective? Only knowing that it would hurt Richard's feelings kept me from tossing the silly thing right out the window.

Aunt Maggie's car was in the carport at the house, but when we went inside, we found that she'd shut herself up in her bedroom. Her light was already out, but I didn't have any idea that she was asleep. I tapped lightly on the door. "Aunt Maggie? We're back. Can I get you anything?"

"No, thank you," she replied without opening the door. "I'll see y'all in the morning."

I looked at Richard, who shrugged. Aunt Maggie

never had been one to pour her heart out, and if she didn't want to talk, no amount of persuasion was going to convince her. So we changed out of our costumes and fed Alice, and went to bed ourselves. Surprisingly, I slept like a rock, and Alice picked the perfect occasion to sleep through the night for the first time.

The next day was just plain awful. Richard and I didn't know quite what to do with ourselves. It was Halloween for real that night, but we just weren't in the mood for it—we'd had enough real horror to last us a while. We halfheartedly discussed taking Alice trick-or-treating, but finally decided that we'd rather stay at the house and hand out candy. She fell asleep before the first trick-or-treater arrived, anyway.

As for Aunt Maggie, she got up and went to the flea market, saying it was Saturday and she had regular customers expecting her. She didn't even come home for dinner. She called instead and said she was going to an auction. I honestly wasn't sure if she was trying to act as if everything were back to normal, or if she was avoiding us. Richard and I weren't scheduled to fly back to Boston for a few more days, but we checked earlier flights, just in case Aunt Maggie wanted us to leave.

When I went to bed that night, I still felt as if I'd completely failed Big Bill and Aunt Maggie, but my subconscious must have put in some serious overtime while I slept. Because when I woke up the next morning, I realized that I was absolutely sure about something. Sandie Herron had not been the one trying to kill Big Bill.

Chapter
Twenty-five

I announced that fact to Richard over breakfast, knowing that he was going to find it a lot harder to swallow than his Cheerios. We were alone with Alice, having woken to find that Aunt Maggie had gone to the flea market again.

He said, "You think somebody else killed Miz Duffield, planted Herron at the Walters place to make folks think Belva shot him, and then got out of there without being seen?"

"No, Sandie killed Miz Duffield, and Belva shot him; I can accept all that. What I can't accept is that a man like Sandie Herron could run around Byerly setting traps. You met him, Richard—do you think he has the temperament for playing a waiting game?"

"Which temperament do you mean? The polite mama's boy, or the avenging son? And who knows how many other personae?"

"That's what I mean—how could somebody as mixed up as he is come up with those clever attempts on Big Bill's life?"

"Shooting at him? Trying to hit him with a truck?"

"Okay, the methods were simple, but the timing was perfect. For the shooting, whoever it was picked a time when Big Bill was alone, and when he didn't get him with that one shot, he held off from trying again. He could have kept shooting until he got him, but he wanted to be sure it looked like an accident, not murder. Same thing with trying to run him over. He didn't just barrel down a busy street. He waited until it was late at night in a relatively deserted spot, and again, when he missed, he resisted the temptation to try again. The trap at the apartment complex must have been set ahead of time, and it could have been an accident, too. What Sandie did sure as heck didn't look like an accident."

"What about the poisoning?" Richard asked. "That couldn't be explained as an accident, either."

"No, but it was done in such a way that there were an impossible number of suspects. The killer planned the first ones to look like accidents, so nobody would look for him, and he planned the poisoning so nobody could find him if they did look. This guy wants Big Bill dead, but just as important, he doesn't want to get caught."

"Most murderers don't want to get caught."

"I don't think Sandie cared. He wasn't exactly trying to hide his tracks, was he? I bet that if he had gotten Big Bill, he'd have gone right back to his cabin and waited for Junior to come get him."

"Maybe," Richard said, thinking about it. "You know, I think you've got a point. It is hard to reconcile Sandie's attack with the earlier attempts."

"Then you don't think I'm just a sore loser?"

"Never, not after the way you changed an extra day of diapers when you lost that bet about *Buffy the Vampire Slayer.*"

"Thank you, love." Then, "Wait! I changed an extra day of diapers? And you didn't tell me?"

The next step was to talk to Junior. I called her and she said she'd meet us at the police station. Aunt Ruby Lee was next on the babysitting rotation, so we left Alice happily ensconced in her lap while Uncle Roger played and sang his way through an impressive selection of Disney songs.

Junior was waiting for us at her desk, and I sat down in the chair opposite her. I'd planned exactly what I wanted to say, so I was able to go through my reasoning and conclusions without any side trips. Once I was done, I asked, "Does this make any sense to you, Junior?" Her face hadn't changed expression once while I was talking, and I didn't know if that was a good sign or not. "Or does it sound like I just won't admit losing?"

"Nobody likes losing, Laurie Anne. I'd guess that one of the hardest lessons you'll have to teach little Alice is that everybody has to give up some time." She paused. "But not this time."

"Then you think I'm right?" I said, relieved. "Have you spoken to Sandie? Did he tell you something?"

"I never got a chance to talk to Herron. He died on the way to the hospital."

"Oh." I'd liked Sandie, even if he had made me nervous, but there was no doubt that he'd killed Miz Duffield and would have killed Big Bill if he'd gotten the chance. Not to mention the injury he'd have done to others if Belva hadn't stopped him. I'd never been in favor of the death penalty, but this time, maybe it was the best thing that could have happened. Sandie was finally back with his mother. "But you do think I'm right?"

"I think you might be, but not only because of what you just told me, as convincing as it was. Something else happened."

"What's that?" Richard asked.

"It was when I went out to Herron's cabin the night before last."

"After the shootings?" I said.

She nodded. "I knew I wasn't going to sleep anyway. I'm always wired after dealing with something like that. Since I was going to have to check out Herron's cabin anyway once things were settled at the Walters mansion, I decided I might as well get it over with. I was looking for something that would link Herron to the other attempts on Big Bill's life, hoping I could tie up those loose ends."

"Did you?" Richard wanted to know.

"Nope. I didn't really expect anything, given the nature of those other incidents, but it was worth a shot. I searched through everything he had, which wasn't much. A couple of changes of clothing. About a month's worth of canned goods if you're not too picky about what you eat. His computer stuff. And all those pictures of his mama. Tell me that wasn't creepy."

"We should have warned you about those," I said.

"Laurie Anne, nothing could have prepared me for that. Anyway, I didn't find anything like what I was looking for. I was planning to lock up the place and stick on some crime-scene tape when I heard something. I can't be sure, but I think somebody was in the woods outside the cabin. When I opened the door . . ."

I started to say something, but before I could, she assured me, "Don't worry; I know how to keep from being a target. I didn't see anybody, but I called out, telling whoever it was to come out where I could get a look at him. I didn't hear anything else for a while, and had just about convinced myself it was just my nerves, when I heard sounds like somebody was moving away at a fast clip. I yelled again, but he or she kept on going."

"Who do you think it was?" Richard asked.

"And what was he after?" I added.

"Those are the ten-million-dollar questions. As fast as

news travels around Byerly, somebody could have heard that Herron was dead, and thought he'd come scavenge whatever he could out of the cabin before anybody claimed it. Whenever you've got somebody living on their own like that, there's always tales about mattresses stuffed with money."

"Or?" I prompted.

"Or maybe there was something out there I'd missed, something that meant somebody else was involved. So I rolled up my sleeves and I went through everything in that cabin again—I tapped floorboards and looked in the septic tank and even made sure every one of those cans of soup was a real can of soup. Nothing. Except that computer."

"It looked like an expensive setup," Richard pointed out. "Maybe the person in the woods was planning to steal it."

"It's possible," Junior said. "Lord knows the computer was the only thing there worth stealing. So I loaded up every piece of it into my squad car and brought it over here to lock in a cell."

I asked, "Have you looked at the hard drive?"

"I was too busy yesterday, what with the mess at the Walters place to clean up and Halloween besides, but I tried to this morning. Unfortunately, I don't have the password to access it. I don't suppose you know anybody who'd be able to get around that, do you?"

I grinned. "Oh, I might be able to round somebody up. Though it would help if I had my laptop."

Richard was already standing up. "On my way."

He must have used some Boston driving tricks, because he was gone just long enough for Junior and me to get some iced tea from the place next door. Then Junior let me into the cell with the computer, and I went to work.

I'd like to say it was genius on my part that got me past Sandie's password protection, or that I used secret hacker software to defeat it. In fact, all I needed was what I knew about Sandie's obsession with his mother. He'd avoided the most obvious choices: the combinations of the name *Eva Marie Volin Herron*, her birth date, and the date of her death. But he'd gone with another obvious one: *NILOVEIRAMAVE*, which was *Eva Marie Volin* backwards.

I hunted through his directories, but there was little there, mostly just applications Sandie had needed to create his web site and a family-tree program that he'd used to record his mother's side of the family for a dozen generations. Then I looked at the word-processing files and found pages of notes about his mother, and saddest of all, some very clumsy attempts at poetry about her.

I also found files of the letters he'd sent to Big Bill, along with letters to several lawyers asking what could be done about his mother's property. Since there was no more than one letter to any lawyer, I figured they'd all told him he had no legal leg to stand on.

Since Junior hadn't mentioned finding any financial records or even cash money, I wasn't surprised to find home finance software that showed where Sandie's money was. If his records were accurate, he'd had enough to fill several mattresses, and I just couldn't fathom why he'd chosen to live in such primitive conditions. Richard had called him a hermit—had he been enforcing his own brand of penance?

I'd saved Sandie's e-mail files for last, figuring that he must have had some sort of life online, and sure enough, he had hundreds of saved messages. I started with the most recent and skimmed half a dozen notes about shared taste in music and the best way to track ancestors, when I found the message that made me stop.

"Junior! Richard! You better come see this."

They were there in an instant, and Junior peered over one shoulder while Richard read over the other. The message was short and brutal.

HOW CAN YOU LET BIG BILL WALTERS GET AWAY WITH WHAT HE DID TO YOUR MAMA? DON'T YOU KNOW HE RAPED HER? AND NOT JUST ONCE. THAT'S WHY SHE SOLD HIM YOUR FAMILY'S LAND, TO MAKE THE SON OF A BITCH LEAVE HER ALONE.

HE'LL BE ALONE AT HIS HOUSE TONIGHT IF YOU'RE MAN ENOUGH TO DO WHAT NEEDS TO BE DONE BEFORE HE GOES AFTER SOMEBODY ELSE'S MAMA.

"Jesus!" I said, staring at it.

"This can't be true," Richard said.

"It doesn't matter, not as long as Sandie believed it. This was what set him off." I couldn't help but be self-ishly relieved that it hadn't been Richard's and my visit that caused him to lose control. "Somebody sent him this note knowing what would happen. That bastard aimed Sandie at Big Bill as if he were aiming a shotgun. He didn't care who else got hurt." I knew that whoever it was, wasn't really a killer—not yet anyway, because his attempts on Big Bill had failed—but as far as I was concerned, he was as much responsible for Irene Duffield's death as Sandie Herron was.

"When did this e-mail get to Herron?" Junior asked.

"The day before yesterday, one o'clock in the afternoon."

"Who sent it?"

I shook my head. "I don't know. The e-mail address is a Heatmail account."

"Which means what?"

"Heatmail provides free e-mail accounts. Anybody can open an account with them, and they don't need to verify names or anything like that, because they aren't charging. You can see that whoever it was used the default address rather than customizing it to their name, so we have nothing to go by. And what do you want to bet that it's a new account?"

"Can you trace where it was sent from?"

I looked at the lines of coded information, most of which was gibberish to me. "I don't know, Junior. This kind of thing can be tricky."

"Laurie Anne," Junior said, "you said you don't like losing. Well, I can deal with losing—every cop has to learn how to do that. Being fooled is different. Somebody is trying to fool us into thinking Herron was behind all the attacks on Big Bill, and I don't like being fooled."

I wasn't real happy with it myself. I looked at the computer again. "If somebody will get me another glass of iced tea, I'll see what I can do."

Between several phone calls to folks I know in Boston who are real hackers, I eventually managed to track down the location from which that awful e-mail was sent. Unfortunately, it wasn't a private line. "Our guy did his dirty work from Gateway Country in Hickory," I announced.

"The computer store?" Junior asked.

I nodded. "Have you ever been in there? They've got a bunch of systems set up for customers to try out, and most of those systems have Internet access. I'm guessing that our guy went in and played around as if he was interested in buying a system. Instead, he sent Sandie that message."

Junior immediately got on the phone with Tim Meyers, a friend of hers on the Hickory police force. Then we had to twiddle our thumbs for a good hour while Meyers drove to Gateway Country to see what he could find out. In the meantime, I explored more of Sandie's e-mail files but didn't find anything else significant.

Next I checked out where he'd been on the web. "Look at this," I said to Junior and Richard. "He found a site that tells you how to disable burglar alarms and telephones."

"That's how he knew where to cut the phone and alarm lines at the Walters mansion," Junior said. "I'd been assuming that he learned it in his wild past—it never occurred to me that you could find that kind of stuff on the web."

"You can find just about anything you can imagine on the Web," I said. "Of course, lots of it isn't true, but I guess the information on these sites was accurate enough."

Finally, Meyers called back, but when Junior got off the phone, she announced, "It's a dead end. A sale started the day before yesterday, and the place was packed, with folks taking turns on those computers all day long. Some of them bought stuff, but most didn't, and I think it's a good bet that our guy didn't leave his name written down anywhere."

"Do we know it's a man?" I asked hopefully.

Junior snorted. "We don't know squat! The clerk in that part of the store was seriously frazzled from partying the night before, and he says he wouldn't be able to reliably identify any of the customers, so a photo lineup would be a waste of time."

"Rats, rats, rats!" I said, wanting to throw the kind of tantrum I never wanted Alice to emulate. "We've got nothing!"

"Not true," Richard said. "We've still got leads. We never investigated all of Big Bill's letters."

"Richard, it would take from now until Doomsday to investigate all those people, and I don't think it was any of them, anyway. Our guy is too good at hiding his tracks to have put anything in writing."

"Okay, forget the letters. We've still got our other suspects."

"Can you see Dorcas or Burt knowing enough to set up a Heatmail account?"

"No offense, Laura, but computers haven't been just for programmers for a long time," he said. "Either Dorcas or Burt could have learned how, and Mike Cooper probably already knew."

"I suppose." I just couldn't see either of them as our killer, and I didn't want to. Maybe it was because I was a new mother, but the idea of Burt killing his own father made me sick to my stomach, and casting Dorcas or Mike in the role wasn't much better. "What about you, Junior? Have you come up with something better?"

She shook her head and in a bitter voice said, "Not a damned thing. I've considered those three, too, but can't find anything to point toward or against any of them. No alibis for the time frames, and all three of them had access to what was needed for the attempts."

"What about the chemical tests and fingerprints and all that?" I said.

"I can't make bricks without straw, Laurie Anne, and I don't have the first piece of a straw." She ticked off the possibilities on her fingers. "We couldn't find the bullet from the shooting, and ballistics would only help if the shooter still has that gun. Then there's the pickup truck that almost hit Big Bill, assuming it was really a pickup he saw. Even he had to admit he could have been mistaken, given the circumstances. Nobody saw the license plate, and since it didn't hit Big Bill, there wouldn't be any useful trace evidence on it if we did find it. There's been plenty of time to wash it anyway. I thought the electrocution attempt was my best bet, but the site wasn't the least bit secure, and it wouldn't take an electrical engineer to know that an open wire in a puddle of water could kill somebody, especially a man as old as Big Bill. Belva and I squeezed the possible witnesses around the apartments as much as we dared, but nobody saw anything, and waving a mug shot under their noses isn't going to change that. Then there was that party!" She threw up her hands. "Charles Manson could have walked in there with Saddam Hussein, and nobody would have noticed either of them, unless it was for wearing open-toed shoes after Labor Day."

"Hey!" Richard said sharply. "If you two don't start showing some optimism, I'm going to start quoting Shakespeare at you, and I won't stop until you cheer up."

"I don't think he's bluffing, Junior," I said with mock alarm. "He's just overeducated enough to do it!"

"Damned straight," Richard said. "So are you two going to pull yourselves together, or do I start quoting?"

"All right," Junior said. "I know when I'm licked. And I have to admit that we're better off than we could have been. After all, that so-and-so came mighty darned close to getting to Herron's computer before we did. If he had, we'd never have known anybody else was involved."

"What about my deductions?" I asked.

"Those helped, too," Junior agreed, "but it's good to have something other than that to work with. Especially since I've got to go to Big Bill and tell him he's still a target."

"In fact, it's even worse," I said. "The killer must know by now that Big Bill was never married to Aunt Maggie, and that he's not sick. Plus he probably knows that you've got that computer, and that there's a good chance you found the e-mail to Sandie."

Richard said, "Does that mean that he'll go after Big Bill right away, or that he'll wait until we're no longer watching for him?"

"Without knowing why he wants Big Bill dead, it's hard to say," Junior said, "but if he's as smart as I think he is, he'll lay low for as long as it takes."

I nodded dispiritedly. The killer was still out there. We knew it, and he knew that we knew it. Unfortunately, he also knew that we couldn't keep him away from Big Bill forever.

I didn't like to lose, and Junior didn't like to be fooled—neither of us was happy that day.

Chapter
Twenty-six

That evening was Miz Duffield's visitation. She hadn't had any close family, so Dorcas had taken charge of the arrangements. I waffled about going but finally decided I owed it to Miz Duffield. Though I knew intellectually that her death wasn't my fault, I couldn't help feeling that if I'd been a little smarter, she'd still be alive. The least I could do was pay my respects properly.

Since the triplets had barely known Miz Duffield, they weren't going to the visitation, and came to Aunt Maggie's house to babysit instead. They were trying to see if Alice could tell the three of them apart when Aunt Maggie, Richard, and I left.

I asked Richard to drive so I could sit with Aunt Maggie in the backseat. It was the first chance I'd had to speak to her since the night of the Halloween Carnival. I was pretty sure she'd been avoiding me, and I thought I knew why.

She confirmed it with what she said first. "I suppose you're right put out with me."

"You mean because you lied to Richard and me, even

when we were knocking ourselves out trying to help you and Big Bill?"

She nodded.

"No, I'm not put out. What I am is royally pissed."

She flinched but didn't say a word about my language, which showed how guilty she felt. I know she doesn't like profanity, and try not to use it around her, but I thought it was justified this time.

"I'm as sorry as I can be, Laurie Anne. You know I'm not the kind of person who likes to lie. I wanted to tell y'all the truth, but Bill said it would be safer if we told everybody the same thing. Not that I'm blaming him—I went along with it, so it was just as much my doing as his."

"Yes, it was," I said, "but that's not what I'm pissed about. I'm not saying that I like being lied to, but I can see why y'all played it the way you did. Honestly, I don't think Richard's and my knowing would have made a bit of difference in the way we went about investigating. So I won't hold a grudge unless you make a habit of telling tales."

"That'll never happen. I'm so embarrassed about this one that I can hardly stand it," she said. "But if that's not the problem, then why are you mad?"

"I'm mad because you shut us out. What happened the other night was so awful, and I know it upset you. Given the circumstances, I can see why you wouldn't go to Big Bill, but I can't see why you didn't come to me. Or to one of the aunts or somebody else in the family. You're a strong woman, Aunt Maggie; they don't come any stronger than you. But even a strong woman needs somebody to talk to in bad times, somebody other than your dog."

"I didn't think anybody would want to talk to me," she said. "Not after I lied to y'all."

"Then you were wrong. We love you, all of us from

Uncle Buddy on down to Alice, and there's not a thing in this world we wouldn't do for you." I made a face like an irate schoolteacher. "You better not forget that again, young lady!"

Aunt Maggie half laughed, half sniffed. "Can I have a hug?"

"Damn straight you can," I said, risking more profanity. It wasn't a long hug, because Aunt Maggie just isn't much of a hugger, but it was a good one, for both of us.

Afterward, she rubbed her eyes as if not wanting to admit that they'd held tears. "At least all this mess is over with now."

I hated to say it, but I had to. "That's the thing. We don't think it is." I told her what we'd found on Sandie's computer, and our idea that there was another killer waiting to get to Big Bill. She was so still and silent afterward that I cursed myself for not breaking it to her more gently.

"Are you all right?" I finally said.

"I'm fine," she said automatically. Then she shook her head. "No, I'm not. I lied to the whole town, including my family, but the only thing I accomplished was to get Irene Duffield killed."

"Aunt Maggie, you can't possibly believe that it's your fault." Not only was I telling the truth, but it was a pointed reminder to myself not to feel the same way.

"Why can't I? If I'd made Bill go to Junior when this all started, Irene would still be alive."

"Nobody's ever made Big Bill Walters do a single thing he didn't want to. If you'd gone to Junior behind his back, he'd have denied everything, and he'd have been that much more in danger. You were doing your best to keep the man you love safe, Aunt Maggie."

She gave me an odd look. "I was trying to keep him safe, but I never said that I love him."

"Oh. Do you?" I winced. "I'm sorry, that's none of my business."

"No, it's not," she agreed, "but I'd tell you if I knew." She sighed. "I was starting to think that I did until Pudd'nhead showed up. Now I'm not sure anymore. I'm too old for this kind of confusion, Laurie Anne."

"It's so hard being irresistible to men," I said in mock sympathy.

She blinked, then snorted, sounding a whole lot more like the Aunt Maggie I was used to.

The parking lot at the funeral home was nearly full already, even though we were early. It made me wonder what kind of arrangements had been made for Sandie Herron. I had mixed feelings about him. He'd been manipulated cruelly, but the fact was that he'd shot and killed an innocent woman because he was willing to believe an anonymous e-mail. I decided I wouldn't want to attend a visitation for him.

"I hear Dorcas booked the Magnolia Room," Aunt Maggie said.

"Really?" I said. The Magnolia Room was the best the funeral home had to offer, and Giles Funeral Home was the best in Byerly. Dorcas really had thought a lot of Miz Duffield.

"Do I look all right?" Aunt Maggie asked. She'd taken time to dress for the occasion and was wearing the same pantsuit she'd worn for her ersatz wedding reception. "This is the only outfit Irene ever saw me in that she didn't turn her nose up at."

"I'm sure she'd appreciate the thought," I told her.

When we got inside, we saw that a receiving line was set up with Big Bill, Dorcas, and Burt. Aunt Maggie took one look and hurried past, not even glancing toward Big Bill. He saw her anyway and followed her with his eyes until Dorcas nudged him to shake the hand being offered to him.

"Have they spoken?" Richard asked me.

"Since their 'divorce'?" I said. "I don't think so."

"Do you think they'll get back together?"

"With Aunt Maggie, there's no telling. I've never known her to be so subdued before. She's never much cared what people thought of her before, but she's just mortified about having deceived everybody."

"I know—I eavesdropped on your conversation in the car. You said all the right things, by the way."

"Thank you."

"Do you think she might also be embarrassed by how she treated Big Bill the other night?"

"It wasn't her fault," I said. "She'd had a big shock."

"So had he."

"I know. I don't think either of them should hold what happened against each other, but I don't know if they realize that."

"Young love," Richard said with a theatrical sigh.

"Young?"

"The love can be young, even if the lovers aren't."

"Shakespeare?"

"Just me."

I saw somebody come into the room then. "What does the Bard say about lost loves?"

" 'Love that comes too late, like a remorseful pardon slowly carried, to the great sender turns a sour offense, crying, "That's good that's gone." ' *All's Well That Ends Well*, Act V, Scene 3. Why do you ask?"

"Because Pudd'nhead Wilson just walked in." He joined the receiving line, and I'm afraid I wasn't terribly polite when I dragged Richard over to get directly behind him before anybody else could. Fortunately, Pudd'nhead didn't see us.

Big Bill finished shaking the hand of a man I didn't recognize, then turned to Pudd'nhead.

"Mr. Wilson," he said as they shook hands. "It's been a long time."

"Yes, sir, it has been a few seasons," Pudd'nhead replied.

"I'm surprised we never saw your name in the sports pages. Didn't you ever make it into the major league?"

Pudd'nhead reddened, but his voice was still polite. "I'm afraid not. Fact is, I wasn't that good a ball player, but then again, even a minor league player looks good next to the yahoos you get in a town like this."

The two men bared their teeth at each other, then Big Bill said, "It was kind of you to come tonight."

"Just paying my respects." He paused, then added, "I'm sorry for your loss." He glanced over at where Aunt Maggie was talking to Aunt Nora, then back to Big Bill, making it plain what loss he was really talking about. He moved on to Dorcas and Burt, who shook his hand but clearly didn't know who he was. Then he went over to Aunt Maggie.

Big Bill kept watching Pudd'nhead until I cleared my throat to let him know Richard and I were standing there.

"Hey, Laurie Anne, Richard. I'm glad y'all came. I just hope y'all aren't too put out at me. I want y'all to know that our deception didn't come easy, especially not for Maggie."

"We know," I said.

"If I'd gotten my way, it would have been the truth, but . . ." He looked at Pudd'nhead, who had his hand on Aunt Maggie's arm. "Not that I've given up, mind you."

"Nobody's ever accused you of being a quitter, Big Bill," I said.

"And I don't ever intend to give anyone an excuse

to," he said. "Which is why I haven't quit looking for whoever it is who's trying to kill me."

"Then Junior talked to you?" I asked, relieved. I'd known that he had to be told, but I hadn't wanted to bring up the subject. "We won't give up, either."

"Even if I'm not your uncle?" he said with a crooked grin.

"Even then."

"Thank you." He shook his head sadly. "It's not right that Irene died that way, Laurie Anne, not when it should have been—"

"It shouldn't have been anyone," I said emphatically.

"Sometimes I wonder. I know what people are saying, that my being in this position is nothing more than chickens coming home to roost. A whole lot of chickens." I started to say something comforting, but before I could, Big Bill patted my hand and said, "I'll be fine. I've got my son and his wife, and that should be enough for anyone." I noticed that he wouldn't let his eyes so much as stray toward Aunt Maggie.

There really wasn't anything I could say to that. Besides, the line was getting longer, and Dorcas was looking pointedly at us. "We'll talk more, later," I finally said, and Richard and I moved past him.

To Dorcas, I said, "I'm very sorry about Miz Duffield. I know y'all had been together a long time."

"Thank you, Laurie Anne. I am going to miss her dreadfully." She took a deep breath. "Now, I know things aren't the way we thought they were, but that doesn't mean you can't bring your little girl over to visit before you go back to Boston. I really do like having little ones around."

"Thank you, Dorcas. We'll do that."

She leaned over to kiss my cheek and whispered, "But don't bring that dog."

Burt's greeting was more perfunctory. He was so busy watching Big Bill that he barely noticed anybody else. He looked half terrified and half overjoyed, and I decided that he was trying to come to terms with how close he'd come to losing his father.

Richard and I had already decided that we weren't going to go into the private viewing area to see Miz Duffield in her coffin. I understood why some people need to see a loved one's body to say a final good-bye, but it still wasn't something I wanted to do.

Aunt Maggie was now deep in conversation with Pudd'nhead, and though I was nosy enough to want to hear what they were saying, I gave them their privacy. Instead, I satisfied my curiosity by staying close to the receiving line while Richard mingled.

That's why I was there when Vasti got to Dorcas in the receiving line and nearly broke down. I didn't hear it all, but I did hear Vasti wail, "I was so mean to her!" before she burst into tears. I would have gone to tend to her, but Aunt Daphine was with her and led her weeping daughter away to the bathroom, where I was sure they'd make the necessary repairs to Vasti's eye makeup. It's not that Vasti wasn't sincere—I was sure that she honestly regretted not having been nicer to Miz Duffield. The thing was, Miz Duffield hadn't been very nice to Vasti, either. I hadn't liked the woman much myself, though that wasn't going to keep me from trying to find out who was really behind her death.

We ended up staying longer than I'd expected because Richard was catching up with some of the people he'd directed in the previous year's Christmas pageant and Aunt Maggie was still talking to Pudd'nhead. They'd been settled down in a quiet corner for a long while when the Walterses decided to shut down the receiving line. Big Bill pointedly stayed away from Aunt Maggie and Pudd'nhead, while Dorcas found a seat with some other society ladies. Burt started off following Big Bill, but when Big Bill impatiently shooed him off, he wandered around aimlessly until I waved him over.

"How are you holding up?" I asked.

"I'm all right," he said. "It's Dorcas and Daddy I'm worried about. Irene had been with Dorcas since before we were married, and Daddy had a mighty close call." He looked over at his father. "First the poisoning and then this, and now Junior says he might still be in danger."

I nodded, glad that Big Bill had confided in him.

Burt almost smiled. "Daddy keeps telling me to quit hovering over him, but I can't seem to help myself. I don't want anything to happen to him, Laurie Anne. He's a mean old cuss, but he's my daddy, and I love him. Maybe I haven't been the son he wanted—"

"Stop that!" I said. "You've been a wonderful son." That was assuming he wasn't trying to kill Big Bill, of course, but I really didn't think he was. "You've done everything a man can do for his father." Then I saw somebody unexpected come into the room, and when Burt started to thank me, I surprised myself by saying, "Come to think of it, no, you haven't."

"I beg your pardon," Burt said.

"You haven't given Big Bill the one thing he really wants, have you? The thing he wants more than anything else in the world is another Walters to carry on the name after you and he are gone."

The blood rushed to Burt's face. "You know I tried; Dorcas couldn't carry—"

"I'm not talking about you having a child," I said. "I'm talking about your brother's child."

The color left his face as quickly as it had come, and he glanced around to see if anybody had heard me.

That's when he saw Mike Cooper, who was shaking hands with Tavis Montgomery.

"Good Lord!" he breathed, and started to move.

But I grabbed his arm and wouldn't let him. I was suddenly angry. No, I was furious. I've never figured out where all that emotion came from, other than the fact that I'd been thinking about my own parents and grand-parents—the way I always did at funerals—and how I wished they'd been able to see Alice. And about Sandie Herron, who might not have gone nuts if he'd been able to make peace with his mother before she died. And finally about Big Bill, who'd suspected his own son of wanting to kill him and was miserable because he saw his family dwindling away to nothing. If Sandie had moved just a little faster, Big Bill would have died with-out knowing that the grandson he'd always wanted was right there in Byerly. Families always have secrets—maybe families need secrets—but I was convinced that Mike Cooper ought not to be kept a secret any longer.

Burt looked at me, shocked, as I held on to him and hoarsely whispered, "You listen to me, Burt Walters. Your father deserves to know about Mike, and Mike de-serves to know about him. If you don't tell them, I will."

"You promised!" he protested.

"I don't care what I promised. I'm doing my best to keep Big Bill alive, but if I screw up again, Big Bill is not going to die without knowing about that boy!"

"But . . ."

"Forget it, Burt. It's too late to stop it now."

Mike had left Tavis and was holding out his hand to Big Bill, saying something I couldn't hear. I don't think Big Bill heard him either, because he was pure-out star-ing at the boy. I'd never seen Small Bill alive, but I'd seen pictures, and Mike Cooper was the spitting image of his father. Mike stopped talking to stare back, and I wondered if he was seeing his father's face in Big Bill's.

Big Bill turned away from Mike to search for Burt, and the question was plain on his face. Burt stared back at his father for a long moment, then slowly nodded. Big Bill looked back at Mike, and tears started to roll down his face.

I finally let go of Burt, and he joined his father and his nephew. Something was said, and Mr. Giles, with the discretion all good funeral directors have, appeared at Big Bill's elbow to usher them away to someplace private. The nosy part of me would have loved to be a fly on the wall to hear what Burt said, but mostly I was just glad that he was saying something.

The visitation was pretty much over by then, especially when Dorcas went to find out what was going on and then didn't come back. So I went to collect Richard and head back to the house. I'd meant to collect Aunt Maggie, too, but she announced that she was going to dinner with Pudd'nhead, and made it quite plain that Richard and I weren't invited. So we went to the drive-through at Hardee's to pick up something to eat.

On the way back to the house, Richard said, "May I safely assume that you had something to do with that reunion tonight?"

"I didn't set it up, if that's what you mean, but I did make sure that Burt didn't prevent it from happening."

"Why did you get involved? Don't you think—"

"I wasn't thinking, Richard," I said, "and I realize that what I did was completely outrageous. Burt had good reasons for keeping Mike away from Big Bill, and I had no right to stick my nose in. But you know what? I'm glad I did. I really think good is going to come of it."

When he didn't answer right away, I looked over at him. "No quote from the Bard about interfering females?"

He shook his head. "Your instincts are usually sound, Laura. I'm willing to believe that it was the right time for it all to come out."

"Thank you, love," I said. I knew darned well that with the personalities involved, it could all have blown up in my face, but I meant it when I told Richard I was glad. Maybe Big Bill had lost a wife or girlfriend or whatever Aunt Maggie was to him, but darn it, he'd gotten a grandson.

Byerly's phone lines must have been burning, because in the short time it took for us to get back to the house, the triplets had already heard about Big Bill, Burt, and Mike going off together and demanded to be told what I knew.

I had to disappoint them. Yes, I'd threatened Burt with revealing the secret, but only to Big Bill. I wasn't about to spread the tale elsewhere, not even to the triplets. I managed to distract them by telling them about Aunt Maggie leaving with Pudd'nhead, and describing the long-ago romance. They seemed satisfied with that bit of gossip, accompanied by some of Alice's messy good-bye kisses.

Though it was past time for Alice to be in bed, it seemed like forever since I'd taken time to play with her, so Richard and I got onto the floor to do just that. It was only after she yawned wide enough to swallow her teddy bear that I fed her and put her to bed.

When Richard and I got back downstairs, he caught me looking at the clock on the wall.

"Are you planning to wait up for Aunt Maggie?" he asked.

"Don't be silly. I was just looking to see what time it is

so I'll have an idea of what time Alice is likely to sleep to. And wondering what's on TV."

" 'The lady doth protest too much, methinks.' *Hamlet*, Act III, Scene 2."

"Okay, I am curious. Those two going off together is just one more bit of craziness in a mighty crazy night. Besides which, I don't think I could get to sleep anyway."

"Is that so? I could help you with that." He leaned over with a kiss, reminding me that playing with Alice wasn't the only thing I'd been missing. Sharing our room with Alice had been a little inhibiting.

"What if Aunt Maggie comes in?" I asked.

"Hey, we're married, which is more than she can say."

I would have argued further, but in a very short period, I was far too busy. Richard relaxed me so thoroughly that he just about had to carry me to bed.

Chapter
Twenty-seven

I didn't hear Aunt Maggie come in that night, but when I got up for Alice's two o'clock feeding, I saw that she was in bed. Not that it was really any of my business, but when did I ever let that stop me?

All of us were up early the next day, though only Alice looked as if she was happy about it. Miz Duffield's funeral was set for that morning, and after yet another drop-off for Alice, we drove to the church together.

It was an elegant service, with a dignified eulogy from Dorcas, and I felt sure Miz Duffield would have approved. Nothing was said about how she died, other than veiled references to her having been taken too soon. To me, the most notable thing was the fact that Mike Cooper was in the front pew, sitting between Big Bill and Burt. Dorcas sat on the other side of Burt, and a couple of times I caught her looking at her husband with an expression of happiness she couldn't hide, even during a funeral.

After the church service was over, we all drove to Woodgreen Acres for the burial. The Walterses had given Miz Duffield a place in their own family plot, and

though I wondered if the deciding factor had been
Dorcas's affection or Big Bill's guilt, I was still touched
on Miz Duffield's behalf. I couldn't imagine that there
was anyplace else she'd rather be buried.

After the preacher said a few words and the Walterses
had tossed handfuls of dirt onto the coffin, Dorcas announced that they were going to be receiving guests at
their home immediately after the funeral. Aunt Maggie
didn't say anything, but I could tell from the look in her
eye that she wasn't ready to go back to the mansion, so
Richard and I dropped her off at her house before
going ourselves. I knew I'd paid enough respects to Miz
Duffield to satisfy propriety, but I had a hunch something interesting was going to happen at the reception.

If Miz Duffield wasn't already in heaven, seeing the
spread Dorcas put out in her honor would have sent
here there. There were no pedestrian dishes of funeral
food like deviled eggs and Jell-O molds. Instead, there
were tasteful hors d'oeuvres, each one a miniature work
of art; shrimp that must have cost a fortune to bring in
fresh that far from the coast; and dainty fruit tarts. In
the corner, Miz Duffield's beloved string quartet played
quietly.

The people there were mostly Walters family friends
and higher-ups from the mill. Junior was there, in a thoroughly starched uniform and freshly polished boots,
and so was Belva, though she looked ill at ease, especially when so many of Byerly's muckety-mucks congrat-
ulated her on her fine work. Ace reporter Hank Parker
looked suitably solemn but was still taking notes, and
Burt's former trio of nurses had come together. Richard
and I, and Vasti and her husband were the only Burnettes
present, which would also have pleased Miz Duffield.

People were starting to think about leaving when Big
Bill rapped a glass with a fork to get everybody's atten-

tion. Since I thought I knew what was coming, I got closer but angled myself so I could watch the other people in the room rather than Big Bill. I couldn't wait to see what the reactions to his news were going to be.

Once the room was quiet, Big Bill said, "I wanted to thank everyone for coming today, and I know that Irene would be very gratified to see how much she was respected. She was an admirable woman, and we'll miss her greatly. This is a sad time for the Walterses." He paused a moment. "And yet, as is so often the case, this is also a joyful time, and I'd like to tell you why. Mike, would you come up here a minute?"

Mike Cooper went to stand beside him, looking uncomfortable and excited all at once.

"I'm sure most of you have met Mike Cooper," Big Bill said. "In a very short time, he's made himself indispensable at the mill, which would be reason enough to recognize him today. But there is another, more important reason. We've recently discovered something amazing about Mike's background, something we'd suspected but, until now, had never been able to determine for certain." He put his arm around Mike's shoulder. "Mike is more than just an invaluable employee; he's a member of my family. Mike Cooper is my grandson."

There was a second of shocked silence, then the room almost exploded in conversation, and I eagerly looked from one face to another. Most of them acted just as I'd expected: with astonishment, disbelief, even amusement. Vasti's eyes bugged out; Junior looked smug, as if an old suspicion had been confirmed; and Hank Parker nearly broke his neck getting to Big Bill so he could bark questions at him.

But there was one face that caught my attention, one expression I hadn't expected: absolute fury. It only lasted a second before those contorted features were schooled back to a look of amiability, but it lasted long enough to make my heart jump up to my throat. The person who wanted Big Bill dead was right there in front of me, and I knew who it was. I even had a glimmering of an idea of why. What I didn't know was how on earth I was going to prove it.

Chapter
Twenty-eight

I was so shaken by what I'd realized that I didn't pay much attention to Big Bill's explanation about how Mike came to be Small Bill's son. I think amnesia and dedicated work from private detectives were hinted at, if not spelled out, but I wasn't offended. The true story wasn't really anybody's business, including mine. I just stood there, and I must have turned white or gone stiff or something, because Richard noticed something was wrong.

"Laura?" he said, looking suspiciously at my cup of punch. "Are you okay?"

"Yes and no," I said. "Just act natural; I want to talk to Junior, but I don't want anybody to hear us."

"Whatever you say," he said, and did a much more credible job of acting normal than I did. Fortunately, I don't think anybody noticed in all the commotion. Eventually, I saw Junior saying good-bye to the Walterses, and I tugged Richard's arm so we could follow her without it looking like we were following her.

Only when we were outside did I quietly say, "Junior, we need to talk."

"Have you found out something?" she asked.

"Maybe, but I can't talk about it here. Can you come over to Aunt Maggie's house? Right now?"

She nodded, and we headed for the cars. Junior must have realized I was worried about our being seen together, because she turned the wrong direction for going to Aunt Maggie's, no doubt planning to go the long way around.

Richard, bless his heart, offered to wait until we got to Aunt Maggie's so I'd only have to go through it once, and even drove, which gave me a chance to go furiously over all the facts in my head, trying to see if my theory made any sense at all. We decided not to pick up Alice right away—the upcoming discussion wasn't one I wanted to have in her hearing, whether she could understand it or not.

Aunt Maggie had gone out, which was a relief. I didn't want to stir her up until I was more certain of my facts. Richard and I got out of our funeral clothes and had cold bottles of Coke ready when Junior got there.

"What have you got?" she said, which showed how anxious she was. A Southerner like Junior would never have skipped the polite preliminaries without good reason.

"It's not much," I warned her and Richard. Starting with what I'd seen at the Walters house, I backtracked to show how my suspect could have done everything we knew about, and concluded with, "I know there's no proof, but if I'm right, Big Bill is in more danger than ever."

Neither Junior nor Richard said anything at first. Then Junior said, "That could be the answer."

Richard was nodding, too. "Now that we've got a name, can't you find proof, Junior?"

"I don't know how," she said. "Belva and I already did everything we could think of."

"This is insane," Richard said. "We know who it is, but we can't do anything?"

Junior corrected him. "We *think* we know."

"Laura's never been wrong yet," Richard said loyally.

"Sure I have," I said, "but I appreciate the vote of confidence."

"I think Laura's right, too," Junior assured us, "but that doesn't give us enough evidence for a trial, or even probable cause for an arrest."

" 'Oft expectation fails, and most oft there where most it promises'," Richard said disconsolately. *"All's Well That Ends Well,* Act II, Scene 1."

"I can't say that this is ending well," Junior said, "but it may be how it has to end. I don't think it would do any good, but I could go talk to—"

"Don't do that," I said. "You'll give us away. This isn't some loose cannon like Sandie Herron—this is somebody who's smart enough to never get caught."

She spread her hands. "What else can I do? I want to get this case to trial so badly I can taste it, Laurie Anne, but keeping Big Bill Walters and his family safe has to come first. If that means letting it be known that we've figured out what's going on, that's what I'll do."

"But Junior, we can't just walk away," I said, not caring how whiney I sounded.

"Sometimes walking away is the only thing left to do." She grinned. "Like when I knew there was something more to Leonard Cooper's murder than was being said."

"I am sorry about that, Junior. Keeping quiet seemed like the best thing to do at the time."

"I understand. I'm just saying that keeping quiet just

might be the best bet this time, too. Don't worry. I'll keep an eye out, in case this one has developed a taste for killing."

I hated it, but maybe she was right. Richard and I had gone into this to protect Aunt Maggie and Big Bill. Aunt Maggie was out of it, but Big Bill wasn't, and we couldn't risk his life just for the satisfaction of winning. Then something else occurred to me.

"Are you going to tell Big Bill?" I asked.

"I have to," Junior said. "He needs to know who to watch out for."

"Then think about it. Is Big Bill Walters going to be willing to just watch his back for the rest of his life? Or is he going to do something on his own?"

She slapped herself on the forehead. "I hadn't thought about that."

"And what happens when Aunt Maggie finds out? Will she just let it go?"

"Not hardly. How am I going to keep the two of them out of trouble?"

"You're not," I said. "We're going to help them get into trouble. And settle this once and for all." I wasn't sure it was Shakespeare, but somebody had once said something about giving somebody enough rope to hang himself, and that's what we were going to do.

It was a lot more easily decided than arranged, of course. If we were going to set this trap, we had to get our bait in place. That was Big Bill, of course, and we decided it would be better for Junior to handle him, since she could talk to him privately on the pretense of clearing up details about Sandie Herron's attack. He was more than willing to go along, and was the one to come up with the right location.

Aunt Maggie came home not long after Junior called to verify that Big Bill was on board and, as we'd expected, insisted on being involved. As she put it, maybe she wasn't really married to Big Bill, but that didn't mean she wanted to be his widow.

We enlisted a few others, but as few as possible. The more people who knew about our plans, the greater the chance of word getting back to the killer or, just as bad, to one of Byerly's stellar gossips. Since several of those gossips were related to me, I knew how quickly they could spread a tale across town.

We did broadcast a little disinformation. First off, Junior gave Hank Parker a nice, long interview about Sandie Herron's death, taking pains to mention that there was no evidence that anybody else was involved in the attempts on Big Bill's life. It was even true—we were going on instinct, not evidence. Since Hank had never met a gift horse whose mouth he wouldn't inspect, he then came to see Richard and me. We played along, giving him details about Sandie's maternal obsession to help fill out the article. I felt a little guilty about blackening Sandie's reputation, but not enough to stop me. Richard made a point of telling Hank that we'd be leaving for Boston shortly, implying that we were satisfied with the way things had ended.

Next, Hank talked to Big Bill, who expressed his regret at not having realized how troubled Sandie was, and told him how distressed he was by the death of Miz Duffield. Then he casually mentioned that in order to help himself come to grips with recent events, he was leaving the next evening to spend some time in his hunting cabin. Alone.

Hank tried to get to Aunt Maggie, too, but she sent him off with his tail between his legs. This wasn't at all suspicious to anybody who knew Aunt Maggie, and besides, she said she'd had a bellyful of lying and wasn't about to sit there and play word games with Hank Parker.

The *Byerly Gazette* came out the next day, and I had no doubt that our stories were spread to the winds by lunchtime. Big Bill arrived at his cabin just after dark, but not before the rest of us were already in place. The trap was set. All we had to do was wait.

Chapter
Twenty-nine

Big Bill's cabin was about the size of Sandie Herron's shack but considerably nicer. Though I didn't get a chance to tour the inside until later, I knew it was made up of one big room that included a kitchenette with the usual appliances, a small dining area, and a living room with a stone fireplace. A compact spiral staircase led to a loft bedroom, and the living room couch folded out into a bed. There was only one bathroom, which made it rough living for Big Bill. Along the front of the house was a long porch with rocking chairs and a swing.

It was cozy for two or three people, but plenty big enough for Big Bill alone. Not that he was really alone, of course. The woods around the cabin were filled with watchers to make sure he didn't come to harm, and to snap the trap closed on the killer.

Aunt Maggie was in a hollow to one side of the house, despite Big Bill's objections. I hadn't been too happy about it, either, but hadn't bothered to say so, because I knew she was going to do whatever she wanted. What had surprised me was the fact that she wasn't alone. Pudd'nhead Wilson was with her. She'd told him all the whys and wherefores of her marriage to Big Bill, and when she let him in on our plan, he'd insisted on lending a hand. Since I no longer considered him a suspect, I couldn't very well argue with him, but I did wonder why he was so willing to defend his rival in romance. It was Richard who figured out that what he really wanted was to guard Aunt Maggie, but he knew enough not to tell her that. Both Aunt Maggie and Pudd'nhead were armed with shotguns.

On the other side of the cabin was Burt Walters, and he'd brought a surprise assistant, too: Mike Cooper. Big Bill had had to tell Burt about the plan, because he'd hit the roof when he heard his father was going off alone to a place where he'd nearly been killed. Once he found out what was really going on, he announced that he was coming, too. Big Bill had tried to talk him out of it, saying he was no use in the woods, but for once, Burt had stood up to his father. I don't know that he'd ever fired the brand-new hunting rifle he was carrying, but from the look on his face, I knew he was willing to try. As for Mike, he must have spent time in the woods up in Tennessee, because even I could tell that he knew what he was doing.

Belva was in back of the cabin, and Junior had the front. They'd argued over which side the killer was likely to come from, and once they decided it was likely to be the front because the only door was there, they argued over who should take the bigger risk. Junior had to pull rank to win.

Of course, between Burnettes and friends of the Walterses, we could have filled the woods as thick as the crowd on opening day at Fenway Park, but Junior said that too many people would make it more dangerous. As it was, everybody had been strictly instructed not to fire a weapon unless they were sure they knew who it was they were firing at.

There were two people who wanted to be in the woods who weren't there: Richard and me. We'd thought long and hard about it, and though it went against the grain for us not to be standing watch, Alice had to come first. We'd promised that we wouldn't put ourselves in danger if we could avoid it, and this was something we could avoid. In fact, it was probably safer for all concerned that we didn't go. Neither of us knew how to shoot, and we were city folk without much experience in the woods.

Still, we couldn't completely stay away, so Junior had stationed us with Trey Norton. We three were in a dark van parked far enough away from the cabin that we couldn't be seen, but close enough that we could hear the radio transmissions from the watchers. Richard and I were officially supposed to provide two extra sets of eyes to make sure nobody sneaked up on the van, but in all honesty we were there because we couldn't stand not to be. Alice, needless to say, was not with us. Aunt Nora had her.

With Byerly's entire police force out in the woods, Junior had had to call in a few favors to get the Rocky Shoals police to cover for them. The Rocky Shoals crew was also going to be our backup, should we need it.

I'd always thought that getting through college, leaving home, and having a baby were the toughest things I'd ever done. After that night, I had to add staying behind to the list. Not that those out in the woods had it any better—in fact, I was sure they had it worse. Though the weather that night was fine, it still couldn't have been any treat to stay hidden all that time, trying to make no more noise than necessary. Every half hour, Junior would use the radio to check on each of them, which was probably as much to keep them awake as anything else.

Big Bill had his cabin to relax in, but I couldn't imagine how he could really take advantage of it, knowing that he was a target. It hadn't been easy for a man like him to put his life into the hands of others, and it couldn't have been easy for him to continue acting unconcerned.

At least Richard and I were relatively comfortable in the van, and safe. We had no bugs to worry about, and we had something to drink, and could even talk if we did so quietly. Still, sitting there and waiting was mighty hard.

It didn't help that I kept thinking that maybe I'd been wrong, that Sandie had been the only killer after all and I was wasting everybody's time by having them wait for a nonexistent danger. Richard managed to reassure me that Junior wouldn't have agreed to set up the trap if she hadn't believed me.

Then I was worried that the killer was one of the people we'd trusted to watch over Big Bill. Could we be absolutely sure that Pudd'nhead, Belva, Burt, and Mike were innocent? After painstakingly going over our logic, Richard finally convinced me that we hadn't misjudged those four.

Next I moved on to worrying that the killer had realized it was a trap and either wasn't coming or had come up with a way past it. Even Richard couldn't get those thoughts out of my head, and eventually gave up so he could take a nap. What with being on duty and worrying about his sister, Trey wasn't interested in conversation, so that left nothing for me to do but to wait and keep quiet. I dozed off a few times myself.

About the time the sky started to go from solid black to deep gray, I remembered one of Paw's sayings: The biggest coon don't hunt until just before dawn. I'd never known what the heck he meant, but after that night, I thought I did. Because it was just before dawn that the man who wanted Big Bill dead made his move. I didn't see it myself, of course, but those who did told me the whole story later on.

The killer crept through the brush on Burt and Mike's side, concealed by the dark camouflage clothing he wore. Aunt Maggie said that from the way he moved, he knew exactly where he was going, so he must have explored the area around the cabin beforehand. Nobody saw him until he was nearly to the porch. Aunt Maggie whispered a warning into her radio, and all the watchers started to move in, trying to move as quietly as the killer. That radio message alerted those of us in the van, too, and we stared at the receiver, waiting to hear more.

Inside, the cabin was dark. Either Big Bill was still feigning sleep, or he really had managed to get some rest. But as the killer stepped onto the porch, an inside light went on. Big Bill later said that he'd sensed something was wrong, but Aunt Maggie said he was fooling himself because there was no way he could have heard anything. Either Big Bill had a sixth sense, or he just happened to pick that time to get up and move.

The killer reacted instantly. The rifle he'd been carrying casually was suddenly up on his shoulder, and he took aim through the window, into the cabin.

Junior's voice rang out through the woods. "Hold it right there!"

The killer was smart; everyone agreed about that. He fired one quick shot into the cabin, and as Junior came at him from one direction, and Burt and Mike from the other, he broke into a run, heading for the side Aunt Maggie and Pudd'nhead were covering.

Everybody went after him, of course, but between

the lingering darkness and confusion of the chase, nobody dared shoot for fear of hitting one of the good guys. Fortunately, the killer didn't stop to shoot, either. He didn't stop for anything, as he crashed through the brush and bowled over Aunt Maggie. He was fast and desperate, and had enough of a head start that he might have gotten away if it hadn't been for Pudd'nhead. The old ball player took careful aim and brought him down. Not with a gun—Pudd'nhead was as worried about hitting a friend as the others were. No, Pudd'nhead pulled his lucky baseball from his pocket and pitched it right at the man's back, knocking him slap over from the impact. As Richard said, never before had throwing one strike been better than a no-hitter.

Junior and the others were on the man before he could stand, yanking the rifle out of his grip and dragging him up. He was wearing a ski mask, and it was Belva who pulled it off him. Then Junior radioed us with the message we'd been waiting for: "We've got him. You were right, Laurie Anne. It's Tavis Montgomery."

Chapter
Thirty

While the others secured Tavis, Burt made a beeline for the cabin to check on Big Bill. Though he'd been cut on one hand by the flying glass from the window, Big Bill was fine and didn't care nearly as much about getting patched up as he did about finding out what was going on. Junior and the others got Tavis back to the cabin just as Richard and I ran up with Trey.

Junior had Tavis cuffed by then, and pushed him toward the cabin, where Big Bill was waiting on the porch.

"Tavis?" Big Bill asked, sounding shocked even though he'd known who we were expecting. "I've never done anything to harm you. Why would you want to kill me?"

"Hold on, Mr. Walters," Junior said. "We've got to do this properly. Tavis Montgomery, I'm arresting you for the attempted murder of Bill Walters." She went on to read him his rights and verified that he understood them. "All right, then," she said to Big Bill. "You can talk to him, but remember, he doesn't have to say anything."

"I'll answer whatever questions Big Bill wants to ask," Tavis said. "I've got nothing to hide. This is all a mistake." He looked and sounded so sincere that I almost doubted myself. "The fact is, I was doing the same thing y'all were doing: trying to protect Big Bill."

"Is that right?" Junior said skeptically.

Tavis nodded vigorously. "Dorcas mentioned that he was coming out here alone tonight, and even though Chief Norton and Deputy Tucker did an outstanding job apprehending Crazy Sandie, I had a bad feeling about it, and I thought it wouldn't hurt for me to come around and make sure Big Bill was all right. I've been watching for a good while now, and was about ready to leave when I saw somebody climb onto the porch with a gun. I was afraid that if I called out, he'd shoot, so I was trying to take him unawares. I was nearly close enough to grab him when I heard Chief Norton yell, and all hell broke loose. Whoever it was ran, and I took off after him."

Junior hefted the rifle they'd found with him. "Then why is it you were carrying this? It's been fired recently, and I'm willing to bet that these bullets will match the one in the wall of the cabin."

"It's not mine," Tavis said. "I almost had the shooter again, and I did manage to grab the rifle out of his hand, but he got away from me. The next thing I knew, somebody hit me in the back and knocked me over."

"That was me," Pudd'nhead said proudly, tossing his baseball into the air and catching it.

"Then you hit the wrong man," Tavis snapped. "It was the other man who shot at Big Bill, and I thank the good Lord he missed."

"There wasn't anybody else around here," Aunt Maggie said, but she didn't sound completely sure. In fact, Junior and I were the only ones who didn't shuffle around a bit. Had we messed up and caught the wrong man?

Tavis must have sensed the growing indecision. "Come on, people, what reason would I have for killing Big Bill?

He said himself that he's never done a thing to harm me." He turned to Burt. "Burt, haven't I been a loyal manager for you all these years? Why would I throw that away?"

Though I'd mentally convicted Tavis just from seeing his expression when he found out about Mike Cooper, I was fuzzy about the motive until that moment. I'd been thinking that it had something to do with Dorcas, and if Mike Cooper hadn't been standing there next to Burt, I still might not have figured it out, but suddenly the rest of the pieces snapped into place. "Tavis didn't want Big Bill dead for anything Big Bill did," I said. "It was for something Burt did!"

Everybody turned to look at me, and Big Bill demanded, "What in the Sam Hill are you talking about?"

"Tavis has been a good manager for a long time, but nobody who knows him thinks he did it out of loyalty. He did it because he was aiming to take over the mill some day. Now, everybody in town knew that Big Bill's will left everything to Burt, which meant that once Big Bill passed away, Burt would have all the Walters businesses to tend to, not just the mill. Since there was no way Burt could do everything, he would need somebody else to run the mill, and Tavis was the logical choice."

"So why kill him?" Belva wanted to know. "Why not just wait for Big Bill to die naturally. At his age and all." To Big Bill she added, "No offense."

I explained, "He would have waited—he'd been waiting for a good while already. Then Mike Cooper came onto the scene, and Burt made it plain that he was grooming him to take over the mill."

Burt looked flabbergasted. "You mean he was going to kill Daddy to get revenge for my hiring Mike?"

"Not exactly," I said. "I think Tavis is too smart for revenge. He just wanted Big Bill out of the way sooner rather than later. Burt had said himself that Mike wasn't ready to take over the mill yet, that it would be a year or two at the very soonest. But if Big Bill died now, somebody would have to run the mill in the meantime, and that person would be Tavis."

"What about when Mike was ready to take his place?" Richard asked.

"I can't say for sure," I said, looking at Tavis, who was watching me with cold, flat eyes. "Maybe he figured he could stall Mike's training, or make him so miserable that he'd quit. Maybe Tavis was planning to move up to another position himself by then."

"Or maybe he intended to get rid of me, too," Mike said.

"You feel like answering any of these questions?" Junior asked, nudging Tavis.

"It's all make-believe," Tavis said. "You can't prove any of it."

"We've still got you for trying to shoot Big Bill, in front of witnesses," I pointed out, "and I can pretty much guarantee that you won't even be working at the mill after tonight, let alone running the place." The expression on Tavis's face made me wonder if he wasn't willing to kill for revenge after all. But other than cursing under his breath, he wouldn't say another word.

"Belva," Junior said, "you and Trey load Montgomery into the van."

"You got it, Chief," Belva said.

"And Belva?"

"Yes, Chief?"

"Stop calling me 'Chief.' "

"You got it, Junior," Belva said, grinning like a cat with a bellyful of canary.

"We're going to go book Montgomery," Junior told the rest of us. "I'll send Trey back in the squad car to pick y'all up." I'd forgotten that since Junior had been the one to ferry us to the cabin, we were about to lose our ride back to Byerly. Since nobody really wanted to ride with Tavis, we were happy to wait.

Once the police contingent had driven off, the rest of us went inside the cabin, and Richard and I handed out coffee and Cokes.

"I don't imagine Tavis knew that I don't drink," Aunt Maggie said, "so I guess he was hoping to get me, too."

I nodded. "Of course, he didn't really care if he only got one of y'all. If he'd killed you, Aunt Maggie, he might have shocked Big Bill into a heart attack, or tried for him later. If he'd gotten Big Bill, Aunt Maggie would then have inherited all the Walters businesses, but since she wouldn't have known what to do with them, she'd have needed somebody who did. Meaning that Tavis would still have been in a good position to get his dream job."

"He didn't care," Big Bill said in disbelief. "He didn't want me dead because of who I was or anything I'd done. I was just in his way, like a slow-moving pickup truck." He sounded oddly forlorn. Big Bill had spent so much of his life being Big Bill Walters, it had never occurred to him that somebody wouldn't care who he was.

"How do you think I feel?" Aunt Maggie said in a disgusted tone. "If you were a slow-moving pickup, I was nothing but a pothole. If I ever get murdered, I want it to be for a better reason than that."

"Y'all stop that, " I said. "Whenever anybody used to call me names, Paw used to tell me to consider the source. Well, you two better consider the source this time. Tavis Montgomery is so blinded by ambition that he doesn't see y'all for what y'all really are. The rest of us do!"

Everybody else nodded in agreement, and Pudd'nhead

said, "It took me a while, but I sure know now what kind of a woman Maggie is."

If I were still in junior high, I'd have described the look he gave her as making cow eyes.

Aunt Maggie snorted, but not as loudly as she usually does.

Big Bill cleared his throat and stood up. "Maggie, now that that's settled, we need to get something else straight."

"Is that right?" Aunt Maggie said.

"If you'll have me, I want to marry you, Maggie. For real, this time."

Pudd'nhead stood up, too. "Before you answer him, I want to say my piece. This isn't the way I planned it, but . . . Maggie, will you marry me?"

Neither Pudd'nhead nor Big Bill looked their best, needless to say. Pudd'nhead had been lying in the dirt all night, and then he'd had a good tussle with Tavis. Big Bill had bags under his eyes, his shirttail was hanging out, and his pants were speckled with blood. But in my mind's eye, all I could see were two knights errant vying for the affections of a fair lady.

Aunt Maggie didn't say anything for a good while, and I held my breath, waiting for her answer.

Big Bill never was known for his patience, and after he'd stood it as long as he could, he said, "Well, Maggie? Is it me or Mr. Wilson here that you want? It's time to choose."

"He's right," Pudd'nhead said. "It's not fair for you to keep us dangling."

"Not fair?" Aunt Maggie said incredulously. "You want to talk about not being fair? How about my saving your life, nursing you back to health, and falling in love with you, only to have you run off to play baseball the first chance you got. Then you don't even so much as send a Christmas card for umpteen years—I didn't know if you were alive or dead until you showed up the other day. Do you call that fair?"

Big Bill had managed to hide his grin but couldn't resist bobbing his head in agreement until Aunt Maggie turned on him.

"And you!" she said. "We lived within spitting distance of each other and worked in the same building for years, and you didn't even notice I was alive, let alone a woman, until we were both ready for Social Security. All that time I was nothing but a mill hand and a union troublemaker, but now you've decided I'm good enough after all, so I'm supposed to run into your arms. That doesn't sound fair, either!"

Now it was Pudd'nhead's turn to be smug.

Aunt Maggie looked from one man to the other. "You two listen up, and listen up good. I'm an old woman now, but I'd have made one hell of a wife if somebody had had enough sense to ask me when I was younger—and I'd have been a good mother, too. But since neither one of you asked then, don't bother asking me now! I'm not going to marry either one of you!"

Pudd'nhead and Big Bill don't look much alike, but at that moment, they had the exact same expression on their faces, as if they'd been struck by the same bolt of lightening.

It was Pudd'nhead who sadly said, "Then you don't want to see me anymore?"

"Or me?" Big Bill said, utterly flabbergasted.

"Did I say that?" Aunt Maggie said.

The two confused men shook their heads.

"I said I don't want to get married. I don't have any objection to letting one of you buy me dinner, or take me out dancing some time. Y'all both know my phone number and my address." Then she turned her back on both of them and went out to the porch. "As soon as Trey gets back, I'm going home to get some sleep," was all she had to say.

Under his breath, Richard whispered, " 'Was ever woman in this humor woo'd? Was ever woman in this humor won?' *Richard III*, Act I, Scene 2."

Big Bill turned and looked at Pudd'nhead, and darned if the two men didn't grin at each other.

"It's like I've said before," Pudd'nhead said, "that Maggie Burnette has a way of catching a man by surprise."

Big Bill said, "Mr. Wilson, you've said a mouthful."

"Call me Pudd'nhead, Big Bill. I think we're going to be running into each other quite a bit from now on."

Chapter
Thirty-one

Richard and I stayed in town a few more days, partially to make sure everybody got a chance to spend time with Alice, and partially to see things start to settle down.

Tavis Montgomery was in jail and likely to stay there until trial. Big Bill knew most of the judges around, and none of them was willing to grant bail. Tavis was still claiming innocence, but nobody was swallowing it, not with the array of witnesses against him. There're people who don't trust the police, and those who don't trust wealthy folks like the Walterses, and those who don't trust regular people like Aunt Maggie and Pudd'nhead. But when they're all agreeing on the same thing, they're likely to be believed.

It was Dorcas who helped us figure out exactly how Tavis had carried out his plans. It was by spending time with her that he'd been able to find out Big Bill's schedule, so he could go after him the first three times. As for the isopropanol, she'd worked with Tavis on a poison information brochure to hand out along with fire-prevention tips at the schools. Dorcas was also the one who'd told him about Richard's and my going through that file of threatening letters, and it hadn't been hard for him to sneak into Big Bill's office and pick through them himself. He'd quickly realized that he could use Sandie Herron to get to Big Bill, especially after looking at Sandie's web site.

Dorcas felt terribly guilty about inadvertently helping Tavis, and Richard and I felt bad about giving him the idea of looking at Big Bill's files, but Aunt Maggie wasn't having any of it. As she put it, only the north end of a south-going horse would take the blame for anything Tavis Montgomery did. The man was a menace, but he was in jail where he belonged, and we should get on with our lives.

Others certainly were, especially Big Bill. In fact, he'd turned over a new leaf. First he gracefully accepted Aunt Maggie's announcement about dating him and Pudd'nhead, and then he set about welcoming Mike Cooper into the family. Next he gave the VFW a much larger donation than expected, and set up a charitable foundation in Miz Duffield's name to promote the arts, particularly string quartet music. Most impressive of all, he finally took the time to go through all those threatening letters and started trying to make up for some of his past mistakes. He investigated Marlyn Roberts's contaminated land more thoroughly, and when he found proof that it was Marlyn's ex-husband who'd caused the problems after all, he spoke to the judge who'd handled the divorce. Shortly after that, their settlement was changed so that Marlyn got a lump sum instead of the useless land. Next he visited Molly Weston's doctor. When he verified that it had been a fifty-fifty chance that her smoking, not working at the mill, had caused her lung problems, Big Bill paid Wynette Weston half the amount of her aunt's medical and funeral bills. She shared it with her siblings but still had enough left for baby furniture and diapers. The bonus Belva got for being made a permanent member of the Byerly police force helped, too.

There was nothing Big Bill could do for Sandie Herron or his mother, of course, but I helped him find a Web-master to maintain Sandie's web site. The rumor was that he'd made sure that Sandie was buried next to his mother, too.

My skeptical side said that he was only doing all that to win over Aunt Maggie, and that a better man would never have made so many enemies in the first place, but there's something heartwarming about redemption. I'd always been taught that anybody can make a mistake; it's how the mistakes are corrected that shows a per-son's worth. Big Bill was proving himself to be a wor-thier man than I'd expected.

Pudd'nhead Wilson, Aunt Maggie's other ardent ad-mirer, never did go back to where he'd been living. Instead, he had his stuff shipped to Byerly and bought himself a house not too far from Aunt Maggie's. To make sure he got plenty of time with her, he'd gotten into the baseball card and memorabilia business and started setting up at the flea market. Aunt Maggie said he was just being a pudd'nhead again, because every-body knew the bottom had dropped out of the sports collectibles market, but that didn't bother Pudd'nhead one bit.

Both men had proposed to Aunt Maggie several more times, so she finally put her foot down and told them that when and if she decided to get married, she'd do the asking. In the meantime, she was being wined, dined, and so thoroughly courted that she complained about not being able to turn around without tripping over one of her suitors. In other words, she was having a wonderful time.

Richard and I went to visit Mike Cooper at the mill one day—he hadn't decided if he was going to keep using the name Cooper or switch to Walters. I wanted to apologize for not telling him what I knew about his father, but he said he understood why I hadn't. Besides, he didn't think he could have handled it if I'd dropped that bombshell on him right after his father's death. What would have been a traumatic shock then was a blessing now, as he got to know his new family. The only problem was that Dorcas had been parading an endless line of eligible young women past him, hoping he'd find one he wanted to marry. She was going to get babies into that house one way or the other.

As for me, I'd decided that motherhood hadn't changed me as much as I'd been afraid of. Richard and I had managed to get rid of Tavis Montgomery and start weaning Alice, all at the same time. I still didn't know whether I was going to go back to work once my maternity leave was over, but I was convinced I could keep nosing around in other people's business as long as I could round up babysitters. Maybe I wasn't the world's greatest detective, but I'd challenge Sherlock Holmes and Dr. Watson any day to solve one of their cases in between diaper changes.

All in all, I was feeling pretty darned full of myself until the day before Richard, Alice, and I were due to fly back to Boston. That's when I was reminded that one of my aunts' old wives' tales about babies wasn't true. In other words, you can get pregnant while you're nursing a baby. The next time Richard and I got involved in a killing was going to be even trickier.

GET YOUR HANDS ON THE
MARY ROBERTS RINEHART
MYSTERY COLLECTION

More Mysteries from
Laurien Berenson

Available Wherever Books Are Sold!

Visit our website at **www.kensingtonbooks.com**